LOVE IN THE TIME OF CORONA

CJ LOOMIS

Copyright © 2020 by CJ Loomis

All rights reserved.

No part of this book may be reproduced in any form or by any electronic or mechanical means, including information storage and retrieval systems, without written permission from the author, except for the use of brief quotations in a book review.

CHAPTER 1

Hayden was startled by his new favorite tune and thought it was strange to have heavy alternative piping through a family store like this. It dawned on him his pants were also vibrating. He grabbed his phone and swiped quickly without looking at the number since the song was nearly to the chorus. "Hi, this is Hayden."

"Hayden, it's Rebecca."

Hayden cringed and regretted answering. Rebecca was Hayden's boss. She was the stereotypical chip-on-the-shoulder type. She needed to let everyone know she was in charge and if they questioned her authority, it was as good as asking for a pink slip. "We've got a fire drill. Sampson's big ad had the wrong dates in it. Their promotion is next weekend and the ad says this weekend and it ran this morning. I don't know what we're going to do, but I need you back here immediately!"

Sampson's was an up-and-coming big box store and the company's biggest account, by far. He was in charge of it. Why shouldn't he be? He was the one who landed it.

Hayden knew advertising inside and out. He couldn't draw a stick figure to save his life, but everything else, was his wheelhouse. Every week Hayden oversaw advertising on behalf of his clients in TV, radio, digital, print, and billboards, which those in the industry called out-of-home. It was a crazy gig, but it was never boring. Hayden loved it. It challenged him on every level.

The good part about having a close relationship with Sampson's CEO was when something like this happened. He could call Kent on his cell, explain the issue, and propose how to fix it. Often Kent would trust his judgment and sign off. Most of the time Hayden would attribute undaunted faith like that to a lack of knowledge or naivety, but Kent was highly intelligent. He and Hayden could have been cut from the same cloth. They never panicked in the face of adversity.

Hayden paused for a moment, assessed the situation, and took a deep breath. "I'll be there in ten minutes. No one call the client. I'll deal with it."

Rebecca barked back, "Okay. I've already reprimanded Alana for the screw up and she had every excuse in the book, refusing to take responsibility. I'm going to have to let her go, Hayden."

Hayden saw red. Alana was the best young talent he'd worked with in his twelve years of marketing. She knew what she was doing, and he would always give her the benefit of the doubt. She had earned that level of trust.

"Rebecca, Alana is on my team and I need to sign off on something like that. Let's not rush to any hasty judgments. You tried doing this with Faith a couple of days ago, too."

"Fine, but you know my thoughts on the matter. Get back here now."

"I'm on my way."

Hayden swallowed the large lump in his throat, calmed himself, and took stock of the situation. He went to his contacts, found Andy's picture, and pushed the phone receiver icon.

CHAPTER 2

"Sloane, what is taking so long?" Her mother yelled from downstairs. Their house was a 1950's rambler and everything on the inside and out screamed it. The exterior was drab with the color of brick, the inside looked even older. The carpet her mother's elevated voice carried over was a worn-down tannish Berber that was at least two decades overdue on a makeover appointment. All rooms were decorated with furniture so eclectic it was damn near retro. It wasn't much.

Rae added another two cents up the stairs, "I've got to get to work and you're going to make me late again! You work at a meat locker. Do you think some guy looking for tube steak is gonna sweep you off your feet? Get a move on, girl!"

Sloane was in the middle of the last chorus of AC/DC's *Back in Black* when she heard her mother hollering from the bottom of the steps. By this point she was usually combing through the wet snarls in her black cherry hair. Today she was running a little behind.

She had mysterious green eyes and the perfect slightly darker skin tone and look that could have pulled off that hipster/goth type, but that most definitely wasn't her. Sloane was old school, at her ripe old age of twenty-six. More Lynyrd Skynyrd, Foo Fighters, and Snow

Patrol. Less Bieber, Lovato, and Gomez. She enjoyed them all. Sloane just loved true rock. Heart was her favorite band.

Sloane Knox hadn't had the easiest of roads leading to this point in her life. Neither she, nor her mother had. Her father was the stereotypical story of a young man not able to handle the responsibilities that coincide with getting a girl pregnant at a young age. He had never paid a dime of child support or sent as much as a birthday card.

The last she heard he was looking for investors in his latest "get rich quick" scheme after he had gotten out of the Navy. Something about a sticker that told you if a fruit was ripe yet. *Yeah, Dad, or you could look at the color of the fruit.* Sloane shook her head, thinking back while applying her mascara. He'd even had the nerve to ask her once to invest when she went to go see him a few years back. He had no clue who she was of course. She made a sly comment about "having too many student loans to pay off since her dad was a deadbeat." He didn't push the matter any further.

She kept her nose to the books and graduated with honors from St. Thomas business school nearly five years ago now with a degree in IT Management. It wasn't irony that she was putting on a hair net and in a business about as far removed from computers as you could get, but it was pretty sucky. Mrs. Morrisette had destroyed the definition for an entire generation. Sloane fully understood what the term meant. If Alanis had sung, "We moved our wedding to an indoor venue because the forecast predicted rain, but the day turned out to be sunny. Ironically, the sprinkler system at the venue malfunctioned and doused the ceremony with water!" Then again, it wasn't quite as catchy. Sloane guessed that was the *Jagged Little Pill* of it all.

Her mom's best friend, Robin, was hard-pressed to find anyone dependable at her butcher shop. Coincidently, about the same time, Sloane was graduating and had fresh student loans coming due.

She didn't want all that hard work in college to result in a low-paying entry-level position. So, she could take the job at Robin's store and hold out for a while.

Eventually interviews dried up. She had been taking online courses at night to keep up with the latest technologies. Unfortunately, she couldn't add that to her resume until she was finished in May. Until then, the future career was pretty much on hold. So, she would work at the butcher shop for a few more months. Then again, that's what she'd said five years ago.

The pay wasn't terrible and she had great benefits with the boss. Like last Friday when she and Justine, her best friend, went out for a spa day to get away from it all. She was in dire need of a manicure. Not every girl gets the combination of cow, pig, and chicken flesh and fat shoved under her fingernails five to six days a week.

PG. How could she describe Justine? Justine was easily her best friend. She was her college roommate from St. Thomas for all four years. Justine Cook was born with a silver spoon in her mouth. In her youth she was always pranced around by her parents in the old court as a little princess. She had the pony that every girl dreamed of. She grew up in the equivalent of a modern-day castle.

When she was six, she got a pony. That she creatively named "Pony." Sloane remembered this because Justine had a little too much rum and tequila one night at a frat party. The nickname Pony Girl was born. A little play on the *Outsiders* character, and then of course, the horse. It was later, not exactly sure when, condensed to PG. For nearly eight years Sloane had been calling Justine that. Hell, her phone picture was of a *My Little Pony* plastic figurine with the first name *P* and last name *G*. PG hated the nickname, but also decided to own it in the hope Sloane would let it go. No such luck. Justine hated the upbringing she had. During her rebellious teenage years, she decided that she was going to make her own way. Despite her mother's best efforts to drill it into her, Justine's first priority was not to find a successful young man, give him a bunch of babies, and sit at home organizing charity events.

They both had boyfriends over the years and when they didn't, they were studying. PG wasn't in IT like Sloane. She was going after her MBA to try to gain a higher-level sales associate job and work her way up the corporate ladder.

Justine pretty much only dated two guys during college. One for all of sophomore and junior year. They kept it pretty light. She knew he wasn't the one, but she had no problem with him being the one for right now. The other she started seeing the last term of their senior year and Sloane never really met the guy, they saw each other a couple of times in passing and exchanged pleasantries.

PG and Sloane hadn't lost touch, they were both busy with term papers, finals, extra classes, and credits to graduate early. So, they weren't growing apart, they were both centrally focused on their futures and that took a toll on their deep sharing and time together. For a while they barely noticed if the other was in the next bed, but they were still like sisters and had each other's backs through everything.

Sloane on the other hand was a serial dater. She always had been. At the age of sixteen when she really started to develop and pubescent boys started to take notice of her filling out in all the right places, she didn't really indulge them. She never found someone that truly challenged her. Not necessarily on an intellectual level, but with quick wit and humor. Either the guys she saw didn't get it, didn't care, or ignorantly laughed to see if it could get them to the end of the night. She never understood what people meant by "the one." What was the enchantment of it all? She decided a long time ago, it wasn't for her.

CHAPTER 3

It took about four rings for Andy to answer the phone. The classic rock blaring in the background was a few decibels beyond that of a jet airliner. *Great,* Hayden thought, *the weekend hasn't even started, and Andy is going to get us kicked out.* There was no way he was going to even bring it up considering the nature of this call.

Andy Ralsted and Hayden Foster had been lifelong friends and classmates growing up in a small town in southeastern North Dakota. Andy moved down to the Twin Cities right out of college. Hayden stayed in town and worked at his family's radio station selling ad space and working on-air.

The whole upcoming weekend was set and there was large-scale, mass quantity consumption to be done. And with it, a lot of fun with friends to be had. He had gone out to the store the other night for all of his necessities in preparation. After all, this was Andy's special day, he had to go big. Andy had done the same for him.

"Hey, Hay!" Andy shouted into his phone. He always thought that was such a perfect greeting for him. "You en route, bro?"

Hayden quickly jumped in, "Yeah, about that..." He couldn't see

Andy's disappointment, but he knew it was there with the pause and sudden muting of the music.

"Seriously, dude?" Andy was hurt.

Hayden's fist was balled up and he pounded it against the store shelf. "Yeah, I've got to put on the proverbial helmet, coveralls, and boots to get this inferno under control."

"Rebecca?" Andy's voice was slightly calmer now. Rebecca had come up in one or two of Hayden's drunken rants. After all, Andy knew Hayden wouldn't miss this weekend if he absolutely didn't have to.

"Yes, Rebecca, you know if I didn't have to go back in I wouldn't. I'm the only one who can handle this, unfortunately. Tell everyone to have a shit ton of fun tonight and tell them I'm sorry I couldn't be there. Technically your birthday isn't until tomorrow anyway." Probably not the right thing to say, though correct. "I'll take off early in the morning and catch up with you tomorrow afternoon, buddy."

The playlist at the cabin must have turned to rap because he could now clearly hear Sir Mix-a-Lot. "You hear that?" Andy shouted again. "That's what you're missing, brother. I'll let everyone know how lame you are. Handle yo bidness and get up here."

"Will do and love you, bro."

"Love you too, man." The phone went dead.

Hayden had a core group of about thirty friends, most of which were transplants from North Dakota. Oddly enough people from their home state seemed to flock to each other. Nearly all of them would be there tonight, but none would ever hold a candle to the thick and thin that these two had. Sure, Andy had an actual brother and sister and Hayden had an older sister, but these two were almost inseparable. They were constantly mistaken for brothers too.

They were classmates and best friends from the age of five and now roommates. Their friendship had been through more ups and downs than most do in a lifetime. Baseball, football, girls, they were even co-workers for a couple years. They had been there for each other for some of their life's biggest events. Andy's parent's divorce, his dog passing, Eagle Scout graduation, even his little sister being born. The one night when Hayden came over during the five-hundred-year storm when the power went out all over town and they stayed up all night filling pails of water because the sump pump had died. Then there was the week straight Andy drove over an hour each way every night during finals when Hayden's mom was tragically lost to a heart attack. It helped him get through that time so much. Just to have someone he could talk to.

Now they were roommates and on the same softball and broomball teams together. They put on two big friend events every year. The "Chilly Cook-Off" because it happened in early February in the middle of the frozen Minnesota tundra. Then there was the annual "Dress Like an Idiot Golf Tournament". Granted most golfers dressed like idiots to begin with, but this was an entirely new ball of wax. Last year the theme was Saturday Night Live characters. While most people were creative and went old school, like Head Wound Harry. Others simply ran a belt through a box and covered up their junk.

Hearing the crew partying reminded Hayden of a few old adages when it comes to NoDaks. One, they can do two things well and the other one is drink. They all work hard and take pride in it. You do the job right and don't cut corners. When you get married, you take those vows to the grave. All of this pride ran through Hayden's mind as he finished what he considered his most difficult task of the night, letting down his best friend.

Well, that was quite the drama infused last five minutes. I don't know about you, but I'm almost queasy from that emotional roller coaster." Hayden heard a feminine voice pipe in from an undetectable location. He knew it was somewhere toward the front of the store. Like a whack-a-mole her head popped up from behind the deli counter. He could only see her from the neck up, but Hayden had to instantly admit, it was quite the neck up.

"Sure you don't need a box of tissues?" She was giving him shit and he picked up on it.

"Why? You got any back there?"

"Will butcher paper suffice?" She smirked.

Wow, she really was gorgeous. Facially speaking anyhow. Even despite the raw meat and juices staining the upper portion of her apron. He never thought the hairnet look could be pulled off, but somehow it didn't detract from her captivating smile and perfectly rounded high cheekbones. Her eyeliner stuck out about a quarter of an inch beyond the norm. It framed her stunningly deep green eyes perfectly.

He stared at the hairnet as he tried to guess what color her hair was for a few moments which caused a momentary lull in their exchange. She got self-conscious for a second. "Oh yeah." She made a repetitive motion with her right hand as if pushing volume into her perfectly coiffed hairdo from the back of her neck. "Like my designer headwear?"

He smiled at her humor.

He decided to indulge her and started slowly walking her direction. "So, do you have any recommendations?"

"In headwear, grilling meats, maybe both? I have a bacon-wrapped filet fedora you might be able to pull off."

For Hayden that sealed it, plain and simply put, this girl was amazing. He tried to keep pace. "I'm more of a boneless bonnet type myself." They both cringed and chuckled. He popped into his radio announcer voice, "Round 1: Stunning Meat Mistress Behind the Counter." He was going to have to get her real name to condense that a little. He was sure he caught a twinkle of satisfaction. She couldn't help but giggle at him.

The phone rang and instantly Hayden exhaled as if he was saved by the bell. In one fell swoop the girl reached out both hands. The left to grab the pen and pad from the counter. With her right she tapped the bottom of the receiver, so the phone jumped off the cradle. She caught it between her shoulder and that amazing cheek. In the same instant she began speaking "Best Cuts." She turned around to begin taking the phone order while Hayden stared at her backside contemplating deeper meaning in the cosmos.

A thousand ridiculous thoughts ran through his head while he leaned over the counter to get a better look. *Why are there interstate high-*

ways in Hawaii? What is another word for thesaurus? When a cow laughs does milk come out of its nose? Maybe that was one for her. Then he realized she had turned around. He snapped back to reality and instantly panicked. More questions raced to the front of his mind. *How long ago did she turn around? Does she think I'm a gawking freak? Even now, why am I still staring?*

He looked into her eyes behind the eyeliner and gave her a warm smile as if to say yep, you caught me red-handed with my mitt in the cookie jar! She winked, put her finger up to inaudibly explain it would be a minute before she could help him, and turned back around. He wasn't sure, but that may have been the first breath he'd taken in the last two minutes. *Pull it together, man!* Hayden was going twelve rounds with himself over this girl.

She hung up the phone and finished jotting the last line when she quipped before looking up, "Anything else I can help you with?" She giggled under her breath.

"Maybe some chicken? I'm trying to offer a variety." Would she let it slide or…

"Sure, are you just looking for thighs and legs?"

Hayden chimed in quickly, "Don't forget about the breasts. Is this a rotisserie or a roast?" Hayden winced and viewed her through slit eyes to see if that one landed.

With a faint closed-mouth smile the woman looked over her shoulder, as if conferring with an imaginary panel. She even covered her mouth and whispered in hushed tones to suggest a private conversation. They were on the same level. She turned back to face him. "Against my advice, the judges are going to give it to you." In her best impression of Hayden's deeper voice, she said, "Horse a piece folks, we've got a tie ball game."

She sensed his uneasiness but had already been laughing at him. "Don't worry, blue-eyes, no offense taken." He lifted his hands in a celebratory fashion. She giggled and then blushed taking notice of his arresting dimples. "Besides, this here…" She swayed her hands both vertically and horizontally presenting her body like Vanna White or one of the Price is Right girls introducing a new prize "…is a prime

USDA choice cut. Not some fatty T-bone. I don't think you could afford it."

As his laughter died down Hayden sensed this concluded their witty exchange. "Actually, I'm here for those liquid heaven steaks." He pointed out the package of marinated wagyu ribeyes and kindly handed over the cash after she rang him up.

"Liquid heaven?" Sloane questioned.

"Just an idea."

"Interesting."

Just as he'd mustered up the courage to ask that nearly impossible question for all young men she looked up. "Hey, don't you have about two of those ten minutes left?"

Hayden jerked to attention. "Oh, man, right, thanks. Hey, can I get a bottle of water too?" She reached behind her to a cooler and tossed one at him. *I don't even need water.* He barehanded it out of the air. "What do I owe you?"

"Free of charge for the chuckle." She slyly winked and he thanked her as he briskly made a b-line for the door. Just before reaching it however she yelled. "And don't forget to put your tongue back in your mouth before you get to work, Becky might get the wrong idea!" She'd given him one more verbal jab before he nodded with a whimsical smile and his back hit the door. In the parking lot he reached in his console for a pen. He grabbed a $5 bill from his change and stuck it under the windshield wiper blade of a Jeep in the parking lot. It was the only other vehicle there, so he had assumed it was hers. Or at least he hoped so.

CHAPTER 4

The building was pretty dim, other than the top floor that Hayden's office was on. The glass doors were already locked, so he had to use his key fab. As he walked through the light pine wood and brushed chrome-accented lobby en route to the elevator bank he thought, *at least the building knows I put in a fifteen-hour day today.*

The elevator doors opened and there was Faith, another girl on his team. She was good, but also new, so still learning the ropes. She picked up fast though. Her mascara was streaming down her face, even now late in the day when he assumed a lot of it had worn off already. Which meant she must have been sobbing pretty hard. Faith was usually a bright light in the darkness of this place. She was short with natural, long blonde hair and hazel eyes. She called him out when he needed it.

Hayden knew what was happening. Becky, as his new meat mistress had coined her, was on the tear. He held out his arms to Faith without uttering so much as a word. It was unprofessional, but they were all rowers in this perilous ship named Rebecca headed toward the rocks daily, so they'd commiserated together on more than a few occasions. He'd wished he had a champagne bottle to personally break over her "bow".

Faith came to him and let the tears flow. After they parted, Hayden looked the other way briefly to allow Faith a moment to wipe the waterworks away. They moved to the lobby chairs a few feet away.

In the process of sitting down she spoke, "I don't think I can do this anymore. She's a monster, Hayden! It wasn't our fault; you have to know that."

"Let me guess, the creative agency put the wrong dates, we forwarded it to the client, and they signed off on it?"

Faith replied, "Yes, I know we should have double-checked it."

Hayden waited for her to finish, barely able to keep his anger in check. "Nope, that's not our fault or job. We are not the intermediary between the client and the creative. It's not our responsibility to check that."

"Tell *her* that." Faith pointed to the ceiling with a flash of frustration.

Hayden assured her he would. He might have included a few derogatory and colorful names for good measure under his breath.

Faith went on to talk about how it was her and her boyfriend Dustin's two-year anniversary and she was already late to meet him for dinner. She told Rebecca that morning she needed to leave right at five today to go home and get changed. That went out the window when the Sampson's "shit" hit the proverbial fan. According to Faith, Rebecca shouted, "I don't care if it's your wedding night! If you want to remain employed here, you'll be here until the problem is solved!"

The audacity of that woman. If she practiced half of what she preached. He hadn't seen her here once before nine A.M. in the last two years.

It was already a quarter to six and Faith's dinner reservation was downtown at a well-known formal dining spot at seven. There was no way she would be able to get home, get cleaned up, and make it in time. Hayden racked his brain and a lightbulb popped. "Wait here for a minute." He ran to his car and dug into his glove box. "Eureka!" he exclaimed and ran back inside where Faith was trying to pull herself back together.

He extended his arm and handed her what looked like a credit card. "Here, call Dustin and tell him to cancel the reservations, tell him to head to Henry's. He won't be upset about the wait when you tell him you have this." It was a $500 gift card for the best steak and seafood fine dining experience in the cities. He had already been holding on to it for a couple of years now. Hayden was waiting for the right girl and the right night. He didn't see it being redeemed for at least a couple more yet.

Henry's didn't accept reservations or have a call-ahead list. You had to wait in line for at least an hour and pray you could get in. For those that were patient enough they were richly rewarded with culinary delights that "tickled the taste buds and scintillated the senses". At least that was their tagline.

"That should buy you enough time to get there and still look like a knockout. Not that you don't already." Hayden gave her a smirk and a wink.

He and Andy each had one of those gift cards that their buddy Ryan had given them for helping him build his monstrosity of a deck last summer. It took over three weeks of working under floodlights every night. He remembered it now with exhaustion. Andy already used his a couple of weeks ago with his, at that time, girlfriend. Hayden remembered bringing it up to Andy in a jovial tone that it must sting considering he used the gift card on an ex. They hashed about it and Andy wished he could get a refund and have his card back. That's how guys got over tough break-ups. They took each other to the bar and gave each other shit. Oh, how Hayden had laughed until he cried about that.

Andy didn't find it amusing at first, but then was a good sport when really reflecting on it. He'd even made a crude joke about how he knows he didn't get $500 worth of compensation from her and wished he would have gone back down her throat to get the food back. Now, Andy would have slight redemption. After all, he at least got to use half of it on himself.

"I-I-I can't accept this," Faith stuttered, all the while still trying to compose herself.

"You have to, otherwise how else am I going to convince Dustin to let you keep working here? I need you, so consider it a fringe benefit donation from the rest of the team."

"I have to stay though, or she's going to fire me, and I can't afford to lose this job."

"Faith, don't worry about Rebecca, I'll handle her. I'm telling you as your boss you are done for the day. Have a great night, and I'll see you on Monday." Hayden held up a hand when she opened her mouth to protest. "You don't have any time to spare, so get a move on."

"How can I ever—?"

Hayden cut her off, "You don't, that's how."

Her face lit up with the biggest smile. Her bloodshot eyes streamed again. She kissed him on the cheek and ran as fast as her little legs could carry her to her car.

One small problem solved, now to lure Rebecca down from the Empire State Building and fix the Sampson's debacle to go.

Hayden felt warm inside, but it wasn't for his altruistic gesture. He pushed the button again, the doors opened, and he ascended to the top floor. He took the two rights and a left until he could see his team standing and discussing. Long before he had a visual on them however, he could audibly identify one individual from the moment the steel doors had opened. He knew that shrill shriek from a mile away.

CHAPTER 5

It was getting to be that twilight hour at the store. Sloane had already begun thoroughly wiping and disinfecting the countertops for the night before dimples strolled in. She still had to mop the floor which took a little more than a half hour if she was uninterrupted.

Just as that thought entered and left her mind, her phone rang. A picture of a little horse with a rainbow cascading overhead appeared. "What's up, P?"

"So now we're shortening it even further? Great, when do we get back to just Justine?"

"Never!"

"What's up, girl? You about out of there for the night?"

Sloane knew where this was going, so her voice took on a slower interrogative intonation. "Yeah, why?"

"Girls night out! Get your azz out of there, get home and get showered. Kristi, Heidi, and I are coming to pick you up."

Sloane had been inclined to say no. She hadn't been out in quite a while and her immediate instinctive response made her feel like maybe she was turning into a bit of a hermit. Sloane had already gotten all of her homework due for Monday done. Heidi had three kids and never got away from the house. The least she could do was indulge her.

"You know what, yeah, I'm in. Give me about two hours and I'll be ready."

"She's in!" she heard on the other end of the line, along with two girls screaming at the top of their lungs.

Great, they've already got a head start, Sloane realized.

"We'll be over in half an hour!" hollered Kristi.

Sloane rolled her eyes as she rationalized mopping the floors in the morning. It would take a little more elbow grease than if she were to get them done now. She was in for a night of babysitting Heidi, trying to be responsible, but also having a few cocktails and fun herself. She hit the lights, locked the door, and headed for her Wrangler. For having all the freedom she thought she had, she didn't get to spread her wings much. Maybe tonight she should do that.

Sloane picked up her phone and dialed Robin's number.

"Yes, Deary, something wrong?" Robin asked with a slight worry in her voice.

"Nope, I closed up the shop and I know this is last minute and all, but do you think you could open tomorrow for me?"

"No problem, I was falling asleep on the couch before you called anyway. Something come up?"

"Yeah, a night out with the girls and I want to get my drink on!"

Robin laughed into the receiver. "Well, it's about time. I've been telling your mom we've needed a margarita night soon too, a little R & R if you know what I mean." Sloane giggled every time she'd used the phrase since they'd coined it years ago. Her mom's name was Rae and her best friend was Robin, it wasn't that difficult of a slogan to land on. "Go have fun, girl."

"I forgot, I didn't get the floor mopped tonight, but I did put the cash bag in the safe with a deposit slip so I'll stop by tomorrow afternoon and run to the bank at least."

"Sloane, I'll handle that, seriously, have some fun for a change. You've turned into such an old maid in the past couple years and I feel somewhat responsible for that. So, the more fun you have, the less taxed my conscience is."

The night had endless possibilities, she cranked the Petty up, and it was Friday night out with the girls. She began plotting. Sloane had a few beers in her fridge the girls could kill and that might buy her an hour. Sloane was a party girl at heart and had some adventurous nights with these ladies in the past, but over the past few years, had become pretty conservative. She could cut loose a little tonight and the prospect of it had her excited.

I've got that LBD in the back of my closet that should still fit. Sloane couldn't recall the last time she'd worn it outside of a friend's bachelorette party last year.

She wasn't in the life she had expected. It wasn't all that bad, but she felt as though something has been missing from her overall happiness. She wasn't in IT or even close to it. It was almost like she's begging for a night off from a butcher store and at times she was downright lonely. She had Rae, but it was a little pathetic how she still lived with her mom. Even if it was by choice.

Sloane's mom had been diagnosed about three years ago now. She was given a few months at the most. Sloane had come back home to take care of her. Yet another reason why the butcher shop made sense. Rae's house was only a few blocks from the store. She wouldn't be more than two minutes away in the case of an emergency. The prognosis to begin with was bleak. Doctors couldn't really get a handle on it. Inevitably they landed on the diagnosis of a rare form of Lupus. However, because she was experiencing other symptoms typically not associated with the disease, it took them too long to diagnose it properly and her kidneys were nearly destroyed. The experts gave her about a twenty-five percent chance of living more than six months and an eight percent chance at living another five years. She had a cane. At times she would use a walker to get around the house.

That stubborn old bird wouldn't give up. Rae was a hero for her daughter and Sloane was Rae's inspiration to keep fighting. Sloane used to tell her mom she was too tough to die. Eventually after the initial shock of it all they were able to discuss it in a lighthearted manner.

Rae had been pushing her daughter to move out on her own now for the past couple of months. Sloane kept imagining the day after she got moved in to a new spot would be the day she'd get a call from the hospital. She'd shared her fears with her mom who chuckled.

"Stop being so damn dramatic! I'm fine, the doctors don't know what's going on anymore. It hasn't matriculated any further. I'm not going to put my life on pause and you shouldn't either. I'm getting on in years, Sloane, you have your whole life ahead of you. Go live it."

Sloane would laugh it off, but she knew she was serious and probably right. "Damn right I'm right" was always one of those Raeisms that would bring a bright smile to her daughter's face. "Thank God you got your daddy's teeth and the rest is me. After all, that is my only imperfection." Her teeth weren't bad, but Sloane's were darn near perfect.

Snapping back to reality, Sloane pulled into her driveway. *I'll wear my black Mary Jane's with the dress.* As if Tom Petty himself was her fairy godfather in a crazy déjà vu moment, Mary Jane's Last Dance came on the radio.

No more than fifteen seconds later she could hear a familiar whoop coming from the moon roof Kristi had her head sticking out of. "Sloane!" She had been hoping for a few more minutes to pick up the house a little. Sloane had barely been allowed to unlock the door when Heidi, PG, and Kristi piled on top of her. It had been a few months already since she'd last seen all of them together. They had a quick happy hour after work and most of the subject of conversation was the latest male risqué showing at the theater, which she hadn't been able to see since she'd been working constantly.

Heidi started in immediately, "B, you should call in sick tomorrow now! Better yet, call in dead. You can only do it once, so we'd better make it worth it."

Sloane was a big Heidi fan. She was a five-foot three-inch ginger with girl next door cute looks. Her personality was off the charts. She was strong and could take on the world all by herself. If Sloane's friend group was a tree, Heidi would be the trunk. She was the glue that held them all together. Heidi always entered scene like a hurricane. She's what you would call the life of the party. She also had a swearing problem. If she liked you, from that point forward she would call you one of two things. Bitch or B. B, of course, was short for Bitch.

"No need, ladies, I already took the day off." They looked at each other with double takes, completely befuddled.

PG chimed in, "What got into you? Whatever it is, I hope you've got more, cuz I'm gonna drink you out of it! Either way, game on girls!"

Sloane yelled from the kitchen, "Make yourselves at home, there's beer in the fridge, and I'm going to quickly get ready."

She'd have to scrub for twenty minutes at least to stop smelling like hamburger. *Maybe it wouldn't be quick.*

She got upstairs and began the ritual. It had been so long she wasn't sure she would remember the steps, but she went to it anyhow. She grabbed the black dress in the back of the closet, leaving it on the hanger. She turned on the shower and hung it on the inside of the bathroom door. The steam from the hot water would expedite the wrinkle removing process. She found the Mary Jane's in their box, brand spankin' new. Other than to make sure they fit, they hadn't been worn. It would be a rough night on her feet with new shoes. Her dogs would likely be barking after a couple of hours. Now was as good a time as any to break them in.

Sloane hopped in the shower and tilted her head up to let the hot water pour through her hair. As she was about to run her hands through her hair to help the water through it, she saw her hands and cringed. *I've got man hands! That's what working with a cleaver and getting calluses all day will earn you.* She closed her eyes and enjoyed a few moments of reflective thought and silence under the soothing cascade. Well, beyond the music the girls had cranked up beneath her. The party had already started. A mischievous smile pursed her lips.

She scrubbed extensively, paying special attention to under her fingernails. Sloane lathered and applied the shaving gel to her legs.

She questioned whether to even apply any to her "lady parts" and thought there would be no real reason, but if booze was involved it was better to be safe than sorry.

Slowly stepping out she dried herself off, wrapped her hair in the towel and started reapplying her makeup. If she was only going to go out once in a blue moon, then she was going all out.

They'd likely head out for a cocktail and appetizers at a nearby bar and grill. Too bad it was the dead of winter, there would be no patio drinking tonight.

Minneapolis, like most of the upper Midwest, was brutal in the winter. There were stretches in January where the temperature would start the day in the double digits below zero for weeks on end. It was a balmy twenty above tonight, so she could throw caution to the wind and skip the leggings. As crazy as it sounds, one does get accustomed to these temps. *I'll bet I'd be one of those jacket people in seventy degrees if I lived in Florida. Oh, to have that wonderful problem.*

After taps and tapas they would likely head out to their favorite dance bar. She wouldn't call it a club per se. Those were now old and annoying to her, that was for the younger crowd. The house mix with a base beat thumping so loud you couldn't hear yourself think. It almost made her sick right now to think about.

King's, where they were probably going, always had a live band. They usually covered classic rock, 80's, some 90's and then a few popular pop/rock/party country songs of today. It was her type of place and her type of music. Sure, maybe they'd have a martini earlier in the night, but when she got to the bar to dance she was a whiskey girl. Sloane was never a mean drunk and really couldn't understand people that were. She was a bourbon on the rocks with a splash of water girl. She was very approachable when intoxicated. Cringing about her past male suitors, sometimes too approachable.

They all hopped in the Wrangler. Of course, she would have to be the responsible one at the end of the night. Then again, they could always call an Uber and Heidi could drive her back down to pick it up tomorrow morning. Strict planning wasn't what tonight was about. Sloane looked to her right at Heidi, who was loudly talking a mile a minute and could tell she was already well into tonight's festivities. She decided tomorrow afternoon would work too.

As they were pulling out of the drive PG yelled, "Stop!" She slammed on the brakes barely missing a car and pedestrian, then skidded toward a light post, missing it by mere inches.

"What the hell, woman!" Heidi screamed. Kristi was now in Heidi's lap on the opposite side of the backseat. It all happened faster than a knife fight in a phone booth as Sloane put it.

Was there a car behind them? Sloane thought she'd looked carefully. PG reached around the windshield and removed a flapping obstruction from underneath the wiper blade.

CHAPTER 6

Rebecca was in the middle of her rant when Hayden arrived back at the office.

She glared at him with thunder in her eyes. "Can't you see I'm in the middle of this huge fiasco? Where have you been? Am I the only one that sees how monumental of a screw up this is? This is my butt on the line and I'm not going down for someone else's incompetence! Where is Faith? We need to go over this red ink to see how much this is going to cost us. It sure as hell ain't coming out of my paycheck!" She started in again on Alana, who was somber with her head down.

Hayden said with a very stern but calm voice, "Rebecca, I told Faith to go home. Please follow me to the conference room. I know how to fix this. Do you want to come to a resolution or vent some more? If it's venting, fine, do it with me, in there." Hayden pointed in the direction of the small side room. He headed straight for the conference room. With the door open he sat down and awaited Rebecca.

Six of the seven people on his team were right outside. Rebecca marched straight into the room and started lacing into Hayden, leaving the door wide open for all to hear.

"How dare you undermine my authority? Why would you tell Faith that's she's free to go home? I need her here, now! Who do you think you are and where do you get off? I've been here doing your job while you've been out gallivanting, and you have the nerve to prance in here and tell me what's what?" The rooms were sound-proofed, but she wanted everyone around to know she was in charge.

Hayden gestured toward the chair opposite him. "Would you like some water?" He unscrewed the cap and handed her the bottle from his pocket. It seemed now that filling her mouth was the only way to end her tirade. Then he began dialing a number on the conference room phone and pushed the speaker button.

After a few rings there was an answer. "Kent, its Hayden. Hey, buddy, sincerely sorry to bug you. I know you're on vacay with the fam."

"Hey, Hayden, yeah, we're having a blast."

"How is Jamaica?"

Kent piped up, "Have you ever been?"

"Nope, but it's definitely on my bucket list."

"Well, next time we come down you and your girlfriend will have to come with, and I mean that." Kent knew he didn't have a girlfriend.

Hayden knew this was a two-fer for him. He could not only send Becky into orbit by acting so nonchalantly about what she perceived to be a crisis, but also the break he needed to show her how real business was done. "Does your wife have a sister?"

He could see the rockets igniting at the bridge of Rebecca's nose. It wouldn't be long before she blew her top, the countdown was on. He figured it was about time to reel it in.

"Hey, so the reason I'm calling is we had a bit of a snafu. I think it's a golden opportunity. So, the creative on your ad for next weekend's big sale was incorrect. It says this weekend starting at eight A.M. tomorrow morning. Since your stores are on the west coast it's only four P.M. there now, right? Can you send one of your infamous mass emails to all the store managers and their assistants? Ask them to put the sale stickers out yet tonight before closing. You can make it a two-weekend sale. There's no specific name given to it. It will also serve as a soft opening of sorts for next weekend's big hurrah. Granted it's going to require you putting down your mojito and jerk chicken sandwich for five minutes. With two weekends and hordes of customers running through your stores, ringing those tills, and racking up the black ink, you may be able to extend your stay there another week."

Kent paused for a moment and there was silence on the phone. Rebecca panicked, but Hayden kept his composure. He knew this was the answer. It was a win all the way around. More sales and revenue for the client and an additional insertion event for the company. Which meant big money for them. Better yet, it was very little effort exerted on everyone's behalf. At most there would be a couple of store clerks that were busier than they anticipated tomorrow morning.

They could hear movement on the other end of the line, likely Kent sitting up in his poolside deck chair. "If this takes me six minutes you owe me a drink." The blood drained from Rebecca's face. Through an ear-to-ear grin Hayden followed with "Deal. Make sure you include me on that so I can organize it with my team."

Kent grew serious. "Hayden, great thinking, really. This wasn't your mistake and here you are rectifying it on a Friday night after hours. I appreciate you looking out for us, buddy. I'll get on this right away. Seems straight forward, right? There's nothing I'm missing?"

"No, I've had some time to wrap my head around it and there aren't any loose ends on this. I've seen all the marketing and in-store signage, this takes care of the problem."

"That's good enough for me, now get out of there and have a story for me next week when I get back."

"Will do, chief." Hayden changed his solemnity into a more professional and sincere tone. "Kent, thanks for taking my call. We appreciate you and your business more than you'll ever know. Have a great night." Hayden pushed the end call button.

A couple of times Rebecca started talking and then stopped herself. She was still trying to wrap her head around all of it. After about ten seconds she asked, "I don't know why you didn't tell me, and I could have handled it."

Hayden was calculated, patient, and good with people. It was this trick he learned called treating people like human beings, with a modicum of respect. Anyone that had spent more than a couple minutes with him in his element could tell you he was damn good at his job.

"Rebecca…" He got up and walked out of the room while he held his finger up as if to shush her. He went over to his team, stood in the middle of them and calmly spoke. "Every one of you, thank you. I appreciate the hard work you put in every day here. This company asks a lot of you and I know that I ask even more. Your trust and respect don't go unnoticed. This is a tough business to be in and we excel better than anyone else at doing it. We, together, working collectively, are titans in this industry and you're my A-team. Don't ever question your abilities, because I don't. You know what you're doing, and I am fortunate enough to not only work alongside you but lead you. I am right here in the trenches next to you and will always have your back if you have mine. Tonight I felt it. Thank you for sticking around and helping me deal with this. I know it wasn't easy. Get out of here and have an awesome weekend. You deserve it." as he was about to pivot to the Queen of Mean and continue, the phone on his desk rang.

His team gathered their things as Hayden walked to his desk. They whispered their goodbyes to him with a couple of "good lucks" mixed in for obvious conversation yet to come.

Though he thought it was Kent calling back with a question, it wasn't. It was Dustin, Faith's boyfriend. Hayden never had the pleasure of speaking with him before. He was sure he was calling to thank him for the gift card, which was completely unnecessary. He let him talk for about thirty seconds. All the while Becky was still in the conference room, likely trying to scoop her jaw off the floor. Hayden was riding a high from the previous phone call until he really started focusing on what Dustin was saying about fifteen seconds in.

"Dude, you screwed me. You screwed me so hard. I can't leave here. I had everything planned out. Now what am I supposed to do?" Hayden's smirk slowly dropped, and his face grew dim.

He had made a grave mistake. He was likely going to need the ladders and the hoses in addition to all the fire gear he already had on for this one. "Dustin, don't worry, brother. I'll handle this. You head for Henry's." Hayden hung up the phone and started running for the door.

"Hey!" shouted Rebecca. "We need to discuss this and go over the details. Why did you send them all home? Did I say they could go home?"

Hayden stopped dead in his tracks, then slowly walked back to her. He wanted to take his time with this. "I have only seven words for you, Becky." He knew by calling her that he was pushing it. However, he also knew that by what he had done, he had all but solidified that corner office. The one she currently occupied. So, he didn't care. He threw caution to the wind and ended with "That is how you lead. You're welcome. Oh, and see you Monday, peace!" He threw up his two fingers, turned around, and ran to the elevator. All the while keeping his ears perked for a response that never came.

CHAPTER 7

The girls were in the three-quarter enclosed warming room while Kristi burnt one. They were concocting a plan for the night. For the entire first half hour while they ate and drank at their high-top Kristi, Heidi, and PG grilled Sloane for the juicy details explaining the five bucks. She'd told them the story in a matter of fact way that would lead them to believe she had little to no interest. She even left out the "blue eyes" detail. It didn't work; however, they could read her like a book. It probably didn't help she smiled and blushed through the entire explanation. Sloane didn't dare ask for the bill back yet. She would wait until the end of the night when PG wouldn't remember or care.

Apparently, the ladies were looking good tonight. In Sloane's case especially, she looked like an absolute knock out in her plunging neckline, spaghetti strap, little black dress. Twice in a matter of two hours a group of guys had bought them drinks. The girls joked but were somewhat serious when one of them made the comment about how it was going to be a cheap night for them. Sloane couldn't recall if it was Kristi or Heidi. It was only eight-thirty, but the finer details of the evening were already escaping them. It was going to be a long night and she had better start pacing herself if she was going to make it to bar close at two. After all, her tolerance was all but gone nowadays. Other than an occasional one after work at home, she wasn't too much of a drinker any more. Back in the day she used to be able to put them down and keep up with the best of the boys, but not so much any longer, she would need to continually remind herself of that as the night wore on and maybe mix in a water or two here and there.

The plan was to hit up a few different spots and end up at King's by ten. That's when things really picked up and the big crowds started pouring in.

PG chimed in, "Do we have to go there?"

Sloane was probably the only one that knew the story behind her objection but didn't say anything.

Kristi and Heidi interjected with a resounding and emphatic "Yes!"

They got the check and the girls walked over to the two groups of guys and thanked them for the drinks.

Only in the last group was there one in the bunch outgoing enough to ask for digits. Of course, it was Sloane's he was requesting. The other two rolled their eyes, it was always Sloane's.

Heidi, who was long married with kids said, "Don't you want my number?"

The preppy, popped-collar Chad that had no clue he was severely out of his depth retorted, "Well, you've got a ring on your hand, you're hitched, aren't you?"

"How do you know I don't put this on to keep the riff-raff at bay?"

"I don't, well then, can I have your number?"

"How dare you hit on a married woman!"

He couldn't find the facial muscles to close his mouth. He had to be thinking, what happened? He tried to collect himself. He puffed up his chest as if it never phased him, a cute facade, but this wasn't their first rodeo and the best part of their little bait and switch was yet to come.

The guy always then came back.

"So, the question still stands then, can I have your number?" As if they were out on a girl's day of fishing, which on great occasion they did together, the bass inhaled the minnow. It was time to boat this bad boy.

Sloane looked at Kristi and PG briefly. "How do you know I'm not married and didn't take off my ring?"

His face contorted like he'd been stabbed in the kidney. "C'mon, we're both here for the same reason, right?"

When Sloane reciprocated, nearly a full second had gone by. "Yeah, to pick up chicks, let's go!" She interlocked arms with him as if they were leaving together.

Both tables of guys that had witnessed the exchange lost their minds with laughter. Thankfully, the girls finished their drinks earlier, otherwise they would have been shooting from their noses. For that young man, his buddies would never let him live that down.

Sloane was known amongst her friends as an artist or maybe even a prodigy at these games of dry humor and wit. It wasn't by chance her silver tongue devilishly charmed Hayden earlier tonight. She had always been quick with a quip, rapid on the rebuttal. Her girlfriends all thought she should use her powers for good with a way to monetarily capitalize on it, like greeting cards, or a gossip column.

It never mattered how Heidi set them up. Sloane was the heavyweight and she never failed to deliver the old one-two combo.

"Good luck, I know when I'm around this many hot women I can't think straight, know what I mean?" She landed the uppercut.

The girls with tears in their eyes grabbed her by the arm and started pushing her for the door. His party posse couldn't breathe through their crowing. It was going to be a long night.

CHAPTER 8

Hayden had circled the block of the restaurant twice. He was running short on time, so he had to pay to park, and it was going to cost him twenty bucks since it was an event night. Harden, Westbrook, and the Rockets were in town playing the T-wolves. He'd have to high tail it over to The American Grille; the restaurant Dustin had originally made reservations for.

Tonight was a big night for the two of them. He wasn't going to be even partially responsible for screwing it up. Dustin had planned the old put the engagement ring into the dessert trick. A little cliché, yes, but it was his plan and his choice. Yeah, he had intended to propose. Then Hurricane Becky came in and decimated everything in its path. Well, when FEMA, a.k.a. Hayden came in with a $500 gift card to another restaurant it doubly compounded the issue at hand. It was now Hayden's job to get the ring, somehow sneak into the back door of Henry's, explain the whole situation to the chef, and see if he could somehow rebuild the island in minutes.

Okay, Hayden, enough with the metaphor. Like earlier with the meat mistress, it was getting way too thin. He shook his head again. *Boneless bonnet, pfft.*

He looked at his phone, she should have seen the Lincoln note he left her by now. Was she playing coy, maybe not interested? He knew he felt the chemistry, surely there had been fireworks for her as well. She did after all notice his eye color. *No time to worry about yourself.* He knew he needed to get a move on and picked up his jogging pace.

Hayden arrived and confirmed there had been a recent cancellation for a Dustin Sharper. He discovered he would need to pay for the lava cake the ring was buried in. It was another twenty bucks! He also burnt his finger nearly to the point of blistering it trying to dig the ring out. He licked off his fingers and shouted over his back "my compliments to the chef!" and was gone. Henry's was only four blocks away, but he had no way to communicate with Dustin and not possibly give away the surprise.

He was calculating the math and time. It took him over an hour and a half to get down here thanks to a pile up from a crash on ninety-four. It took twenty minutes to park and get to the restaurant. By the time he parked it was already nearly eight thirty. He got the ring, cleaned it thoroughly, and was out with a nearly boiled off appendage by ten to nine. It should have taken an hour for the line, but with the ballgame people probably came early tonight.

"Damn," he exclaimed.

If he only had to wait say half an hour that put them right in the middle of their main course if they had an appetizer first, which he's assuming they did. Then again, maybe Dustin couldn't eat. Hayden knew he wouldn't be able to with all the somersaults his gut would have been turning. It's a stressful night for a guy, or so his buddies had told him. I'm hoping he bought me some time with wine or champagne. Lord knows he had enough money to cover it. *Hayden, you're over analyzing this. Get there and deal with it as it comes. You need to relax sometimes.* He started to sprint.

Hayden ran to the alley behind Henry's, making sure to steer clear of the line out front. He could see they weren't in line. He had been hoping they were still waiting to get in. Out back there were two cooks smoking. He walked up to them and by picking up on their conversation he assessed that unfortunately neither spoke English. So, in his broken Spanglish they were able to point him through the door.

He walked in and it was a bustle of a dozen or so people running around like heads with their chickens cut off. He didn't know much about the culinary arts, but he figured starting with the guy who had the tallest hat was a good place to start.

He explained his predicament and luckily the chef was more than happy to help. Actually, his exact words were, "Are you kiddin' me? Sappy love stories are my life." He had Hayden point out the couple and then turned and yelled for Tony. A guy that looked like a Tony came over to talk to the chef. Tony was waiting tables six through ten tonight. Chef asked him where they were in the meal. Tony said he had just handed them their dessert menus. Tony and the chef, Hayden never did get his name, started to conspire.

Tony walked out into the dining room. He asked them if he knew what they wanted, because if they didn't, he had a fantastic recommendation that he would make special for them and then winked at Dustin. He picked up on the hint. Luckily, Faith did not. So far, so good.

There was only one little hiccup, Faith had her mind and palette set on the restaurant's twist of a pineapple upside down cake. It was one of their specialties and very popular amongst returning patrons, but definitely not ideal for their situation. There was no real way to shove it inside without demolishing the delicacy and pretty much giving away the surprise.

Tony looked in Faith's direction. "Are you sure you don't want the Baked Alaska?" It was easy to put the ring in the meringue, there was a lot of it, and it was a quick wipe down of the jewelry after. He had done it many times before.

Politely, but also unfortunately, she wouldn't budge. "I've heard great things about the pineapple upside down cake. My girlfriend said it was to die for."

"Well, it or you, may kill me." Tony whispered under his breath.

"I'm sorry." Faith leaned toward him. "What was that?"

Tony came back "The upside-down cake it is." He returned to the kitchen and reported the failure. Luckily, the chef concocted an ingenious back-up plan.

. . .

Since their cakes were premade every morning, it required a finishing chilled vanilla drizzle on top for that artistic flair. It looked good. Tony brought it out to the couple along with two forks to share. Tony was the stereotypical short Italian guy with dark facial features and even darker hair. He had a thick bushy mustache and hair that was out of control from wiping sweat from his brow all night. As he put the cake down, the pineapple was placed on the bottom of the delicacy.

She asked, "Isn't the fruit supposed to be on the top? Isn't that why it's called upside-down cake?"

Dustin saw this whole little production unfolding. He slowly slithered out of his chair and proceeded to act as if he was tying his shoe. Meanwhile Tony was acting frustrated and buying Dustin time. She didn't see him move. Hayden was watching the fiasco through the small circular window in the door with every finger he had crossed.

Tony then made a big scene and boy could he act. It may have been academy award-worthy. He flew off the handle, "Miss, I think I know how our specialty dessert is supposed to be served! You want it upside-down? Then fine, you'll get it upside down!" At that moment he took the plate and flipped it, smashing it on the tabletop food down and plate on top. "There, happy?" With that he took the plate with him and headed back to the kitchen with his nose in the air.

By this time everyone in the restaurant had witnessed the scene unfold and were silently glaring at the two of them. It was as if she couldn't register what was happening and why he had become so upset. A blank look crossed her face and then she looked down and saw the fruit on top of the cake, on top of the table. And on top of that, was something else.

She picked it up with a baffled expression and someone grabbed her hand. It was Dustin, he was on his knees. *Why was he...?*

"Oh my God! Oh my God, oh my god, oh my God! Yes, yes, yes Dustin, yes!" She jumped on him, showering him with kisses and hugging the life right out of him before he could even open his mouth. People all over the dining room applauded.

Tony brought her a replacement piece of cake with a mischievous smile to boot.

Hayden exhaled.

CHAPTER 9

A sweaty mess. That's what he was. In addition to the sprint to the restaurant and the stress of that whole charade, it was really sweltering in a restaurant kitchen. That was why they have the old adage. He was on the cusp of not being able to handle the heat. Hayden proceeded to shake the hands of the entire cast of their little play, each bowing in turn.

Hayden then retreated out back to the alleyway. While breathing a sigh of relief all he could think was *I need a drink!*

Not only did he think it, he stated it out loud. The two smokers that directed him earlier pointed to the bar with the familiar neon sign next door and one of them said the single best Spanish word in the English dictionary. "Cerveza". *Well, if it isn't in Merriam-Webster, it should be.*

Yep, that was where he was headed and stumbled, as if peeling off imaginary coveralls and a helmet. The day was over, and the infernos were officially doused.

All-in-all, it was an amazing day, but physically and mentally he was beyond spent. He bellied up to the bar, held up his hand, and vegged out to the Timberwolves game over head. It was nearing the end of the third quarter and they were down by twenty-two, *typical*.

It was after ten now and he knew he should be home in bed. Especially if he wanted to get up early and head for the cabin.

Hell, I'm all packed. I'll finish my beer, take off now, and surprise him. Andy and I can hit the slopes at the crack of dawn like we planned.

His adrenaline was still pumping from the fire next door. He would probably be tired, but awake. After all, it was their tradition to be out on the slopes first. It's a well-known fact that the early morning powder after a fresh snowfall is the best and the forecast called for that in Lutsen tonight.

There was a band in-house tonight. They had been on break in between sets when he walked in. On any other night he would be down, but tonight he needed some peace and quiet. He slapped a five down on the table and waved so long to the bartender.

He was probably half way up the block when someone ran out of the bar, it was the same bartender. He yelled to Hayden, "Hey, you shorted me four bucks!"

It had totally escaped his mind he was downtown. *I can't catch a break. Can anything go my way tonight?*

He trudged back to the bar. Hayden apologized profusely and paid him not only the four he'd shorted him, but another fiver on top to show him he was a good sport and wasn't attempting to dine and ditch, or drink and dodge in this case.

"Now you come up with the wit," he murmured under his breath.

As Hayden was getting up and putting away his cash two loud girls stumbled up to him in time to peek at the stash in his wallet.

One of them hollered, "Well, hello, Mr. Moneybags, are you all alone?"

Great, just what he needed to cap the day.

CHAPTER 10

They had hit Grumpy's, J's, and The Acropolis. They were lame and lamer. Those were Heidi's words, not Sloane's, but she couldn't argue with the assessment. They were pretty dead. A jukebox and a few stragglers here and there. The ladies were out tonight for the two Ds, dancing and drinking! Not necessarily in that order. It was time for the main event, King's.

PG said she was ditching out after buying them one last beer at J's; claiming she was buzzed and needed to get home because she had to work tomorrow.

Kristi said, "Oh sure, now you buy a round once it's two for ones and it only costs you eight bucks!"

PG's responded. "Mama didn't raise no fool."

Sloane knew the real reason why she was done for the night. King's was her ex-boyfriend's regular spot. Coincidently it was where she had met him. PG was afraid she would run into him and wouldn't be able to look him in the eye after what had happened. She left before the Acropolis to not raise any suspicions.

Kristi had thought one of the boys at the Acropolis was cute. Apparently, *she* was out for a third D. She was getting to the point of agreeing to go home with him when Captain Cock Block flew onto the scene.

Heidi tied her coat around her neck, jumped in between them, and shouted her new title in his face. "Rookie mistake, not buying her friends drinks to grease the rails, that's straight up bush league! Captain Cock Block says no soup for you!"

A combo of random idiom, Ron Burgundy and Soup Nazi, impressive Sloane thought. She was crying so hard she nearly peed herself.

The combination of cold and Sloane's need for a restroom had them shuffling their little designer footwear as fast as they could to King's. Kristi was almost incoherently hollering at Heidi, "Why didn't you let me go with him? Over a drink?"

"Of course not. Who knows what that muscle-bound ape and his buddies were going to do to you tonight, I love you and you're my sister. We've gotta watch out for each other!"

"So, the drink?"

The biggest smile crossed Heidi's face. "I mean come on, you're not even gonna move up to double A ball cheating the game that way!"

Kristi was doubled over in laughter. Sloane wanted to laugh but didn't dare. They had a lot of booze tonight and twice as many laughs.

"This is what it's all about!" Kristi shouted as she brought them both in for a hug. "These are my sisters and I love them all!" She may have had one too many too.

Before they got to the door, they made a pact. If a guy was alone and bought both her and Heidi a drink, Kristi could go home with him. She was at the horny stage of drunk and once she was there, there was no stopping her until that thirst was quenched…or she puked.

The bouncer outside checked their IDs and stamped them. Even though they had gotten there a little earlier than expected the place was already hopping. The room had a light stale smokiness to it as it had been a favorite dive bar to many a smoker. Until legislation put an abrupt end to it. There was tight red plastic fabric pulled over all the booths and stools. It was everywhere. Gold flairs accented all the trims throughout the place, including the rivets in the red plastic.

They were going for an eclectic late 60's to early 70's diner aesthetic. It was nearly pulling it off. This place's appeal had nothing to do with the décor. People of all makes and models were dancing in the middle of a giant wooden parquet floor. The band sounded great and they needed a drink.

Sloane headed straight for the powder room. Heidi and Kristi were circling the bar trying to find an open seat where they could grab a drink and wait for Sloane. A tall, dark, handsome, yet disheveled young man stood up and started combing through a stack of bills.

"Hey Heidi!" Kristi waved emphatically trying to get her attention. "Look." The duo made eye contact as Kristi pointed at the dude with the devilish dimples. "Two birds, one stone!" she exclaimed.

They walked right up to him and Kristi shouted so he could hear her over the band, "Well, hello, Mr. Moneybags. Are you all alone?"

"Yes, but you can have my seat, I was headed out." He smiled at them as he held his arms out to their sides.

"You're going to flash me those piercing peepers and leave?"

"I tell you what," He grabbed another twenty out of his wad of cash and laid it down with the other five. This night was really running up a tab for him that he personally wasn't taking advantage of. "Here's a few bucks, have a couple on me."

Kristi looked right at Heidi, who rolled her eyes. Heidi checked the time on her phone. She would bite and play "wing-woman" one more time.

Heidi stepped up. "What about me, aren't you going to buy me a drink?"

"That should cover at least one for both of you..." He leaned toward her and tilted his head slightly.

"Heidi," she yelled over the roar of the bar crowd. "My name is Heidi."

"Well, Heidi, I know this sounds a bit forward, but I'd love to offer you a ride home since I was already leaving."

"What makes you think I'm going home with you?"

"I'm sure your husband would appreciate a sober driver for his wife to get home safely, right?"

"How do you know I'm not wearing this ring to keep away the riff-raff?"

"I didn't even see the ring, but there's no way a catch like you isn't already taken. I bet you even have a couple of adorable rugrats at home. I'd even go so far as to guess that's your family picture on the lock screen of your phone."

Busted.

Hayden Foster was six-foot-four and had a perfectly symmetrical face. In high school he was boney and gawky looking. A couple of years ago he had grown into those features by adding contours and muscle definition to his now fit frame. His nose was slender and there was a gentleness to his smile which perfectly complimented his rugged good looks. Hayden had a short beard, but more than a simple five o'clock shadow. His Danish heritage was obvious. Had he trimmed the side of his head, Hayden would have made a gorgeous Viking. In a few years he would be the perfect nominee for a silver fox award. All of this with that black hair, those killer indentations, and painfully piercing blue eyes. It created a perfect package. It seemed he was packing one of those as well. In tight dark gray dress slacks and a light blue button up dress shirt, what wasn't to like?

"I'll go home with you." Kristi shouted above the loud venue.

He laughed wholeheartedly. "That wasn't the offer. Where are you ladies most nights when I'm down here on the prowl? Yes, by the way, that's my way of saying I come here often. Actually, I'll take both of you home if you need a ride, where do you live?"

Heidi wobbled. "Nice try, Mr. Smooth Operator, but the second we get in the car with you we're all headed back to your place, right?"

"That would be a wonderful scenario for me in theory, but I don't think either one of you would be awake when we got back there. Besides, I know if you were my wife I would want to think there were guys out there who didn't necessarily have an agenda and could give a beautiful woman a ride home without any strings attached. Chivalry isn't dead."

They wanted him, they both did, equally. Heidi stammered, "Okay, we'll go home with you, but you have to have me back to my house to make pancakes for the kids by eight at the very latest!" They all had a good laugh.

Hayden turned to Kristi and asked for her name. As she was about to give it somewhere in the back came "Hayden?" Kristi looked at him and sputtered "I didn't say that. That's not my name!" She whirled around and saw her friend. "Sloan-e!" Kristi waved excitedly.

"Come here and meet this handsome young gentleman. We never did get your name stranger." Kristi was now on the full court press.

Hayden dramatically perked up scanning the crowd for the origin of his name. There were a lot of heads behind them. Kristi hugged someone and they both approached.

Hayden realized why he couldn't pick out the head that had hollered his name. Because last time he hadn't seen it either. It had been in a hairnet.

It's her. Her hair was a very dark red. It completed the retro, cherry-dress, 1950's pin-up look. She had on a breathtaking little black dress on with a small slit up the side that revealed what appeared to be a long side-body tattoo. Of what he really couldn't make out, but he already knew he liked it. Here he was looking like a slob, likely with sweat stains on his shirt, which was untucked, and she looked... *She looks more stunning than I ever could have imagined under that apron.*

"You know," she said, "every time I see you it seems like you're salivating over a piece of meat." This time she was referring to Kristi.

Heidi was completely and utterly dumbfounded. Kristi was intoxicated and in la-la land.

"Hi, Hayden," came the sultry voice of Sloane.

"Hayden?" Heidi blurted. "As in $5 Hayden? Wow, boy, she didn't do you justice. You were downplaying the hell out of him, you saucy minx!"

Sloane turned a shade that resembled her hair and gave Heidi the laser eye stare as if to say, "Shut up!"

Sloane piped up, "Did you get your inferno extinguished then, fireman?" The slightly deep, smooth, and alluring way she'd said it nearly dropped Hayden's jaw to the floor.

He chuckled nervously and looked away. There were those intriguingly sexy dimples she remembered. Sloane was transported back to five hours ago when she'd felt like a lovesick teenager ogling over a celebrity heartthrob.

"Funny you should bring that up, I think I got some smoke inhalation from the blaze I put out next door." Came in here to clean my system so as to not incur any long-lasting damage. I heard alcohol is good for that. Health first you know."

Sloane stood a few feet away. Hayden could physically feel the distance as if it were a canyon he would have to shout across. Sloane was in front of him. Heidi was to his left and Kristi was all over him. *Don't screw this up, remember, you've got a leg up here Hayden.* Thankfully, she'd obviously been drinking all night so hopefully it had slowed her sharp-witted reflexes.

Sloane jabbed. "I've found extensive mouth-to-mouth helps clear the lungs." *Nope, that idea flew out the window, she's still sharp as a tack.* Hayden was hoping there would be a round two to their repartee and there were no ifs, ands, or buts about it. She was flirting.

Hayden instantly started fake coughing into his fist. "Do you know of anyone that could help me with that?"

She smiled shyly and looked at the ground while working the toe of her cute black shoes in a small circular motion. He picked up what she was laying down. She was toying with him.

She fired back, "Kristi seems more than happy to help you out there." Before she could finish the sentence, Hayden realized Kristi's hand was rubbing his chest. Heidi smacked her hand and Hayden's chest incurred some collateral slap damage.

Kristi howled. "Ow, what was that for? Remember, we had a deal and he bought you a drink. What more do you want woman?"

Heidi's eyes lit up, "Kristi, this is Hayden."

Kristi shot back, "Yep, we've already established that!"

Heidi grabbed her by the arms and shook her while yelling at her like she was slow; one foot from her face. "Kristi, remember earlier, Hayden?"

At that moment Hayden realized what was going on here. Sloane was under the impression that he was hitting on Kristi and being the great friend that she was, she didn't want to interfere. After all, how could she know that he didn't randomly give out his number to any girl that would take it?

Hayden needed to set the record straight. *This isn't going to be one of those chick-flick back and forth will they/won't they moments. Only for them to eventually hook up in the final thirty seconds. I hate those movies.*

Sloane was far too amazing to be limited to half a minute. Too incredible not to be direct and honest with. He was always playing the game by holding back. He didn't want to do that here, not with her, not now. He was desperate and he didn't care if she knew it. Especially since he'd blown it earlier today. At least he had to try. He wasn't going to let this moment escape him so he could regret it for the rest of his life.

"Ladies, my name is Hayden Foster. It's a pleasure to meet you Heidi, Kristi, and Sloane, was it?" He subtly winked at her at the same time. "I am the gentleman that had the privilege of meeting your girl earlier tonight. Just so you know Sloane, I was offering to give your friends here a ride to their homes. I wasn't trying to pick them up. I'm sure they're amazing. Besides, I think they were having fun toying with me."

Both ladies flushed.

"I should have asked you for your number earlier today and had every intention of doing so when you reminded me I needed to rush back to work. You absolutely captivated me, and maybe that's sort of corny, but I really thought we had something there. Hopefully, you felt it too."

He paused to let the words linger in the air as if searching for an answer that wouldn't come. "You are impressively witty. I would love to verbally spar with you in the future. But for right now, tonight, and especially after the day I've had; I will not beat around the bush. I like you, Sloane."

The three girls looked at each other like wide-eyed new born pups.

Hayden persevered. "And not in an 'I like you tonight' sort of way either. I'd love to get to know you or hell, learn your last name. I realize that your ability for word play can likely be attributed to a defense mechanism. I want you to know candidly, upfront, I would love nothing more than to sit and talk to you."

The trio stared on, as if riveted by him. Hayden writhed as the silence made him queasy. He had spilled his heart and soul onto the floor, and he hoped someone would say something or at least help him mop them up.

Heidi was the first to respond, "Well, I'm sold! I hope your dirty laundry pile is near your front door. Because my thong is soaked!" That more than cut the tension.

Sloane stopped and peered intently at him. "Are you for real?"

"Yes, Sloane, completely real and standing here with my guts hanging out." Only then did she realize she had said that out loud and blushed.

Kristi chimed in, "Please tell me you have a brother."

Sloane had no response, none at all. No quick comeback, no verbal jab, she stood there staring at him. That was the second time he'd done that tonight. He needed to work on his communication skills. Hayden felt more vulnerable than he had ever before. That was probably the most honest he'd ever been with a girl and he had only known her for maybe a total of ten minutes.

"Can you say something, please?" Hayden pleaded.

"How about I do?" Heidi spoke up. "Kristi, let's go find that guy for you to go home with out on the dance floor. You know, where the guys are using childish cheesy pick-up lines and not crossing the boundaries of comprehension and ridiculous honesty. Before we do though, can I say thank you?"

"You're more than welcome for the drink. If you hadn't come up to me, I might never have seen her again. I couldn't have been that lucky twice in my life. So, let me instead thank you."

Heidi interjected, "Not for the drink. For restoring my faith in the male gender."

Hayden grew beet red. Heidi had Kristi in tow. They leaned against each other whispering undoubtedly about him and looking back as they headed to the dance floor. Hayden half-heartedly watched them for an excessive amount of time before gathering the intestinal fortitude to turn and face the firing squad. The girls were already "getting their groove on" with a couple of guys by the time Hayden turned back to Sloane.

He had the shakes. One beer couldn't have affected him that bad. *C'mon, Hayden, get it together. You can do this. You have conversations with forty different people every day. What's one more?* He was frightened out of his mind to face her after what he had said.

Sloane appeared to be truly struggling. She was always guarded, always had to be. A few different sharp comebacks formed on her lips, and she bit her tongue and swallowed every one of them. She stared at his face from top to bottom and straight into those arctic blue eyes.

"By the way," he said, "I've never done that before."

Finally, Sloane thought, *something I can work with.*

"Bought meat?" she quipped. He could tell she was still holding back. She instantly saw it in his face. "I'm sorry, Hayden, it came out. It's a natural reflex." Looking down, she whispered, "I'll have to work on that."

"Sloane," he said with a put-you-at-ease timbre in his voice and she loved the way he said it. "It's fine, I don't want you to feel like you should be anyone other than yourself around me. I want to meet the real you." He stalled for a moment. "I know this is going to sound like a line, but I promise it's not. I think there's a lot to you and I would do anything to learn it all. Hayden stopped because he heard exactly how cliché that sounded. He gritted his teeth and balled his fists in frustration. *Why was this so hard?*

He wanted to hand her his heart on a silver platter. *Here, it's yours. Do with it as you please.* Then again, that would have freaked her out and she would have run for the hills. *I want to blurt everything out, and yet I can't.*

"I saw that." Sloane had seen him stop himself and retreat.

He was so vulnerable. "Saw what?" He swallowed hard.

Sloane's face softened. Her nose that had been scrunched in confusion now relaxed. "I saw you stop yourself, please don't, not on my behalf. Look, I'm sorry, and that's the last time I'm ever going to apologize to you." Hayden cracked a smirk. "Can I first say, wow? I don't mean that in a 'you're a weirdo and frightening me because you've overshared' way. I mean wow as in, how did you do that? How did you open yourself up to a perfect stranger? I could never do that." She paused. "Or at least I thought I couldn't."

He saw her eyes moving rapidly left to right as if sorting through all of this, looking for validation from him.

Hayden sensed she was dipping her toe in the water to test the temperature and confirmed, "I want to talk. If you want a drink, I'll buy you one, but not for any reason."

She raised her hand between them. "I'll take a water."

They moved over to the corner of the bar and sat down in a booth across from each other. He reflected for a minute trying to gather what he had wanted to say. He stared down at an overlapping boomerang like pattern that graced the diner style tabletops strewn around the place.

"This doesn't have to be like dead serious conversation. I wasn't trying to be overly dramatic. I am tired of the games. I don't want this to be cheap and meaningless like that. Does that make sense?" – Hayden asked.

"Yes, it makes complete sense." She saw him exhale in relief. "Outside of this conversation I would have said you were nuts or trying out some new angles to pick me up, but I think I can sense your sincerity. I'm not necessarily hesitant, I don't know where to start. This is totally uncharted territory for me."

"Huh." Hayden chuckled. "Me too. This may be hard for you to entertain, but I've never left my number on a strange girl's vehicle. I don't do that. Sure, I've tried to pick up girls before, but I want your number, not your digits. It all sounds rehearsed or contrived when I say it to you, and I feel like I keep coming across that way."

She jumped at her chance to reaffirm that she was feeling what he was, "It doesn't. At least I know what you're trying to say, even if it does have a slick pitch."

"Blame it on the day job I guess."

"So, wait, you're not a real fireman?" A salacious little smirk crossed Hayden's face. Somehow she could be entirely sincere, yet a smart ass at the same time. She briefly covered his hand with her own. "Really, I'm genuinely interested, what do you do?"

Over the next three hours Sloane Knox and Hayden Foster sat in that corner booth and they were the only two people on the planet.

Equal in passion, they craved to learn everything there was to know about one another. Through Hayden's ever-deepening infatuation he knew it was going to be tough to honor the strictly verbal promise he made. Sloane couldn't keep a straight face anytime he smiled. He was literally melting her. They talked. Like really, truly talked. They hadn't looked away from each other in hours other than a couple of restroom breaks. Sloane and Hayden discussed where they were from, family and friends, funny stories, everything really. Including her last name. They had laughed so hard they couldn't find their next breath numerous times. Sloane couldn't remember having had a better time, relating to another human being, ever. She practically pissed herself, so she'd said, when Hayden told her about his crazy day. Then the way he verbally illustrated Faith's face and how happy she was had Sloane swooning.

She was more than a little smitten. He was still handsome, but no longer a stranger. Looking back now Sloane realized a lot of time must have passed since she and Hayden had covered so many topics. Their ability to lose themselves in one another was positively simple.

Heidi came over near their table one time a couple hours ago and mouthed "Are you alright?"

Sloane had looked so serious at the time. She was stone sober by now after seven consecutive large glasses of water and nothing else.

She nodded with a look in her eyes that said, "I'm more than alright." It was almost the same look that means "Holy Shit!" They were darn near interchangeable.

It seemed as if no more than twenty minutes had passed and the bouncers were shouting, "Last call for alcohol! You've got time for one last song and drink."

They both stood up as if to leave. Hayden put his jacket on. Sloane picked up her scarf, then promptly abandoned it again on the tabletop; as the first few bars of the song's acoustic guitar began. She took three steps toward the dance floor, pivoted, then turned back to him. She bowed and extended her right hand in invitation. He eagerly threw down his coat and accepted. She led the way, holding his hand behind her. As she approached the edge of the dance floor Hayden placed his hand on top of hers and lifted both arms above their heads to twirl her around into place for a slow dance.

"Look at you, Mr. Astaire."

He gave her a cheeky grin. "Oh, I don't know about that, but I do love this song."

Sloane laughed and shook her head. "Of course you do." It landed on him in a way that left him questioning whether to be offended by the comment. He opened his mouth to refute her assumptive judgment as she tilted her mouth within an inch of his left ear and began softly singing the first few bars.

Hayden's head jerked back from her. His astonished look made her laugh. She yanked him back to where their cheeks nearly met, needing a barrier between her and his eyes if she even stood a chance of continuing. She whispered the last line before the chorus, with a seductive emphasis on the word "explodes".

"You're going to make me explode, woman!" He jokingly retreated about a foot from her. "Leave room for Jesus, ya trollop!"

She backed away from him and put her hand to her mouth as if offended. Then doubled over in laughter.

Hayden pulled her close again. They swayed in unison.

Her head went to his shoulder. "Trollop?"

He couldn't help but grin. "It was a choice."

"What was the other option?"

"Strumpet actually."

"See, there you go. I'd much rather be a strumpet than a trollop!"

"Aren't they the same thing?"

"Not even close. You could never confuse a trollop with my favorite brass instrument! While you're at it you might as well strap a boneless bonnet on me and…" She got cut off by Kristi as the lights came on. "Sloan-E! They ended with a cover of your song!"

Sloane blushed at Hayden. "That *Pogues* song is a favorite."

The bouncer hollered, "You ain't gotta go home, but you can't stay here. Everybody out!"

The two girls now hollered at them, both heaving and sweaty. They were still talking about their fun, the guys, and how loaded they both were. Heidi whispered to Kristi.

Kristi snuggled up to Hayden and put her arm around his waist in a lighthearted manner. "Hayden, baby, can we schtill take you up on that ride —" *hiccup* "— home?" Sloane almost bust a gut.

Hayden held out both elbows out to offer as an escort for the drunken twosome. "It would truly be my honor ladies, it's a little bit of a jaunt back to my vehicle, but the fresh air will probably do you good."

Heidi spoke in a sarcastic tone, "So jus whashes that mean, you think we're, I'm drunk?" She could hardly get it out without laughing. "K, so mayyyybe we're a tittle bit lipsy."

The two girls stumbled in front of them on the sidewalk back to the parking garage. All the while Sloane and Hayden talked through chattering teeth.

It was nearly a quarter after two when they arrived back at Hayden's Yukon. Had it been summer it would have been the perfect night to roll down the windows driving through the now nearly empty city streets. It was about as far from summer as you could get though. At present it was maybe ten above.

Hayden dropped Kristi and Heidi at Kristi's house up in Maple Grove, about a half hour from downtown at this time of the night. They were both passed out within five minutes of entering the front door. Sloane was down in Plymouth by the shop he had met her at earlier.

As they were backing from Heidi's driveway Hayden scratched his cheek. "How did you girls get downtown?"

"I drove," explained Sloane, "but don't get any ideas, mister."

"I wouldn't dream of it." He smirked.

"I wanted to have some more investigation time to make sure you weren't a serial killer." She smiled.

"Your idea was to trust a complete stranger you met a couple of hours ago when the fewest witnesses are out in public?" Hayden chuckled.

"I wouldn't say we're exactly strangers anymore, would you?"

They both flushed in embarrassment.

Hayden reached over the console and touched her hand. She wrapped her fingers around it, lifted his hand up and kissed the back of it. He was on cloud ten and couldn't wipe the expression from his face. Sloane caught it out of the corner of her eye. Bemused, she thought, *this must be what content feels like.*

CHAPTER 11

❄

Hayden was headed back to the interstate when he drove right past the on-ramp.

Sloane pointed. "You know you missed 494, right?"

"Yep, I did." He laughed.

She cocked that gorgeous eyebrow again as he turned into Perkins. "If you're thinking you're going to ply me with pancakes and I'll put out…" she said it with fervor.

He leaned in. He was no more than six inches from her face and grinned. "We have to have our first breakfast together sometime."

She was in a lot of trouble. *Can men really be like this?*

They sank down opposite each other into yet another booth. Hayden was looking at the décor. They'd used about every hue of green possible in the carpet. There were only two other tables with patrons. *I bet they're all here to soak up the night's booze to lessen the blow come hangover time tomorrow.* Hayden's assumptions were likely correct.

Sloane was rifling through the menu and specials. The two of them sat and drank coffee, and both ordered large breakfasts. She had shoved a huge bite of her short stacks into her face when she looked up with a full mouth and saw him staring at her with a contorted face.

"What, don't you like a girl with a healthy appetite?" Somehow, she was able to get the words past the spongy decadence.

Through a giggle and a look of adoration he stated, "I love them, I was wondering how you breathe. Is it like a snake thing and you unhinge your jaw?"

"Oh, you've got jokes! I can't help it, I'm starving. All I had all day yesterday was some appetizers. I had annoying guys hitting on me all day in the store and didn't even have time for a stick of jerky."

"So, there was more than one? Not surprising, I hope you verbally assaulted them too."

"Why do you think we have a ticket dispenser that says roaster? It ain't a line for cooked meat."

There's that saucy banter I love so much.

They continued to share and entertain each other. Once she allowed him to open up and relax, he didn't disappoint. He was smart, funny, and charming. Hayden lifted his straw and ripped the end off.

"Don't. You. Dare." Sloane's eyes widened as she looked around, anticipating a paper projectile popping her in the face in the not-too-distant future when she was least expecting it.

"Relax, it's not what you're thinking. Care for a friendly competition?" With that he picked up her straw as well and tore it.

With an inquisitorial look she held out her hand and Hayden gave her the clear plastic portion while he shimmied the paper slightly to allow for air.

"Loser buys."

Sloane was a gamer. Not an actual console video game gamer. She was competitive and loved playing games. "Ooo, I like it! What are the terms?"

"Purely distance."

"Here I thought you were going to make it interesting and I'd get a kiss or something if I hit Flo in the perm over there." She blushed. Hayden's loud cackle embarrassed them both.

He skipped over the comment as if it never happened to ease the tension. "Longest distance gets a free meal. Ladies first."

As she puffed her cheeks after she had filled her lungs a busboy came out of the kitchen and cut off the path she had chosen. It caused them both to roar. After regaining her composure, she adjusted her trajectory and launched it. The girl had pipes. The paper dart traveled a good twenty-five to thirty feet across the restaurant unseen and landed under a row of tables.

"Alright, you're up, Skippy." Sloane liked this banter they had going. It was easy and she appreciated it.

He shot back a look of distaste like a toddler being forced to eat broccoli. "Skippy?"

Sloane shrugged. "It was a choice."

Hayden inhaled and exhaled quickly through puckered lips. The breath he expelled was a bit too concentrated. He blew the back of the wrapper out. A dud.

"Poor guy. I hope that's not indicative of other things." She winked and laughed.

"Stunning Meat Mistress two, blowhard sleep-deprived slob one."

Sloane picked up the menu "what section do you think the caviar is in?"

He winced in pain. "Nothing like rubbing salt in the wound."

Their flirty banter was easier than breathing. She was completely engaged and hung on his every word. He had this storytelling quality about himself that caught her having to remind herself to close her mouth. She thought, he must be good at his job because she could listen to him read the phone book for hours. Her favorite of his stories included Andy. He sounded like quite the character.

She cut him off mid-conversation, "So, Hayden Foster, what is wrong with you?"

The question caught him off guard. He knew what she meant. There had to be a silver lining.

He pondered for a good bit. "Two things," he responded. "One, I've been heavily focused on my career and didn't want anything serious getting in the way of that." He paused again.

"And two?" she asked with a furrowed brow.

He loved the way her lips pursed when she said the word two.

"So, you are listening?" He thought he was hilarious, and Sloane had to admit, he was. "I have been trying. Andy and I…" She felt like she'd known Andy for years. "We've gone out to the bars and clubs and hit on women or if we've been lucky enough, they've hit on us. This is going to probably sound a little conceited, but here goes. Every time I start talking to them, they…I guess, disappoint. There isn't that connection. I wholeheartedly believe in a spark. It's that perfect culmination of everything that makes up a person."

Hayden searched beyond the window for answers to her question and a better explanation. Shockingly, he found it. "Take this snow falling outside. So, a boy and girl meet and it's a snowstorm at first. It's a wild blizzard of passion. But when the howling wind and swirling powder have subsided what have you got? This peaceful accumulation. For me that's love. It's a blanket of snow. Maybe I'm rambling incoherently due to a lack of sleep, I don't know."

Sloane snapped out of her trance. "Yes, and I'm loving every minute of it." She was giving him her doe eyes unintentionally. To have her sense of humor and intelligence and to be single.

"Wait," he swallowed and frowned. "Do you have a boyfriend?"

With a quizzical stare, she answered, "I don't anymore." She laughed shyly. "No." She looked away in embarrassment, but not before she caught Hayden's face lighting up upon her answer.

Sloane sensed every one of the questions running through his head. "Want me to answer those?"

"Answer what?" he retorted.

"Your inquisitive mind." It was astonishing how she could read him already. He was supposed to be mysterious, dark, and unassuming. She already had him pegged dead to rights.

"Sure."

"Well, Hayden Foster…" She liked his name, it was strong. She loved when guys had two first names. "I was raised by my mom who has a pretty dark viewpoint of the male species. I was taught to never need someone and to always be self-sufficient. So, I have been a loner of sorts, independent. When it came to relationships, I always kept it light. You can't get hurt if you don't allow yourself to truly invest. I'm uncomfortable feeling vulnerable. The thought of putting my heart in someone's hands, it's always been inconceivable. So, I guess yes, in a sense my lack of a father figure hardened me. I put a barrier of wit and sarcasm between myself and anyone that attempts to penetrate it. It is a defense mechanism and I know that. Can I say something I've felt for a few hours now and feel I need to share?" She didn't wait for his answer, it was rhetorical. "I trust you."

It was a longing to explain himself and expel all of these emotions and platitudes. It turned out all along, he wanted to earn her faith. Now he had it, he would never do anything to jeopardize it. He opened his mouth, but nothing would come out. What could he say or do to comfort the vulnerability she was displaying?

"Thank you." Perfect.

Sloane canvassed his eye line. "Do you trust me? Because this is all kind of scaring the shit out of me. This could all be one hell of a long-con."

"From the moment you recommended the bacon-wrapped filet fedora. I've always been an Indiana Jones fan by the way, and well, let's face it…" Hayden picked up a crisp piece of bacon from her plate and took a big bite, "You can't go wrong with bacon."

"Aww, a man after my own heart and stomach."

"And to affirm your concerns, yeah, I'm petrified right now. It's exhilarating and yet constricting to the point of suffocation. How has my 'play it cool' acting been so far?"

"Has anyone ever told you that you have a way with words? Because you do, and I love listening and relating to you. You say what I'm thinking and feeling, and it puts me at ease. My background tells me I have to be skeptical and on my toes, but with you, I guess there's no other way to say it other than I believe you," she complimented.

"I need you to know I'm sincere Sloane. I want to blurt all these things I'm feeling to you all at once and yet I know I have to hold back or it's going to freak you out."

She exhaled deeply. "Then I'm not alone, that's all I wanted to know."

"Never. I have one more question for you and then fair Cinderella I will take you back to your pumpkin. Can I not kiss you tonight?"

"Huh?" He had caught her off guard. "I'm perplexed. Did you not...?" Her voice trailed off and her face depicted hurt.

Hayden witnessed the emotions he had caused and forged ahead. "Allow me to expand a little. See, we're going to get to the parking lot. I'll walk you to your car, and there will be this awkward moment where we both feel like we need to kiss, to seal the perfection. Then we'll both overanalyze the lack of kiss and what it meant. I don't want a single thing from you tonight, like I promised. Heaven knows I want to more than anything, but I need you to know exactly how true my intentions are. I'm sure..." He would have continued, but his lips stopped moving. They were covered by hers from across the table.

Having a wide slab of wood between you wasn't conducive to kissing. *Then again sometimes it's great.*

She broke the lip lock and quickly slipped from her side of the table to his. She leaned in close while alternately looking at his lips and then his eyes and back again. This time he leaned in.

Sloane was attempting to devour him, one small nibble at a time. His lips were soft and subtle at times and then aggressive as if he was about to ravish her. He was gentle, yet commanding. Hayden was the boss now and considering she was the one that initiated the kiss, she obliged. Sloane pawed desperately at him. To say Hayden's kissing was good would be a gross understatement. She had dated many guys and kissed a lot of frogs. She's had ample experience for comparison. He would play with her upper lip, then move in sideways and deeper. Then tease and lightly suck her lower lip before he withdrew. He would move slowly and linger and then speed up when the passion of their intertwining called for it. His fingertips would play at the back of her neck and then he'd lightly caress her ear lobes. Hayden held her face in his hands. Right on the edge of her jaw and his thumbs would encircle her cheekbones. He could have been a professor of foreplay. Her entire body sank into him. If this is what he kissed like, imagine...

Hayden hadn't wanted to push this, but since she instigated it, there was no way he wasn't going to partake. With pure abandon for anyone else that was in that restaurant Hayden now expressed to Sloane exactly what he hadn't been able to say all night. What he had been suppressing. What he held back verbally he now communicated through his lips. The opportunity to convey his longing for her with some resonance rose to a crescendo in one of those life-defining moments. You don't care who or what else is around you. There is nothing or no one else. There is you and her and the chance at a long-lasting impression.

She was on fire and reciprocated his movements perfectly. If he was her ying, she sure as hell was his yang. He could easily imagine himself kissing these lips for the rest of his life.

Two people that hadn't known each other for more than twelve hours in a lip-lock in the middle of a nearly empty Perkins in Maple Grove, Minnesota. He pulled away to say something, but she grabbed his face, pulled him in, and continued where she felt they had left off. He retaliated in turn and pulled her back into him. He wanted to kiss her until his lips were chapped. They were both intensely desperate. He pictured picking her up, setting her down on the green tabletop, dropping the spaghetti straps from her shoulders and…that's when he felt her tongue.

She. Was. Perfect.

CHAPTER 12

"Ahem," someone cleared their throat from the end of the table. "Can I get you two any more coffee?"

"Um no," he said in a cracking voice. "I think we're more than good. If I can get the check please."

Sloane giggled, straightened up, and tried to get ahold of herself. *Right, like that's anywhere near possible after that earth-shattering, knee-buckling moment.* It was a good thing she was sitting down.

"Well, my liege, no more chivalry necessary. This damsel ain't in distress." She winked.

"Yeah, I can see that, you nearly knocked me off my horse."

She gave him an embarrassed smile. He tried smoothing his clothes and combing down his hair with his fingers. Somehow, he also needed to figure out a way to tuck "himself" under the elastic band of his boxers. It was rather uncomfortable, and it appeared as if he was trying to erect a tent in his pants. He was probably hard enough to support the table.

"Wow" was all Hayden could muster.

She looked up from digging into her purse with a playful smile. "Well, I'm glad we got that out of the way." Sloane began applying lip stain and attempted to play it cool. She politely excused herself to head for the ladies' room. She was going to need to "freshen up" if she didn't want him to know how deeply to her core he had rocked her world.

By the time she had gotten back she had pulled herself together but did flush at the sight of him. Hayden had paid the check and left a rather generous tip as if to say to the waitress, "Sorry about the embarrassing moment, but thanks for your discretion."

They walked out, with her in front of him and he grabbed both doors on the way. Sloane hid her smile by looking at the walkway as they made their way back to his vehicle. Hayden reached out his pinky and linked it with hers and they walked to the passenger door. He opened it and helped her up. They hadn't talked since she had returned from the restroom. There was no need to. Talking had its time. Right now, silence was golden. Sloane rested her head on the window as they picked up speed to hit the interstate.

Sloane was deep in thought. *Had last night happened? Did men like him actually exist?* She came to an agreement of sorts with herself. It had only been a handful of hours that she had known him, but she was going to give him the benefit of the doubt. If he did inevitably disappoint as all the others before him had, then no harm, no foul. *It was only one night, right?* Sloane replayed the evening's events in her mind and hoped that it had meant nearly as much to him as it had to her. She looked over at him. He yawned despite the four cups of coffee he'd had at breakfast.

"You're not going to fall asleep on me now, are you?"

"Whoa now, aren't we getting ahead of ourselves a little bit? I figure it's going to be at least a few more dates before I fall asleep on you."

There was that rapier wit, even tired he was still challenging her, and she loved every second of it. She shook her head and went back to staring out the window. Through the reflection she caught his little Cheshire cat grin.

After a couple of minutes of quiet, he realized he needed something to interact with. Otherwise his eyes would get too heavy. Hayden reached for the radio. The faint chorus to U2's *With or*

Without You perked his ears and he reached for the knob. She assumed it was to turn the channel and before she could get out the words "Don't change that that" he had already turned it up. "This is my favorite band." She realized Hayden had a beautiful soul and also fantastic taste in music. Two very redeeming qualities.

They arrived back at the parking lot and he saw her Jeep. It wasn't difficult, it was one of only a handful of cars left in the lot. Hayden put the SUV in park and turned it off. She started saying her goodbyes, not sure exactly how to end a night like the one they had shared. He opened his door and jumped out as she was mid-sentence. *That was rude*, she thought. He walked around to her side then opened her door and helped her out.

"Still trying to be my altruistic knight in shining armor, I see."

"Blame it on the upbringing. At least I've moved up a bit on the ladder from 'meat hat guy.' I hope so anyway." She giggled at him.

Sloane hugged him. She rested her head on his chest and never wanted to leave. As far as hugs went, this was a great one Hayden thought. With all the cars driving by on the busy streets there was that feeling again, nothing and no one but her. After an indefinite amount of time she reluctantly withdrew.

"Hayden, wow okay, where do I start? I'm going to go on a rant here for a few minutes. You've been completely honest with me." She reached for his hands with hers. "Last night… Well, last night meant a lot to me. I hope it did to you. I like you, whatever you need or want me to say to confirm that your feelings are reciprocated, I do." Hayden's lips parted and his mouth opened. As it did, she put her finger to his lips. "Please, let me get all of this out before I lose my nerve." He closed his mouth. "I had no clue what I was in for when you—" She couldn't talk any longer. If she had, it would have been into his mouth. It was his turn to cut her off. His tongue tangled with hers. A couple of seconds into the kiss she pushed him away and with attitude started again, "I'm not fin—" He was all over her again. She decided they could finish later. They grabbed and pulled at each other as if the only way to quench their thirsts would be if they were one.

Their mouths melted together, and they slowed down the insatiable rate they were going at. With one last peck, they broke.

Her eyes were closed, and she lingered with her lips and head slightly upturned and tilted.

"Can I say that you are exceptionally good at that? Whatever I was saying, for some reason it has escaped me." She grinned.

As if he read her mind, he lifted her face with his bent finger from under her chin and looked her straight in the eyes. "Thank you for the most amazing night of my life Sloane Knox."

It was the perfect end and sentiment to a perfect night.

He opened her door for her. "So…can I have your number?" It had caught Sloane by surprise. She had to pause for a moment to think. It was a *great* kiss. She rattled it off through a smile that wouldn't quit, and he put it into his phone under the name "Meat Mistress".

CHAPTER 13

The Yukon idled while he waited to ensure her Jeep reluctantly came to life. She waved back as she pulled away. He was still reeling from everything that had happened in the last twelve or so hours.

It was nearly six thirty A.M. He was parked in an outdoor parking lot before it technically had opened for the day. He no longer needed to worry about falling asleep. He was riding a high that would keep him pumped for hours to come. He decided he was going to head north.

He had a four-hour drive in front of him and then he could finally rest for a few. At this point, he had been going nearly thirty hours straight. Math was a little fuzzy at this point too.

Hayden was a little over an hour out of town and he already needed to stretch his legs and replenish his caffeine. Hayden pulled over at a convenience store in Hinckley. He topped off his gas, relieved his bladder, and grabbed some joe. This was a straight black type of morning. He got back into his vehicle and out on the road when he noticed his phone had a missed call from Andy.

Andy was likely continuing their tradition without him and was hitting the first powder after the storm. Hayden pushed the Bluetooth button on his steering wheel and spoke loudly to his hand's free system, "Call Andy." It rang once and then connected. "Hey, I was about to leave you a message, what…?"

"Is this Hay?"

It was only three words, but he knew the voice wasn't Andy's.

"Yes, who is this?" Curiosity and fear percolated in his mind.

"I don't know how to explain this, so I'll just tell you. My name is Dave Tipton. There's been an accident. This guy was in an accident."

Instantly you could hear that soft metal on metal tap of a gas pedal hitting the floor. Hayden wanted to get to Andy as soon as possible. His mind was a blur. Time and life had stopped on a dime and he was going ninety-five miles per hour before Dave could get out the next sentence.

Hayden could hear pain and panic in the man's throat and knew something was seriously off. "I understand you're emotional right now, sir, but I need to know where Andy is. Is he alright? What happened?" Hayden had no idea where that calm voice and commanding tone came from. He was hysterical and yet he was outside of himself somehow compartmentalizing all of this in real time. His subconscious was in control and asking the pertinent and vital questions to obtain concise answers, but it was as if he was on autopilot and didn't have control of asking them himself. There were three people in this conversation. He, Dave, and an alter ego that snapped to attention and handled the calm interrogation.

"I, I don't know, I'm not sure. My family and I came out here and we were headed to a blue hill. My little boy's ski got caught. It sent him down a black diamond that was next to us. Your friend, Andy is his name?"

Hayden answered before Dave could continue, "Yes, Andy."

"Andy pushed my son out of the way of a snow groomer he was headed for, but only got to him at the last second." Dave was having trouble speaking. Hayden could hear him choking on his tears.

Hayden's face and emotional state went gray. He was lingering on this stranger's every word. *Get to the point Dave, tell me what I need to know.*

"Dave," there was a choking emotion in his voice, "is he alright?"

"He went under the tracks. I got to him in less than thirty seconds and there was blood. There was a lot of blood. I didn't have my phone, but he had his in his pocket. The first number I called was 911. He was conscious for a few minutes. The EMTs were here within ten minutes. They started CPR. I'm not sure if he regained consciousness again, but they put him on a stretcher. Then I thought I'm sure he has people that needed to know so I dialed the last number on his recent calls list and got you."

"Okay, I know you're hysterical right now and probably in shock Dave and I am too, but I need you to focus. Where is Andy?"

"Mayo is sending a life-flight to pick him up at the local hospital and they're supposed to be here in forty-five minutes."

Hayden slammed on his brakes. Mayo Clinic was in Rochester, about an hour and a half south of the cities, the exact opposite direction he was currently headed. Right now, he was about an hour and a half north of Minneapolis. He was trying to multitask at a time where singular rational thought was beyond comprehension. His fingers yanked the steering wheel left and he whipped the SUV around in one fluid motion. At the same moment he hit the gas again to optimize his turning radius without losing speed. He headed for the ditch.

He learned this maneuver of fishtailing and countering with Andy. Driving like reckless teenage idiots on the back-country gravel roads of North Dakota. Hayden's dad used to always say, "If you can learn how to drive a stick with the road moving underneath you, it will be a piece of cake when it ain't."

Hayden learned in an old 1960 Custom F-100 pick-up; it was his grandpa's. He had passed it down to his son when he needed to teach Hayden how to drive and the plan was to pass it onto Hayden if or when he had a son. Of course, he would lend it to Andy for his son, they'd already discussed this.

Hayden's grandpa Lester would take them fishing and they'd ride in the truck bed on the way back. Those were great memories of early childhood together for them. Car seats didn't exist. It's obviously better now that they do, but still, there was freedom in growing up that way. You weren't coddled, you were made to learn by doing and had to fend for yourself.

Dave snapped Hayden out of his wandering mind, "Does he have any family I should contact?"

"I'll take care of that. Thank you for calling me, Dave, I really appreciate it. Is your son okay?"

"He saved his life. Please let me know if there's absolutely anything more I can do."

"I will, take down my number from Andy's phone and I'll stay in contact with you. Right now, you need to take care of that little boy and I've got to get to the hospital and call some people. Thanks again." The line went dead.

Hayden turned off the radio. His conscious caught up with his subconscious and it hit him all at once. He had lost the ability to process for a while and drove in silence for what seemed like hours, entertaining all the worst possible outcomes.

He came to about ten miles down the road, when he passed a law office sign that asked, "Have You Been in an Accident?" He quickly realized he had responsibilities to take care of and depressed the green phone button on his steering wheel. With a trembling voice Hayden spouted "Marna".

"Hay, long time no talk, how are you?" Hayden guessed she assumed he was calling for some Andy birthday related issue. Hay was like Marna's 3rd son.

"Unfortunately, not too good, Mrs. R."

"What happened?" Her voice took the same immediate turn that his had no more than fifteen minutes ago.

"I'll be quick and to the point because that's how I wish that I had heard it. Andy was in an accident up at the ski lodge. I'm not positive of his condition. It happened maybe a half hour ago. He is being life-flighted…"

Hayden continued as well as could be expected under the conditions, but he was starting to fail. He relayed everything Dave had told him. He probably should have gotten his number now in retrospect. Obviously, he hadn't been thinking clearly. Near the conclusion they were both crying into the phone. Hayden was apologizing that he wasn't there, now his guilt set in, he should have been there. "I'm so sorry Marna, I am on my way to Mayo and I should be there before eleven. You probably need to call the rest of the family and get them there as soon as possible. If I have any more details, I'll call you immediately."

"Thank you, Hayden. If you see him at all before I get there please tell him how much I love him and to hold on." If desperation had a tone, hers would have been it.

"I will, Mrs. R." With that the call ended.

Call after call he made and by the time he got off the phone with Corrie back at the lodge his throat was sore and he could barely see out of his swollen, bloodshot eyes.

Within a half hour of Hayden making the call Corrie had everyone at the ski lodge back on the highway headed south. By that time the helicopter had already picked up Andy and was winging its way to Rochester. The ski cabin caravan wouldn't make it to Rochester for at least six hours.

It was now after nine and Hayden saw the water tower for Little Canada. He called friends to share the news as he drove through their respective cities, remembering who lived there. He was hoping he was making way more out of this than he needed to, but based on Dave's words on a loop in his mind "a lot of blood," he doubted it.

Hayden's mind drifted for the last couple of hours of the drive. It went to all the memories that now appeared fleeting. The countless number of Lutefisk suppers they'd worked together for church. Christmas Eve mornings when they would pick up the absolute best fresh Norwegian hand-rolled lefse in the U.S. from Jacob's in Osakis while heading back home to see their families in North Dakota. The softball and kickball games and the list went on and on. Hayden's foot hit the floor again.

Before he knew it, Hayden was taking a parking ticket for the lot of Mayo Clinic's Emergency Care facility.

CHAPTER 14

❄

It was the dead of winter and the sun wouldn't be up for at least another hour. *This must be what it's like to live in Alaska.* The footprints Sloane had left behind were perfectly undisturbed reminders of how calm and peaceful things could be, even in a bigger city. It was that perfect time of morning when it was still and dark and the sun's light is shy of touching the horizon.

The light snow continued its silent decent. The wind slowly swept it across the roadway. It passed to and fro and danced eloquently over the blacktop like a cloud whisking her from the enchanted evening she had shared to her bed, which was calling her name.

She was grateful her mom didn't have a dog, despite Sloane's repeated attempts to convince her that it would be a great companion when she eventually moved out. "They're another kid to clean up after and I'm too old to be a parent again, but a grandparent…" She would leave it open ended for Sloane.

"Yeah, yeah."

"Well?"

As the door quietly squeaked open the smell of caramel reached her nostrils.

Busted.

"No use in attempting a mission impossible, girl, get your butt in here. I already poured you a coffee when I heard the snow crunching in the drive from your Jeep." There really was no pulling one over on her mom. There was also no reason to. They were mother and daughter, but friends too. They shared everything and after the past couple of years and medical issues, there were very few boundaries between the two.

Sloane sat in the seat of their breakfast nook as her overly perceptive mother flipped the caramel rolls and cookie sheet completely over so the caramel would ooze down over them. Rae started tearing off a piece on to a second small plate for her daughter when Sloane piped up, "No thanks, I already had a big breakfast."

"Good, then I don't have to wait. Alright, girl, time to dish."

"What?"

"You would be a terrible poker player. Robin told me you called her out of the blue and had a girl's night out. Were you okay to drive home?"

Ever the parent.

"Yes, Mom, I'm sober as a judge."

"I'm going to guess that you had a fun night?"

"You could say that."

"C'mon girl, don't make me pry it out of you. What did you do? Where did you go?"

"The usual spots. J's, Acropolis, Grumpy's and King's."

"What was so good about the night? Wait, did you stay at PG's?" Even her mother called her by her nickname.

"Nope." The corner of Sloane's mouth lifted, and she knew Rae saw.

"Now it's all making sense. What's his name?"

Sloane weakly refuted her mother's assumption. "Who said anything about a guy?"

"Well, then what's her name?" They both cackled at the quick response.

"His name is Hayden, Mom, and I don't want to make too big of a deal out of it. I'm trying to be cautiously optimistic."

"Why not make a big deal out of it?" Rae quipped.

"Because they all eventually disappoint, right?" Sloane fired back.

"Where did you get that from?"

"You and my personal history."

"Oh honey, I don't..." Rae trailed off to collect her thoughts. "Just because I've had bad luck with men, and it's only been one man, don't think you're destined to be let down by them. Besides, that one man gave me you and it's the best thing that could have ever happened to me. There are great guys out there, I know there are. You're going to meet one of them."

"I think I met one of them tonight." Rae walked over and gave her daughter a big hug.

Over the next half hour Sloane divulged every detail to her mother, holding nothing back.

"You're sure you didn't dream this guy up? Is his last name Charming?" Rae wasn't skeptical, just sarcastic.

"You see," said Sloane. "He seems too good to be true."

"I have a little advice for you, don't hold back. If there's one thing that this has taught me." She gestured toward her cane. "It's that life doesn't give you enough time to make good on regrets. I'll promise you now that he isn't perfect, but perfect for you?" and she let that thought linger in the silence.

"I had a very long night, so I'm gonna head up and hit the hay for a few hours."

"Alright, Deary, go get some rest and you and I can talk some more and maybe hit up a matinee this afternoon?"

"That sounds awesome mom, good night! Or good morning, whatever."

"Sweet dreams princess." Rae giggled as she raised her coffee mug to her lips.

Sloane didn't even have the energy to take a shower, or the gumption to put on her pajamas. She peeled herself out of her dress and fell into bed.

As sleep was about to take her, the phone rang. She looked at the name, pushed the button and said, "What?"

"I tried calling the other two before you, but no one answered." It was PG.

"That's not surprising. They were smashed and got to bed only a few hours before I did."

"When did you get to bed?"

"Oh, I don't know, about three minutes before this phone call."

"Sorry, E." That was Justine's nickname for Sloane. "I wanted to find out what I missed out on."

"If you would have stuck around you would have found out."

Justine frowned as she shook her head. "You know why I couldn't, right? I didn't want to awkwardly run into him. Not until I've had the time to think of what I want to say."

"It's been nearly a month." Sloane was calling her out.

"How was I supposed to know he was going to ask me to marry him the same day I'd taken a job in another city?"

With a sympathetic tone Sloane inquired. "Did you ask him to come with you?"

There was a soreness in PG's throat and a tightness in her chest. "No, it all escalated too quickly before I could say anything after I'm moving."

"See, this is why you need to talk to him and not avoid him at all costs."

"Yeah, yeah, Mom, enough with the lectures. I feel like we should be having this conversation at the club house. I did leave him a message that I wanted to sit down and talk at the coffee shop next week and told him to call me back. I wasn't ready to run into him randomly at King's. What if he would have been there with someone else? I couldn't have dealt with that. So, changing the subject, what happened?"

"Right, well, um, quite a bit actually."

"Well, spill it already."

"You remember Hayden?"

"Who is Hayden? Oh, wait, that was the guy's name on the money, right?"

"Yeah, well we randomly ran into him."

"Get out and drop dead! What happened?"

"Just the greatest night of my life, you know, the usual…"

"Seriously?"

"Seriously."

PG commanded, "Tell me all, omit nothing, now."

"I know this is going to seem selfish, but I'm dead tired. Can I call you back in a few hours?"

"You do know you're killing me here, right?"

"Yeah, so I get to cop some Z's and torment you, looks like this girl's on a bit of a luck streak. Speaking of, do you still have that $5 with Hayden's number on it?"

"You didn't get his number?"

"No, I gave him mine, I figured…"

A few second passed and Sloane could hear rustling on the other end of the line. "Holy crap, E, no, I'm so sorry, that must have been the money I bought the last drinks with. Don't worry though, he'll call. Start making it a habit over the next couple of days of answering calls from numbers you don't know. Hey Sloane, I've got another call on the other line. Call me back when you wake up and tell me everything!" The phone went dead.

Sloane turned on her side and began daydreaming about Hayden. At long last, peace, quiet, and sleep.

CHAPTER 15

According to the nurse that Hayden had been pumping for information the past few minutes, Andy had arrived unconscious due to some brain hemorrhaging. The doctors had to drill a hole and drain some blood. In addition to the head trauma they didn't know the full extent yet. He had four broken ribs, an arm broken in several places, a few other sprains and minor fractures. He was in surgery right now and had been for a couple of hours already. Hayden was told it would likely be a couple more. He couldn't get a read on the nurse to see if she thought he would pull through this or not. She told him that she would check back in a couple of hours. "Thank you, Amannnnnda," Hayden stretched her name through a long yawn, "Sorry, I appreciate you taking the time to sit down and talk me through this. Please let me know the minute you hear anything more, good or bad, I need to know."

"By the looks of it you need some rest. There's a much more comfortable cot in our lounge than the chairs here in the waiting room if you want to lie down and rest. I'll come and get you when I get an update from the surgeon."

"You're amazing, Amanda, above and beyond the call. Thank you again."

Amanda showed Hayden to this tiny floor cot that looked like a king sized Posturepedic mattress at the Hilton with thousand count luxury sheets. He wanted to stay awake in case something changed in Andy's condition or if there was a problem in surgery. He also knew friends and family would be showing up in the next few hours and he needed some rest to deal with it all. As he started imagining the worst, sleep overtook him, and Hayden was out like a light.

* * *

"Hayden, Hayden, honey." Hayden had been in the middle of a deep dream and Sloane was nudging him with a familiar voice that wasn't hers. He smiled for a moment until he kicked awake.

It was Marna, Andy's mom, who had been trying to shake him back into the land of the living.

He was trying to get his bearings and he must have only been sleeping for a few minutes when she shook him. "What time is it?"

"It's a little after two."

He realized he'd been out for nearly three hours and he jolted into the present as soon as he remembered where he was. "Marna, how is Andy?"

"I've been in contact with Amanda off and on over the past couple of hours on the trip down. Andy is in the ICU and still hasn't regained consciousness and they're not sure when he will." She looked down, probably in an attempt to keep herself from crying any more. "I don't know what I can do. I feel completely helpless."

Hayden stood up and hugged her as tight as he could.

"Hayden, that's my baby boy in there. I can't lose him. You guys are too young to understand the love a parent has for their children. I didn't understand until I became a mother." Tears streamed down her face. "If I could go into that room right now and trade places with him I would without a moment's pause. That stupid, stupid boy, what was he thinking? I raised him better than to be so foolish and crazy!" Mrs. R was becoming hysterical.

Andy's dad, Marna's ex, Jim grabbed her and tried talking some sense into her. Jim was one of those fit dads. Always into cardio and running. He had light hair, but dark eyebrows. It was a strange combination. He owned his own tanning bed, and everyone could tell. Andy was really nothing like him. His dad had only been around until he was eight. He was trying to help, but without much of a leg to stand on.

"We don't know anything right now, Marna, there's no reason to jump to conclusions at this point and assume the worst."

"How can I not?" she screamed. "Why did he have to be so careless?"

Hayden knew she was in a state and needed to be tactful, but at the same time he knew he needed to intervene in the conversation. "Marna, sit down here, I need to talk to you."

She sat on the cot and he beside her.

"That boy of yours in there, saved a little boy's life today. When I talked to his dad on the phone a few hours ago, I heard the love and concern you were talking about that only parents have. Without a second's hesitation Andy selflessly and heroically threw himself in front of that groomer and officially made me more proud of anyone than I have ever been in my entire life. Not to mention, do you know what kind of story this is going to make when we're trying to pick up chicks for the rest of our lives? Playing wingman is going to be a piece of cake!"

Hayden's face depicted a shit-eating grin and a face full of tears. Marna released a deep laugh you wouldn't think possible considering the circumstances. They all howled together.

"I have always loved you, Hayden, you know that?"

"Besides, Mrs. R, my best friend in there, he's indestructible. At least until I get ahold of him and kill him for putting us all through this. Andy will pull through this because he knows how much we need him."

Hayden grabbed Marna to hug her again and the whole family was around them now silently weeping. He reached over and put an arm around Andy's dad and whispered to them both, "If this ain't a Christmas card opportunity, I don't know what is."

Andy's dad smiled. "See, Hayden is right. We're all going to sit in here, pray, and remain optimistic. After all, Andy needs us to be positive for him right now because that's all we can do. The rest is in his hands."

Hayden excused himself for a minute to run to the restroom and hopefully pop an energy drink in the cafeteria. He needed to get his bearings and call his friends to find out where they were.

"Hey, where are you at?" Hayden asked Corrie.

"About twenty minutes away. What do you know?"

"I passed out about three hours ago here and his nurse hadn't given me any updates. According to Marna he was still unconscious, and we are in a game of wait and see."

Corrie responded, "Okay, well, we'll be there shortly. We're all a little worse for the wear, but we called ahead and rented a few hotel rooms and we'll all come right now and then go back there in shifts."

"Good idea, I think we're all a little out of it and drained right now."

"I'll see you in a few."

"Love you, Hay."

"I love every one of you, too."

With that the call ended.

Hayden went inside and paced the halls searching for Amanda.

CHAPTER 16

"Sloane, I think it's time to get up, girl."

Groggily Sloane reached for her phone to see the time. It was after four. It seemed like her mom was always yelling at her up those stairs. That would be one thing she wouldn't miss if she moved out.

Since her phone was already out, she had a few items on her agenda before she put it back down and entered the land of the living. First off, sign up for a Facebook account. Then cyber-stalk Hayden and eventually call back PG. Sloane was the "loner" type, she never had any use for the "likes" of social media. She didn't need anyone cyber-stalking her. During her programming courses, she became a little over-informed about all the "tea" that "the man" was gathering on everyone and at the center of it all was social media.

Searching through Facebook, Sloane was able to put faces to the names in the stories from last night. One or two of them even seemed familiar, like they could be friends that she would have hung out with. She could see herself fitting in with this group. A twinge of jealousy struck her every time she saw Hayden with his arms around any girls.

Sloane was contemplating the add friend button when her phone rang again. It was Heidi. "Hey, I was about to make the call rounds to you girls. How are you feelin'?"

"Shhh, stop yelling into the phone."

"I'm taking it the kids didn't get their pancakes this morning?"

"What?"

"Never mind, what's up?"

"Yeah, I crashed here at Kristi's. How did I get here by the way?"

"You don't remember? You *were* in a state. Hayden dropped you two off there."

"That's why I was calling, we didn't get to talk at all last night. Loverboy bogarted all of your time at King's. Well, that and to ask you if you've talked to PG?"

"Yeah, she called right when I got home this morning. I was supposed to give her a call when I woke up, so she was next on my to-do list."

"Hopefully you have better luck than I did. Tried calling and left a couple of voicemails for her and no reply."

"Beats me, maybe I'll wait until after the movie mom and I go see."

"Forget about that, come on, E, what happened?" Heidi was dying to find out and for some reason her memory of last night had a few holes in it.

"See, that's what you get for drinking too damn much you crazy chick!"

"Still have to say, totally worth it. You know how much I get away from Ben and the boys."

"Oh, I get it, I said you are crazy, Captain Cock Block."

They both laughed.

Heidi started rubbing her temples. Her throat and mouth were the Sahara and her head felt like it went about fifteen rounds with a jackhammer. "Stop being funny, damn it! My cranium can't take any more pressure. We've been talking for five minutes now and you still haven't given me the goods."

Sloane finally gave in. "We dropped you off, which you don't remember, then he took me out for breakfast at Perkins."

"Ooo, big spender!"

"It was convenient and pretty sweet, not to mention I was starving!"

"Actually, Perkins sounds awesome right now. Cheesy hash browns slathered in gravy with a country fried steak, mmmm."

Sloane rolled her eyes. "You know it's like dinner time right now, right?"

"Not for me!"

"We talked, and I kissed him." Sloane still blushed just talking about it.

"Sloan-E!"

Sloane covered her mouth in embarrassment, though she was all alone in the confines of her own bedroom. "Girl, I was all over him! He was smooth in this awkwardly weird and funny way. I don't know what it was, but it all worked. He wasn't going to kiss me, so I laid one on him. Then I moved over to his side of the booth and attempted to suck his tonsils out."

"E, you're getting me all hot and bothered over here! Kristi, Sloan-E was a hoebag last night!"

Heidi pushed the button for speakerphone and Kristi chimed in from the background, "At least someone got some action." Sloane assumed the comment was directed at "The Captain".

Kristi took over the inquisition yelling from the back. "Keep going girl, this is getting good!"

"Well, that's pretty much it. He was chivalrous and opened doors for me on the way out. He drove me back downtown to my car and—"

"Hold on, back this train up, I need deets girl. How was the kiss?"

"Best I've ever had, no contest."

"That's a pretty damn bold statement."

"I know, right? The things I wanted to do to him. Hell, the things I wanted him to do to me!"

"This is unbelievable, Sloane, I'm so happy for you. Then he drove you downtown and what?"

"We said goodbye, he kissed me again, we hugged, and he waited to make sure I got off okay."

"Aww, sweet." They were fawning.

"It was too good to be true ladies. He can't be this good." She was blushing so hard.

"Hey, he burps and farts like the rest of 'em I'm sure, but if you find one that knocks your socks off and you can't fathom living without, you hold onto that with everything you've got!"

"Thanks for the gross advice."

"Anytime. So, when's your next date?"

"He's got my number. I'm trying to play it cool….and have a feeling I'm going to fail miserably. I already wish he would have called."

"No worries, E, he will. Well, let me know if you get that hag to answer her phone."

"Will do. Thanks for calling, Heids."

"Yep, later hoebag." All three giggled.

Click.

Sloane walked down the stairs and found Rae in the living room. "So, did you find a flick for us this afternoon?"

"Afternoon, where, in Japan?"

"Funny."

"I thought this would be even better, we can do dinner and a movie tonight."

"Great, it's a date!"

CHAPTER 17

❄

The last bars of *How Great Thou Art* rang through the bitter air as one of Andy's cousin hung onto the final note for as long as humanly possible as if prolonging the song would somehow also extend Andy's life for at least a few additional, albeit precious, seconds. The pastor, donned with a black pea coat, walked over to the closed coffin with a vile of dirt and sprinkled it in a cross pattern atop the casket. The beautifully ornate hand-crafted and polished rosewood coffin was underneath a three- quarter enclosed tent to block the bitter cold elements. The only sound to be heard now was the crunching of the officiant's boots in the snow; along with the sniffles of attendees attempting to hold back tears. During this time of year, they wouldn't be able to put Andy in the ground until the permafrost thawed. In a sense it was all a show until his body could finally be laid to rest in the spring. In the north, when a death occurred between November and at least March, a family had to go through the grieving process twice. It was excruciating one time. Twice seemed inhumane.

Frigid cold accompanied by hopeless despair and utter emptiness with no solace in sight. That horrific combination was what Hayden Foster felt.

Hundreds of Andy's closest friends, family members, and former co-workers showed up. They all gave funny and relatable stories of the memories they had with him the night before at the prayer service. They spoke of how he would be missed and was now in a better place in the hands of the almighty.

Dave Tipton was an impressive man. Probably early fifties if Hayden had to guess. The type that wore a three-piece suit even on leisure days. His black hair was perfectly slicked back with the right amount of product in it. He looked like a bank president. That is typically what he looked like. Today was a different story. Superficially he looked the part per usual, but as he approached the podium, he was a shell of a man. Dave stood before them with tears constantly streaming over and down his cheekbones and a seven-year-old version of himself standing in front of him with his father's hands clad in old school dark gray Isotoner gloves on his shoulders. He explained in detail what had happened, to the best of his recollection, about Andy's last ten minutes on earth. Then Dave walked to Marna and reached for her hand in front of the rest of Andy's immediate family.

"For the rest of my life I only have one goal as a father." He had to stop for a long moment. Just as it appeared like he would be able to continue on; he fell to the ground. Dave shook and sobbed uncontrollably.

Marna knelt with him, covering his body and convulsions with her own. She spoke to Dave, yet loud enough that all could hear. "I know it was an accident. I know bad things can happen in life. It's impossibly hard to accept, but I know."

Dave covered her hand with his in acknowledgment. She must be destroyed, yet this amazing woman was showing compassion. He was on the ground, unintentionally making this about him. It wasn't, so he sucked it up, for Andy. It was the least he could do. He stood and collected himself.

Dave's voice cracked. "I will consider myself the proudest parent on the planet if I can raise him..." Dave gripped his son's shoulders tight, "half as well as you did Andy." Andy's mom grabbed him hard to pull him in for a hug. They held each other's shaking frames extremely tight for a long time.

After Dave retreated and returned to the front of the funeral. He was committed to making sure his son understood he'd be living for two and that he had a great responsibility to be an extraordinary human being, the likes of which Andy would be proud of. Dave was a millionaire many, many times over. He then announced he had already set up a college fund in Andy's name. There were enough funds to be sending kids on full rides pretty much wherever they wanted to go for decades to come. Even in Hayden's opinion, it was something he didn't have to do, and yet Mr. Tipton was adamant.

The despair set in. Hayden didn't want him in God's hands. He didn't care about other kids' futures. He wanted Andy here, in the bedroom next to his. He wanted to revert to childish, selfish ways. Andy's best friend wanted to yell from the mountaintops at the benevolent creator, fate, whatever entity or reasoning that was behind Andy not being here next to him. He wanted to demand an answer as to why and be given a legitimate response…as if one existed.

It was Thursday morning and Hayden had been numb since Nurse Amanda had finally sought Andy's family out. Hayden was the first to lay eyes on her. He knew people. He could read them instantly. By their movements and demeanor he could infer whether they were in a good or bad mood. It took less than a second to read Amanda as she approached Marna.

The next five days had been a blur. He wanted to help Andy's family and the rest of his friends, but that alter-ego never kicked in. The consummate professional was missing. In perfectly coincidental fashion Hayden's phone vibrated in his pocket. He sent it to voicemail. He had been avoiding all calls save for a few pressing ones from Kirk at work. In his haze he had managed to call Kirk's voicemail on Sunday night and told him that he'd be out for personal reasons for the next week. That's all he had said and hung up. Kirk was Hayden's number two. He was the guy who could pick up the ball and keep running with it. He was likely the most vital member of Hayden's team, and he was including himself.

The onlookers appeared as a black mass through blurred vision as they slowly crept away from what was to become the eventual final resting place of Hayden's best friend for life. They all headed for warm retreat within their automobiles. Next the procession would slowly meander back down the hill making their way to the church basement for a light lunch.

Hayden's friends one-by-one departed from his side. Each of them asking if he needed a ride back or if he wanted them to ride with him. With a large lump in his throat and his face looking straight up to the heavens he slowly shook his head. He had wanted to stay here, at this place, with his best friend and brother, alone for a while.

Everyone had gone now. Everyone was going to now continue with their lives. Everyone but one other person, a woman Hayden thought based on her almost non-distinguishable features at the angle he had behind her. She was on her knees sobbing uncontrollably.

Curiosity got the better of Hayden and he leaned down and placed his hand on her shoulder. The weeping ceased. "Are you okay?"

"No!" came a shout. "No, I'm not okay!" She looked up with mascara streaming and Hayden recognized her instantly.

CHAPTER 18

It was Thursday morning and Sloane was beyond frustrated. She understood he was likely sleeping Saturday afternoon, but was still hoping he'd at least texted her sometime that night. Then her thoughts drifted to worry. *What if he fell asleep behind the wheel?* Hayden had her number, but she didn't have his. She thought he wasn't into games and didn't want to play them with her. *Then why the obligatory multi-day wait? It was the typical "guy" thing to do. Act like you don't really care that much, wait a few days, then check the line to make sure the fish was still on.* Sloane was no sucker. If/when he did eventually get around to finally calling, he could leave his pathetic excuse on her voicemail.

She'd decided later tonight, after her shift, to read a book in a hot bath. Anything to take her mind off everything that was going on, or rather a lack of going on.

Sloane didn't like being slighted. It was difficult for her to comprehend in today's day and age how people couldn't get back to you in a short period of time. There were so many options for communication. Call, text, social media, and Hayden hadn't accepted her friend request. She decided to take the leap and push the button last night to thank him for the fun time on Friday/Saturday and to find out what the heck happened to him. Surely there had to be a reason. Unfortunately, she hadn't heard anything back.

Instead of being frustrated, she decided to do something about it. She went digging in her closet and found an old notebook in the far back under textbooks that should have been thrown away at least ten years ago. It still had scribbles in it from her high school days. She recanted the meanings of the doodles and partial notes she never got to pass in class. After her short jaunt down memory lane, she opened to a fresh unused page close to the back.

Sloane wrote page after page of diatribe and drivel that caused her to rip out, wad up, and toss sheet after sheet. Every time she started discussing her feelings the writing would turn accusatory and downright mean. *Damn him for making me care this much after only one night. He's proving me and my insecurities right.* She wasn't positive that he was blowing her off, but how could she help but feel that was the case? Sloane would be naïve if that wasn't her initial assessment of the situation, right? She started again. By the time she was done she had six full pages front and back written. It was a happy compromise of trying to give him the benefit of the doubt and unleashing holy hell at him on paper. It was heartfelt and candid. She added wit and humor in spots to try to make it a little more lighthearted than the theme of the letter in its entirety. She had let him really know how he'd hurt her, and she thought that maybe he was different from all of the other men she'd met before. In summation, this was a plea for him to explain. For as much time as they'd spent talking that night, she had a thousand more questions now. She'd built her walls back up again. She wasn't going to let her guard down any time soon.

She really wished PG had saved that $5 bill.

CHAPTER 19

Now as Hayden sat hugging Justine in the most unbearable climatic and emotional conditions he had no words of comfort. He helped Justine to her feet and asked her if she wanted to go somewhere and get some coffee. He didn't really feel like following the procession any longer. He had formally paid his respects and now he needed some time to do his own thing and grieve in his own way. Hayden had known Justine for a couple of years now and they'd become pretty good friends. At least up until she and Andy had suddenly broken up the night his best friend intended to propose. He'd heard Andy's drunken version of the split all too many times He knew that if anyone understood how he was feeling and the complete loss he couldn't come to grips with, it would be her.

She followed him in her vehicle, and they arrived at the shop at the same time. Her eyes were bloodshot, and her makeup was a mess. He walked up to her and held out his arms again. "You look like shit."

She laughed. "You know just how to sweet talk a girl."

They sat down at a table and started talking about the good ole' days and the times that they'd had together. Laughing about Andy and how crazy and stupid he was sometimes. No one could find humor faster than Andy, no matter the situation. Justine had always loved that about him.

"So, I've heard his version of your break-up, what happened?"

"Oh, I'm sure you have…or did." She started convulsing in deep gasps. "It wasn't over! It's not supposed to be over! I'm supposed to have time to make amends; to explain where I was coming from and what I meant." Hayden realized somehow this was even harder for her. Unfinished business and undealt with emotions are the cornerstones of regret. She calmed herself the best that she could and forged ahead. "I didn't know he was going to ask me to marry him. He said that he had big news and I told him so did I. He told me to go first so I did and told him that I was moving for work. Hay, he looked like I'd ripped his heart out. He slammed the ring box on the table and stormed out before I could come to terms with exactly what was happening. His response and lack of excitement for me pissed me off, so much that I couldn't run after him to tell him that I wanted him to come with me. I was so stubborn and expected him to call and tell me that he'd overreacted, and he was sorry. When he didn't it seemed as if too much time had passed."

"You wanted him to go with you?"

"Yes, of course I did. I wanted to spend the rest of my life with him Hay, but he huffed off like a little petulant child before I could get out another word. I love him so much. I'd never felt love like that before. He was everything I wanted. We were going to move to Chicago for three years, get married, and start a family. I had it all planned out. I guess I should have shared that with him. My boss told me about the position that day and I needed to give him an answer on the spot. So, I said yes, knowing Andy could do graphic design from anywhere. It wasn't fair to him, it wasn't fair to me either, but I didn't get a chance to tell him all of this and now I never will." Hayden extended his arms and she gladly accepted her friend's shoulder. She clutched him so tightly she could taste the lint of his coat.

"Yeah, the story I heard was a lot different than that."

Through her sobs she asked, "What did he tell you?"

"That you rejected him and were leaving. Other than that, we're guys, we don't go into much detail. I know we had a lot of shots to numb the pain. I'm not saying this to rub salt into the wound, I promise. I'm trying to be forthright here. He knew he needed to get the engagement ring back from you. He wanted closure and to get you out of his system. He told me that he planned to meet you sometime next week."

"Yeah, I left him a message asking him to meet me here. I didn't think he was going to. I made up my mind on Friday night when I was out with the girls that I wasn't going to give him the ring back."

"Really, why?"

"Because I was going to say yes…Chicago or not." Justine looked down and the tears silently started to dot the cedar table top. Hayden handed her a few napkins from the dispenser.

"Damn, I guess he didn't waste Henry's on you."

"What?" Justine's forehead scrunched and her nose bunched up in confusion.

"Never mind, inside joke." Hayden's head rose and he spoke haltingly, fighting back the tears, "I don't even know what to do now."

In a daze, Justine replied, "I haven't been able to process this yet. Do you know what I feel more than anything else right now?"

Hayden shook his head. "What?"

"Anger. Anger at the world, people, and time. They're all going to move on. They're moving on right now. It's like all of them don't realize how important he was Hayden. I want the world to stop!" she yelled the last word in the tiny, quiet coffee shop. Hayden lifted his hand to the rest of the store that non-verbally said "I know, I know and don't worry, everything is fine, I got this."

Justine continued. "I have friends, family, and work I've been avoiding."

"Me too. I've been ignoring it all like they don't exist." Probably for the same reason. "Well, Andy would tell us to 'Suck it up, you sad sacks' and to 'start picking up the pieces'."

Justine's eyes were tracing the floor as she sniffled. "I don't know where to start."

"Me neither," Hayden said. "But right now, we have each other, so let's start with that. How about we head home and rest for a couple of hours, change, and you come over to our…my place later. I'll grill us up something."

She tilted her head at a forty-five-degree angle, her chin dimpled, and her eyebrows dropped into her eye line. "It's the middle of winter." Justine articulated with a tone in her voice that questioned his sanity.

"Yeah, and I have a lot of unused steaks that are going to go bad if they don't get eaten. Don't suppose you like cigars?"

"Eww."

"No? Didn't think so."

"I always told Andy I thought it was gross and stuff like that was eventually going to kill him." They both laughed wholeheartedly. "You know what?" she said with a change in her tone. "Yeah, I'll have a stogie with you."

Hayden shrugged as he had a brief internal chuckle at her conceding this one time. "Great, then it's a date. We'll wallow in each other's misery." Hayden gave her a half smile and opened the door leading back to the parking lot for her. "How does three sound?"

"Perfect," replied Justine.

Hayden and Justine got in their vehicles, checked their faces in their mirrors, saw each other checking their faces in their respective mirrors, laughed, and then drove off. Justine headed home; as the wheels of Hayden's Yukon slowly bit off the first few yards of his guilty journey toward the butcher shop.

CHAPTER 20

Hayden was more than a little disappointed when an older woman had helped him at the butcher store. He knew after days of not calling Sloane he was likely on thin ice. He had decided to talk to her in person. He also knew it wasn't until now that he had his act together enough to not break down in front of her as he explained. It would give Andy's death a finality he wasn't emotionally prepared to embrace yet. All the same, he needed to see her, in person. He searched the aisles for some sides.

Tomorrow would be a new day, he kept telling himself. He would explain everything at work and start putting together his presentation for the meeting with the CEO next Monday. Dan was nice enough to allow Hayden to reschedule to a week later. He would stop by to see Sloane, if she was working, on his way home. As he'd been looking for sides and his eyes had landed on vegetables he avoided the skewers with peppers. Andy hated peppers. He stopped for a minute and caught himself in realization. It hit him like a ton of bricks. He even had to grip the store shelf to keep his world from crumbling again. He wasn't going to be able to keep it together. He felt the beginnings of a panic attack. Then a voice chimed in.

"Hey, can I help you with anything?" He took a few seconds to collect himself.

"No, I'm okay. Had a rough day, but thank you for the offer. I'm just looking."

"Nothing solves a bad day like a perfectly marbled tomahawk." She held up and waved the colossal rib bone with the gargantuan piece of meat attached to it.

"I don't suppose Sloane is around? She usually helps me out."

"No, she had a pretty heavy load of homework, so I took this morning's shift."

He could sense that she was more than comfortable making idle chit-chat and that was the furthest thing from what he wanted right now. "Okay, well thanks anyway."

"I know my way around the store pretty well, is there something you're in the mood for? Need a recommendation?" She was extremely helpful and very chipper. All fantastic qualities when dealing with customers. Not this one right now.

"Not really, but I appreciate the offer."

Please, stop talking to me. Leave me alone! Can't you see that I'm a shell of a man right now?

"Look, it doesn't take a rocket scientist to realize you want to be left alone, let me know if you need anything."

Well, that was impressive, he had to give her credit. Apparently now he needed to feel guilty for two reasons. Hayden was having the worst last few days of his life.

Hayden meandered over to the counter with his kabobs silently paying and exiting.

"Hey, buck up, buddy, she'll be back tomorrow."

He smiled as he exited.

Justine got to her house. She walked through the front door and stood zoned out in the entryway for at least ten straight minutes. Justine was shocked back to consciousness from a notification sound from her cell phone, which she'd been avoiding since Saturday when she received the news. It was as if she didn't dare pick it up again because it could only lead to more despair. It was the initial bearer of

Andy's horrific tidings and now she glanced at it as if it were a monkey paw and nothing good could come from the contraption. As she drew it close, she could make out twenty-seven missed calls, sixteen voicemail messages, and over fifty texts. Tomorrow she would deal with reality, tomorrow she could attempt to return to the world. Tonight it was friends, wine, a Kleenex box, and if Hayden was smart, he had Ben & Jerry's.

CHAPTER 21

❄

Sloane finished the letter and stuck it in a business envelope with his name on the front. Her stomach growled and she recalculated her next move. She was starving and yet didn't feel like making anything. Rather than figuring out how to get ahold of his address, she folded the envelope and pocketed it. She jumped into her Jeep and bee lined for the Korner Konvenience store.

Between finishing her homework and drafting the letter, she was emotionally spent and mentally drained. Sloane wandered aimlessly past the shelves of snack food. They had about every type of fried food available in the warmer, but she wasn't here for any of that. She knew what she wanted. Korner Konvenience was the only c-store in the cities that stocked frozen Pizza Corner pizzas, her favorite. Also, if you added Arizona Gunslinger hot sauce to their taco pizza, it was the best thing ever. As she began eyeballing a hostess apple pie for dessert, the jingle of another customer entering the store caught her ear. The bell here sounded identical to theirs at Best Cuts and by pure instinct she looked up. There was PG. The only person in her life she really wanted to talk to that had also been avoiding her.

Rather than confronting her, Sloane decided to figure out exactly what it was that she was doing. She brilliantly hid behind the automotive/pharmaceutical aisle and texted her friend. She watched as PG reached into her pocket after feeling the phone vibrate, she pushed a button on the screen and returned it to her pocket.

She knew it, she was avoiding her, but why? She followed PG at a safe distance around the store and saw she'd picked out a few items and was now headed for the cash register. Sloane ducked out behind her back through the entrance as another customer entered. She hurried to her Jeep to hopefully avoid PG's detection.

Sloane was going to get to the bottom of this here and now. She jumped in, pulled around to the side of the store, and waited for her friend. She watched her with laser focus as she collected her change, smiled at the clerk, exited, and hopped into her car. Sloane put the Jeep in first gear and waited patiently for another car to pull in between them. As luck would have it, someone did, and she now had a safe tailing distance.

She followed her friend's burnt orange and black Mercedes CLA down a couple of back streets into a residential area. Sloane knew the vehicle well. Justine's parents realized their tactics of constant nagging about PG's life choices weren't panning out. So, in their new tactic employed a few years ago, they had moved up the moral totem pole to now buying her love. Sloane herself had driven it several times. She had lost the car buffer a couple of blocks back so she was hoping that PG would be reaching her final destination soon. Otherwise Sloane would be detected.

Finally, Justine's car started slowing and came to a crawl just beyond the driveway where a familiar SUV sat.

No, it couldn't be. She prayed it wasn't. *The chances it's the same Yukon in a metro of three and a half million people are astronomical.*

PG carried the convenience store sack up to the front porch step and rang the doorbell. Low and behold no more than ten seconds later the largest lump she'd ever felt in her throat cut off her air supply. Her eyes widened and a sharp pain emerged in her chest. Even from nearly a hundred yards away, she knew it was him. He came out and gave Sloane's now-former best friend, a long hug.

There was no rationale, no reasoning, she couldn't comprehend.

Why, how, who, every inquisitive word was all coming to the question party currently raging into a migraine at the forefront of her mind. *She didn't use that $5 after all! That lying no-good — how could she?* There was no other explanation. She called the number on the bill and stole Hayden right out from underneath her. If PG thought she was going to sit idly by and allow that to happen with no repercussions, she had another thing coming!

Without hesitation she threw open her door, slammed it shut, and stomped towards them. Just as she got out the words "You bitch!" she saw two bright lights out of the corner of her eye; juxtapose of one another accelerating in her direction.

CHAPTER 22

❄

Justine and Hayden looked up in the nick of time to recognize where the profanity had originated. The pickup's four-wheel-drive must have synced, and the truck righted itself on the road. In slow motion Sloane's face contorted from hurt and anger to terror as she unsuccessfully attempted to dive for safety. In doing so, she hit her head on the curb, hard.

Hayden started sprinting toward the lifeless body in the road as the final last second of the truck's horn finished sounding and sped off. Apparently, they didn't care if they hit her or not, they weren't going to stop to find out and suffer any legal ramifications. Justine sat in shock as Hayden tore after. Then she looked past them to the Jeep parked nearly a block away and dropped the sack she brought from the store.

"Sloane!" she screamed. "No, no, no, no!"

Her feet were propelling her forward in a faster motion than she knew she was capable of. Time stood still, again. The world became unescapably surreal. Everything outside of the three of them was muffled and drowned out. There was only the immediacy of getting to her best friend and helping her. It didn't dawn on her for even an instant that she might lose both the love of her life and her best friend in a matter of days. Hayden was almost to the unmoving body when he heard what Justine had yelled. He looked beyond the body in a heap on the ground. He wasn't processing this. Then he also saw the Jeep.

Hayden got to Sloane's body and knew it was her. She was on her side and there was blood coming from her head. From where he couldn't tell right now. He took off his coat and propped it under her head and took off his shirt and started searching through her scalp for the source of where the life was spilling out of her in crimson form. Justine started screaming. "Hayden, turn her to her back!"

"No, we can't move her, I have no idea how bad this is. Call 9-1-1 and give me the phone." Finally, his silent and steady co-pilot had returned and in the nick of time.

He ripped his belt from his waist and strapped the balled-up shirt over the wound and cinched the belt around the shirt and her head.

Justine said, "Hayden, here's the phone!"

"Hi, my name is Hayden and there's been a hit and run outside my house. I need an ambulance here immediately, she's unconscious."

Justine was sobbing uncontrollably. She appeared desperate. Notwithstanding, there was nothing she could do.

What seemed like an eternity later, but was likely only a couple of minutes, the two of them saw flashing lights. Hayden was over Sloane continuously whispering to her, "Please stay with me, please stay with me." He said it repeatedly as if the more he wished it aloud, the more likely it was to come true.

He repeated it as Justine sat down next to him bawling.

The paramedic had to physically remove his shirtless form from her. "We've got it from here, sir, can you tell me what happened?"

Hayden's autopilot kicked in and he recalled the information that he had as best he could under the circumstances. Justine stopped one of them taking Sloane's blood pressure, looked him square in the eyes and said, "She's my best friend, please do everything you can for her."

"We will," was the only response she got before they counted off and lifted her onto the backboard and then in the same sequence the stretcher.

It was only then that Hayden came out of his lackadaisical state and realized what Justine had been saying and with sharp focus the exact phrase she had said. "Best friend?"

CHAPTER 23

It was bright, but not a piercing brightness like the sun, it was a soft warm white. She had no sense of the vastness of where she was, nor was she concerned with it. She had no inclination to go anywhere or do anything. She just existed in the place where it seemed as if time didn't exist. There was pure nothingness around her. A very low-lying dense fog at her feet, almost comparable to dry ice creeping along the ground, but thicker. She couldn't see her feet below her shins. Sloane looked around in every direction and there was nothing but white. As brilliant as the butcher paper she worked with every day, but all of that seemed so far away and insignificant. Slowly she started to wander, but without a sense of purpose or destination. It was mystical and yet there was no sense of threat from the unknown, just peace.

Sloane's hand was outstretched as if she were trying to touch the color, or rather lack thereof. It was as if it was directly in front of her, yet it could have been miles away. She tried to think of how she would explain this place if someone were to ask her. It was as if she were in a warehouse. There was a sense of enclosure, yet no distinguishable walls or ceiling as far as the eye could see.

She called out, "Hello?" As if it were a soundproof room, there was no echo. "Is anyone here?"

Again, no response. She wandered some more, still attempting to get some compass or bearing for where she was and what she was doing here. She wandered for what could have been hours or merely a few minutes. Again, she wasn't sure.

Sloane thought she'd heard something. She couldn't be sure since it was so faint. "Is someone there?"

A diminutive murmur materialized, "I'm here."

She made out the faintest whisper and yelled back, "I heard you, where are you?"

Still barely audible came the reply. "I'm right here."

There was a shadowy figure with no discernible features. It was a hazy silhouette of what appeared to be a man maybe a couple hundred feet from her. She blinked and opened her eyes. Instantaneously, as if by enchantment, he was transported to her. "Who are you?" There was no response. "Where are we?" It was a man, about her same age. His previously expressionless face now furrowed and sharpened. Still, he offered no answer. Finally, Sloane asked, "What am I doing here? Do I know you? You seem familiar."

"So do you," he finally responded. "My name is Andy. What's yours?"

"Sloane."

"To answer your other questions, I don't know. I'm not sure where we are, or why we're here."

"How long have you been here?"

"I'm not sure. The last thing I remember is it was my birthday and I was skiing."

Sloane's inquisitive nature began thirsting. "Where are you from?"

"Minneapolis, you?"

"The same, well, Plymouth."

"It can't be a coincidence we're both from the same place," Sloane suggested.

"I'm sure not."

"Why are you sure, do you know something I don't?" She rifled through all of the questions that came rushing through her mind as if she may only have a few moments here with him to resolve them. There was a sense of immediacy now. When she believed she was all alone none of this seemed to matter. Now having company, she began to gain some clarity of her situation. Even with the lack of answers he had.

Andy spoke. "No, it stands to reason though, right?"

"Where do you work?"

"I am or was kind of in between jobs."

"What do you mean by was?" Sloane asked.

"Right." He paused. "The initial euphoric sense of peace."

She stood no more than a couple of feet from the man. Her mind was foggy and disjointed. "What does that mean?"

Andy responded, "That I've been here for a while now and the longer you're here, the more your bearings come back to you.

He continued, "The last couple of minutes since you showed up it's all starting to sharpen. I'm remembering a lot more. Eventually you come down 'out of the clouds' so to speak. Then it finally sets in. Now I feel like there's something I have to do."

Sloane agreed, "It's starting to happen to me, I think. Guess I'm not really sure of anything right now."

In an overly dramatic fashion Andy exhaled. With arms at his sides he peered at her and braced himself. It wasn't going to be an easy conversation.

"Think about it. All of your life you've been told stories of a bright light. It usually only coincides with one thing."

Then Sloane's demeanor changed considerably. "Wait, what are you trying to say…?" Her chin and bottom lip quivered.

"Yeah, I'm going to give you a minute because the second I came to the conclusion it hit me like a freight train."

Sloane's eyes welled up, she opened her mouth as if to speak and then closed it again as though she'd asked and answered her own question in a few seconds. "No, this can't be right. I was at a convenience store and I was following PG."

"PG?"

"Oh, right, sorry, Pony Girl. It's a nickname I gave to my roommate back in college."

Now Andy was the overly curious one. "Where did you go to school?"

"St. Thomas."

His forehead crinkled and his eyebrows flew up. "Me too, I knew I've seen you before, that must be it. What was your degree?"

"IT Management."

He shook his head. "I didn't really know any nerds."

Sloane smirked for the briefest of moments. "Very funny. What did you study wise guy? Liberal Arts?"

Andy scoffed. "Close, Graphic Arts."

"Ooo, impressive."

Now it was Andy's turn to give her a knowing glance. "Not all too apparently, I was unemployed, remember?"

Sloane heard him again use the past tense and the lump in her throat doubled in size. "Andy, we can't be dead. I refuse to believe we're gone. I have no reason to believe that. Shouldn't I remember how I died or at least the moments leading up to it? I was driving in my car and had parked."

"Wait, I thought you were following someone? Maybe you were struck by another car?" Andy suggested. "I've heard stories of people being in traumatic accidents that couldn't remember days before it. That's what I thought happened to me anyway. Like I said, I had got to the top of the mountain and 'poof!' the white powder turned into 'Washburn'."

"Washburn?" Sloane asked.

"Yeah, you know the Gold Medal Flour sign?"

"Obviously," came her somewhat sarcastic reply. It was a huge staple of the Minneapolis skyline. It was right up there with the Grain Belt bottle cap or the Cherry Spoon.

"Well, Gold Medal Flour used to be called Washburn's Gold Medal Flour. Until they bought up a bunch of other mills in the area and became…?"

"General Mills?" She honestly wasn't sure of that answer, but it was a decent educated guess.

"Bingo. My Mormor..." He was cut off, not by her voice, but scrutinizing look. Andy rolled his eyes, "Sorry, my grandma. Anyway, she used to have an old Washburn's tin on the countertop she'd always keep her flour in. As a kid I would climb up to get it when we made cookies. Look around, it's a softer white than snow and it feels denser, like flour. So, I nicknamed it 'Washburn'."

Sloane caught something there, she wasn't sure of exactly what. "Wait, you were skiing? I met a guy a few days ago who was going up there for a friend's birthday party. Oh my—" She cuts herself off. "Do you have a friend named Hayden Foster?"

"Only all my life."

"You're Hayden's Andy?"

"First of all, I'd like to think he is Andy's Hayden."

Sloane laughed, then shut up because she knew they were on to something here and didn't want to lose course or momentum.

"Secondly, yes, Hayden Foster is my best friend. Well, was. He and I were more like brothers and yeah...it was supposed to be my birthday party weekend." He paused momentarily. "So, how do you know Hayden?"

"I hung out with him at King's on Friday night. My name is Sloane Knox." She extended her hand at him.

He took it. "It's a pleasure to meet you, Sloane Knox, my name is Andy Ralsted." A strange look of confusion washed over his face. "Wait, he was supposed to come to the cabin Friday night. He said he had to work."

"Oh, he did, I didn't catch up with him until late that night. Hold on, why am I defending that slimeball?" Sloane's disappointment and anger had transferred to Washburn. She was seething.

"What? Who? Hayden? Sweetheart, you must have the wrong guy because Hayden is by far the best guy that I know. I'm actually offended."

"Sorry, Andy." There was a sarcastic tone in her voice. "I call 'em like I see 'em...and not even my mom gets to call me sweetheart."

"Okay, chill out. Let's get to the bottom of this. Why are you calling him a slimeball? What happened?"

"Just broke my heart is all."

"Hey, Chica, I thought you said you met him Friday night? How long have I been here? I'm assuming since you referred to the day rather than date that it can't be more than a week."

"It's impossible to explain without sounding absolutely ridiculous and like some lovesick teenager. It was the best first date I've ever had. By the way, I have a name, it's Sloane, remember?" She huffed.

"Yeah, way to go Hay!" Andy punched the air and a huge piggish grin appeared.

"Not like that you Neanderthal!" Sloane rolled her eyes and crossed her arms.

"So, no bump n grind? No hoochie coochie? No horizontal mambo?"

Sloane wanted to be mad at Andy right now, but her laughter betrayed her. "No, none of that. Sorry to disappoint," she raised her chin in the air "but your boy only made it to first base."

"Hey, he's been in a slump lately, so getting in the game is a monumental improvement."

"So, he's a player?"

"About as far from it as you can be, but it doesn't mean we hadn't been trying to make the team." He chuckled. "It's actually not surprising."

"What isn't?"

"Well, you're his type."

"He has a type?"

"Not to be that guy and appear to be hitting on you; though I'd say my chances should be good with that whole last man on earth scenario. But I'd guess that you're most guy's type." *Good recovery,* he thought.

"Am I your type?" Even in the afterlife she was still quick.

The three distinguishable lines on Andy's forehead raised. "Sorry, no, I'm not in that place. Still getting over someone."

"You didn't stand a chance anyway." Now it was her turn for a cheeky smirk.

Andy laughed. "Ahhh, that feels good. It's been a while since I laughed. Not much to find humorous here all alone. So, getting back to how you were so wronged?"

Sloane answered, "Yeah, well, your buddy was snuggling up to my best friend before I ended up here."

Andy's thumb and forefinger touched his chin. He rubbed his jawline with them. "Let me see if I've got this straight. The two of you were together Friday night."

"And Saturday morning." She didn't want Andy downplaying and dismissing her like some dumbstruck love nut.

"Whatever, I'm trying to establish a timeline here…and you're not helping your case with those two cents."

Sloane snarled, he was right.

"He said he was coming to the cabin Saturday when I talked to him." Andy stated.

"Wait that was you on the phone that he was apologizing too at the butcher shop?"

Andy's head and neck jerked back. "Yeah, how did you know about that?"

Sloane perked up. "That's how I met him, I overheard his conversation and then interjected my 'two cents' as you so adequately put it. Then I randomly ran into him downtown later."

Andy's posture stiffened. "What was he doing downtown?"

She responded. "One of the many fires he needed to put out." Andy smiled and nodded.

Sloane went into detail about the entire encounter and the meeting and re-meeting of Hayden. Andy especially liked the part about giving his co-worker the gift card to Henry's and interjected, "Ha-ha, suck it loser, you blew yours too!"

Sloane hadn't the foggiest as to what that meant but continued. She rehashed all the way up until he dropped her off in the downtown parking lot. "He said he was taking off for Lutsen right from there." She hadn't mentioned any of their "canoodling." She didn't want her appearance with Andy tarnished by Hayden making her into an even bigger fool.

Andy urged, "What time was that?"

"Between like six and seven that morning, I think."

"Well, I got up before everyone else to hit the slopes by myself first thing before the sun even came up." In a soft and shaky voice of disbelief Andy spoke. "Poor guy."

Sloane took a step back. "Poor guy? Sorry if I don't share your sympathy."

"No, you don't understand, think about it. He lost his best friend." Andy had a sense that he'd been self-absorbed with all of his own questions that he hadn't taken into account all the loved ones he'd left behind. It felt as if he had perpetual cobwebs that made it nearly impossible to connect the dots of his memory. "Oh man."

Sloane's eyes perked. "What?"

"I thought about my mom, this must have destroyed her."

Sloane looked up. "Mom!" She was blindsided. "My mom needs me. We can't be dead, Andy, I have to get back to her." She was frantic.

"Sorry, Toots, I don't think there's any redoes…I mean, Sloane. I'm not trying to be insensitive here, I am trying to be a little lighthearted in the middle of an obviously dark situation."

"You call death a 'dark situation?'" She regained her feet.

Andy apologized. "Wrong choice of words?"

"Yeah, like not in the same dictionary of terminology wrong choice." Sloane was flustered.

"Look, somehow you being here with me is jogging my memory. I hadn't thought of anything other than the same questions you first asked me since I got here. Now it's like the mental fog is starting to dissipate."

She nodded. "I know what you mean. I'm starting to remember more too."

Andy shook his head. Then he held an outstretched arm to her gesturing back at the floor. They sat a couple feet apart from each other crisscross apple sauce style.

"Okay, let's get back on track here. So, you were with Hayden, he lost his best friend, me, and then what happened?"

"I caught him red-handed cheating on me with PG after ghosting me for several days." Andy could hear the break in her voice. Hayden had really done a number on her. This couldn't be right. That wasn't Hayden. Not once had he made a misstep in character like the one she was describing.

His mouth finally opened, "So he was supposedly in the arms of another woman a few days later? That doesn't sound like Hayden. I'm sorry, but I refuse to believe it."

"Look, it wasn't any woman, it was my best friend!"

"Right, we've established that I think, firmly. Well let me ask you this, what did she look like?"

"She's box-job blonde, about five foot five with dark brown eyes."

With a quick bark of laughter Andy continued. "What's that mean? Is that a girl thing?"

"It means she's been dying her hair since college when it was dark brown." She was delivering all of this in a negative tone and connotation as her anger for her friend was once again welling up inside her.

"Ha," Andy cackled. "Sounds like Justine."

Her eyes flickered back and forth past his pupils, processing, as they had Friday night with Hayden when he'd been so honest.

"What? You seem like you figured something out."

"Shut up for a second." She said it with a commanding tone.

Under his breath, in passing, however he couldn't help himself. "Wow, pushy broad, maybe you are my type."

Sloane reeled through everything. She silently put the pieces together. Standing up she paced and looked off into the distance and then suddenly stopped in her tracks and walked quickly right back to no more than a foot from Andy's face, now level with hers. She searched his eyes again as she was deep in thought. Instantly everything once again snapped into sharp focus. As if she was working a Rubik's cube and suddenly solved it. She grabbed both of Andy's forearms with her hands and gripped tight. "Oh no…I got it wrong. I got it all wrong. Now there's no way I can make it right!"

The tears formed in the corners of her eyes and kept coming. It was a disturbingly silent steady streaming. Obviously, Sloane had swiftly come up with some answers, but he wasn't about to interrupt her. "Hey, it's alright, we'll figure this out." He put his hand on her shoulder.

"That's it, I already did." She pulled away.

"Come again?"

Sloane punched Andy in the shoulder hard.

"What the hell? Ow!"

"Don't you mean what the Washburn? That's for dumping Justine."

Now the look of realized shock hit his face. "How do you know Justine?"

"She's my best friend, dumbass! That's who we've been talking about here."

"I thought you said her name was PC or something?"

"No, PG, that's the nickname I gave her. Her real name is Justine Cook."

"How is this possible? I'm totally confused." His gaze clouded and he'd gone distant.

"I knew you looked so familiar to me. We've met, albeit briefly, before. You dated Justine at the end of senior year, right?"

With sudden intuitive realization Andy exclaimed, "You were her roommate!"

"And her best friend since freshman year and you left her with a broken heart because you were a stubborn little boy who stomped off on a tantrum before she could explain."

"What was there to explain? I asked her to marry me and she told me she was moving to Chicago."

"She was going to ask you to go with you, numbskull! She had to give her boss an answer on the spot. She never imagined that you wouldn't be a part of her future you moron!"

Andy looked toward the ground…or where the ground should be. "She was?"

"Yes, she was trying to figure out how to ask you to marry her when you two finally met up to talk!"

"Damn." It was one solemn word, but its meaning was pretty comprehensive.

In perfect reciprocal fashion Andy's lightbulb brightened. It was his turn to have an epiphany. "What exactly did you see that night between Hayden and Justine?"

"Nothing, that's just it. I put together the same thing that you did. He was merely trying to comfort a friend. They were hugging. They both lost you, the love of her life and his best friend. I literally made a grave mistake and made overarching assumptions that were completely inaccurate and unfounded. That's why Hayden hadn't called, and Justine didn't answer my calls, they were grieving…for you."

Andy and Sloane both stood in this place staring into each other's tear streaming eyes silently. Andy leaned forward to her and put his arms around her. She fell into him and spoke into his shoulder. "The worst part is…now look what I've done to both of them." They stood there holding each other through nose sniffles and weeping. It was the type of hug of lifelong friends comforting each other despite the fact they'd known each other for no more than a few moments.

CHAPTER 24

❄

They jumped into his SUV and took off like a bat outta hell after the ambulance. They spoke through choked up voices. Justine had just figured out he was the Hayden from the $5 bill on the windshield. She should have figured it out. It wasn't like she knew multiple Haydens. Well, she knew two, but the other one was her RA from freshman year. He was skeazy and Sloane wouldn't have anything to do with that guy. Hayden confessed to her how he'd met Sloane and their night at King's. Justine explained how she went home before that to avoid running into Andy. She of course remembered it was his birthday weekend but hadn't known that he was out of town.

As they arrived at the hospital, he was instantly taken back to a few days ago when they were in the same scenario. He was pleading now and asked Justine out loud, "God can't do this to us, right? He can't take them both away from us like this. There's no reason, no fairness." Then he yelled at the top of his lungs to no one and the entire world all at the same time, "You can't do this!"

Justine grabbed him and sat him down in a chair in the waiting room. "I thought you only spent one night with her?"

"Soulmates, love at first sight, fate, whatever you want to call it

Justine, I felt it. I don't know if she did to the same extent, but I know it was that overpowering for me. Seriously, I don't know how much more of this I can handle."

"Tell me about it." Justine said through bloodshot eyes and a cracked voice.

Justine called Rae, Heidi, Kristi, and some other friends of theirs. The girls all remembered Hayden. They hugged him for a long time and inquired as to what happened. They all sat in the waiting room talking as Sloane was no more than a few hundred feet away in surgery holding on for dear life. It was there that Hayden met Sloane's mom.

According to her, Sloane had shared the same feeling he had. Rae said she had been on cloud nine Saturday morning when she got home. She made sure to rib him about the time she got there of course. Rae had good reason to be upset with Hayden; to ream him a new one for being the cause of the situation, yet she didn't.

Hayden begged Justine to tell him stories about Sloane to take their minds off all of this. He listened to tale after tale of the misadventures of Sloan-E and PG. Including the night the nickname was coined. Hayden was a *big* fan of that one. Periodically they'd get up to get a cup of coffee.

Since Hayden only knew Andy's side of how they met, Justine told Hayden her version of the story and how they'd broken up for a while and then eventually gotten back together. When they had, Hayden knew they were pretty hot and heavy. It didn't come completely out of the blue when he'd asked Hayden's opinion on him asking Justine for her hand. Coincidently Hayden and Sloane were about the only people that really knew they were together again. They hadn't spent a lot of time this go around socializing in groups. Instead, she and Andy had wanted to make sure it was for real and that they weren't lapsing into old habits. Sloane had only met Andy once and it was years ago.

PG laughed. "Maybe he can take care of Sloane up there."

Hayden hugged her and whispered in her ear, "Don't you dare give up hope yet."

Hayden meandered down the hall with no real destination. He

needed to be alone for a while. Maybe he'd go get another cup of coffee for Rae. He and Justine had already had a few cups each. He was looking at the walls when he came across bulletin boards full of children's artwork and thank you cards, staff rummage sale notices, and random items for sale and give away. In between a couple of them was an open door. He peeked his head in to find a small chapel.

In the room it was dark aside from two small recessed lights at the front. He could still make out chestnut wooden pews, a lighter modern carpet down the aisle, and an exquisite mosaic piece hanging from the ceiling in front. The combination of obviously hand-carved wood, metal, and stained glass were inspiring. It was the cross with flames, and what he perceived to be some sort of representation of the Holy Spirit ascending. It was stunning.

He walked in and sat down in the front row. Hayden was raised Lutheran, but he hadn't been to church aside from the standard once a year for Christmas in many years. It had the fold-down kneeboards of a Catholic church. He lowered the kneeler and dropped. He recited the "Lord's Prayer" out loud.

"Andy, buddy, I know you're up there. I need you to do me a favor bro. I know this is asking a lot and I have no idea if you have the capacity to help me, but I'm going to ask either way. Maybe you're like a genie now and can grant wishes. If so, I'll think of two more, but for now, I only know of this one for sure."

Hayden collected his thoughts. "I'm not positive how to explain this. So, there's this girl. Isn't there always? She's like my Justine I guess you could say. Her name is Sloane and coincidently," he chuckled, "she is Justine's best friend. Of course, she is, right? By the way, did you know she has a nickname? Yeah, PG, crazy, right?" He was getting off topic. "Back to what I was saying. Sloane, right. I met her on Friday night when I was supposed to be at home getting some sleep before I came up to the cabin to join you guys."

A deep exhale escaped his lungs as he plunged. "I'm pretty sure she's the one, man." That statement sunk in deep within his psyche. He had never felt this way before. "Except there's a little snafu. She's in the other room fighting for her life. So, if you see her wandering around up there, boot her back down here, would ya? Oh yeah and hands off. I know how you like to touch the merchandise." The left side of his lip tugged upward.

Hayden started welling up again. "It's only been a minute, but I sure do miss you brother. I'm sure you've already got a new best bud and you're making them crack up constantly. This all has been a lot to take in and I haven't had the time to even process you yet and now Sloane. Do you think you could possibly have a word with the boss up there and tell him to give a guy a break?"

"I'm not sure that's how it works." Came a voice from behind Hayden.

He quickly whipped around. "Oh, sorry, I thought I was alone."

The stranger gave a short light laugh under his breath. "Yeah, I gathered that."

"I didn't mean to interrupt."

Hayden responded, "No problem." His eyes finally focused enough through the darkness behind him to make out a male figure. Hayden stood up and began walking in his direction.

The man was older, yet had a definitive and immediate softness to him. He thought it was his kind eyes that gave him the overall soft aura to this point. Though he was a larger man, he had an approachable demeanor. His appearance transmitted a teddy-bear like quality. If he was pushed to guess Hayden would have thought mid-fifties. He had darker hair and glasses. His cheeks appeared damp and his hair was disheveled. Like he'd been weeping. If ever there was a place to do it.

Hayden sat a comfortable distance away to give him his personal space as the man then motioned him closer with a sweeping gesture. Hayden scooted down so there was but a couple feet between them now.

The mysterious figure pressed on, "I've never been one that believed he speaks back to you. Directly, through a bush, or by signs. I've always thought of church as more of a place to think and collect yourself and your thoughts."

Hayden said, "I'm not really sure what I believe anymore."

The stranger laughed out loud. "After hearing what you're dealing with, I'm not sure I'd blame you. I would say that's one lucky girl waiting for you in that other room over there though."

"Hey, I've got nothing better to do," Hayden replied.

The man turned to Hayden. "How about this, what if we're each other's sounding boards?"

"Sounds good to me. It seems like you already know what I'm dealing with…other than the fact that I wasn't talking directly with the big guy up there, I lost my best friend a few days ago, I was hoping he could be of some help."

"I see. First, I'm very sorry for your loss."

"Thanks."

"It's a pleasure to make your acquaintance. Horrible circumstances, but a pleasure nonetheless."

"Likewise."

"So, tell me about your friend."

"Andy, his name is…" He caught himself and corrected, "Was Andy."

"Let's hear about Andy then."

Hayden started from the very beginning. He explained how they grew up together, were basically kin, and had each other's backs through thick and thin. When he was done more than twenty minutes had gone by. Moisture again welled. Now it did in Luke's eyes as well. There were already bags under them, but now they were even more discernible.

"Hayden, wow, that's a lot for a young man to take in."

"Tell me about it."

With a crack, Luke quipped. "I did." They both laughed through their tears for a moment. Then Luke forged ahead. "And the girl in the other room?"

Hayden again commenced storytelling mode and told Luke how he'd met her when he was supposed to be with Andy at the time. He told him he hoped there was some way Andy could know the circumstances of everything so he wouldn't have been too upset with him not being there when he died like he was supposed to be. The guilt of that fact always hit him hard. Had he been there he would like to think he could have possibly prevented the tragedy.

"He was your best friend, right? You knew everything there was to know about each other?"

"Yeah."

"Then rest your mind son, he knows. I'm sure of it."

"I hope you're right."

A nurse walked into the chapel and sat down with Hayden. She told him she'd like to talk with him outside. Hayden kindly interrupted her and said, "This is Luke, I'm fine with him hearing everything. He already knows all there is to know anyway."

The nurse shrugged and continued, "I've already shared this news with Sloane's mother, and she wanted me to tell you, she's pretty beside herself at the moment. Miss Knox hit her head very hard. She has ICT, intracranial pressure. Some of it was relieved after we drilled, but there's still too much swelling. I won't go into the technical jargon or specifics, but there's a new experimental procedure that we'd love to try. It's expensive and still not covered by insurance companies. So, it's an unlikely option, but we're trying to give her family all of the information and options. If she doesn't have this done in the next couple of hours, she'll likely die."

Hayden's worst fears were once again validated. His jaw was slack and nothing but air came out of his mouth.

Luke leaned over to him as he saw his newfound friend was currently at a loss. "May I?"

Hayden nodded. "Ma'am, is this the only option, and if so, what kind of odds does this give her?"

"Like I said, it's very experimental. This is only the first step, but in the cases to date, most have been successful."

He looked at Hayden, "Do you have any more questions for the nice lady?"

"No," Hayden muttered with a tight chest.

"Thank you, nurse."

She smiled at them both, got up, and somberly left the room.

CHAPTER 25

They had put together all of the pieces and somehow the puzzle seemed distorted or incorrect. As if one edge didn't fit exactly right and there was no way to complete the enigma.

Andy spoke first. "So, what exactly happened to you, how did you end up here? Have you figured that part out?"

Sloane released the embrace that she and Andy had shared. "Yeah, well, most of it anyhow. I followed PG to a house and saw a vehicle like Hayden's. Turns out it was his. I saw her walk up to his porch and then they both hugged. I overreacted and thought the worst. When in all actuality, they were comforting each other because of you. They knew each other. Do you know how well?"

Andy paused thinking of how to explain the relationship. "We'd hung out a number of times all together. She absolutely loved Hayden and he loved her too. They were like cousins. Not exactly siblings close, but they got along great. He was always a little leery with past girlfriends, not that I've had many, but that was the protective brother side of him. Probably my favorite side and one of the best parts of our bromance."

"You two sound like former lovers or something." She laughed.

"Don't knock it, we were best friends, still are, and I love that guy with everything I have."

Sloane understood. "PG and I too. Did she ever talk about me?"

"Of course, but you were always busy, and she wished you would lighten up and have a little more fun in your life. How did she put it? 'Like Sloan-E had the weight of the world on her shoulders'."

"Yeah, I could see that. Looking back, I wish I would have lived more in the moment." She started sobbing again. "Andy, I felt like Hayden was going to give me that. I know it was only a couple of days, but I was so happy, like I was getting a new lease on life and anything was possible. You know, the initial butterflies that come with new love? I'd never experienced that before. It probably exponentially heightened those feelings."

"Wait," Andy said, "you've never been in love? How is that possible?"

CHAPTER 26

Luke put his arm around Hayden's shoulder and lightly and briefly rubbed it for comfort. "Well, champ, what do you think?"

"I think we need to get you a dictionary if you think I even slightly resemble a champion."

Luke cracked a smile for the briefest of moments. "About the experimental treatment?"

Hayden knew what he meant, but as always with him, his first defense to cut tension was humor. "I don't know, what do you think? Jeez, I realized something. Here I am selfishly going on and on with the drivel that is my life and I realized that I hadn't asked you why you're here."

"Of course, she'd pick someone like you." His right hand went to his forehead covering it like a visor and rubbing both temples in a sign of deep pondering that could have been misconstrued as a painful headache.

Hayden's face contorted in confusion and he shook his head back and forth as if dazed by an imaginary punch. He wanted to dismiss it, but it was too specifically aimed to not have been intentional. "What?"

"Let's take a walk outside."

Puzzled, but highly inquisitive, Hayden struggled to his weary feet. *Man do I need some decent sleep.* His weak knees found it difficult to perform the simple task.

Outside, past the lobby entrance, was an enormous enclosed and heated atrium with a circular tranquility garden. It connected all the medical buildings of the hospital's campus. Not exactly a place one would picture two "dudes" hanging out. It was magnificent and tranquil. It was multi-tiered. The concept was very much like the steps used in Asian agriculture. On the top level were gorgeous flowers and shrubbery. There were purples and pinks and blues and all hues that connected them. At the bottom and in the middle was a gigantic fountain with crystal clear water and what appeared to be a copper bottom. Upon closer inspection it was lined with pennies. Likely visitors had been making well wishes for patients staying in the surrounding buildings. In the middle tier was a grass terrace that was mowed down to the level of a pristine golf green. It was simply a walking path.

The man's eyes went to the top of his sockets and slowly returned to Hayden's. His arms had been crossed. Now one untangled and he gestured with it toward him. "My name is Luke, I'm her father."

At that very moment his phone rang. The man that had completely dumbfounded Hayden checked who it was from, looked at Hayden and said, "I know, we need to talk, but I have to take this. I'll be a couple of minutes." He hurried away, swiped his phone and started talking. The classic maneuver everyone used when a conversation wasn't for prying ears. "Hey, Marcus, what's up?"

Hayden was attempting, though pitifully, to understand what this man had confessed to him. From the short amount of time he and Sloane spoke that night, he hadn't gotten the inclination that this was a good man. While he was sorting this all out Luke was wrapping up his brief phone call. He paused for an instant, as if scanning the horizon, and turned back toward Hayden.

Under his breath, he muttered, "Of all the times of my life." It was a confusing statement to Hayden.

Luke used his phone to point at Hayden, started walking in his direction, and finally officially introduced himself by extending his hand. "My name is Luke Harder. I'm Sloane's father. Have you heard of me?" The handshake was firm on both ends.

Hayden answered simply, "Yes."

"Judging by your…shall we say "efficient" response, I'm going to go out on a limb here and guess it hasn't been anything good."

"Not really."

No matter if it was common knowledge or not, it still stung. "I never did catch your name."

Still a nervous wreck meeting his first date's dad, Hayden said. "Hayden, sir, Hayden Foster."

"Well, Hayden Sir Hayden Foster, let me tell you a quick little tale." They shared a smile.

"About two years ago I invested in what most people thought was a get rich quick type of thing. I don't blame them because, well, I've gotten involved in multiple similar 'opportunities' before. Whether it be a pyramid scheme, a new invention, or whatever you want to call it. I've been hoodwinked and stolen from multiple times over due to my gullible and admittedly somewhat lazy optimism. I never could commit myself to the grind of a desk and a nine to five with a steady paycheck. I guess, in a sense, karmically I deserved it. As painful and pride swallowing as that is to admit. It explains on several levels why I was all wrong for Rae and Sloane."

Hayden was wide-eyed and not about to interrupt.

"This isn't an excuse, because what I have done to those two women in there is, well, it's beyond excuses. I'm merely giving you an explanation, so you understand the current circumstances and predicament completely. Now, hear me out because this is going to get a little technical and may be hard to understand. Are you with me?"

Hayden nodded. Hell, his mind was still reeling from the first bomb-drop. He doubled his effort to concentrate. He could tell what Luke was about to tell him was important.

"This most recent 'endeavor,' was a sticker." He put air quotes himself around the term. Hayden's eyes got wide and Sloane's father anticipated an eye-roll coming. "Hang with me here, Hayden, please."

He gave Luke the benefit of the doubt and remained somber and focused. Any way you look at this, it's a difficult conversation that would have seem contrived by anyone. Well, anyone a week ago. Now it seemed as if the improbable was the mundane in Hayden's everyday life.

Luke lingered momentarily. "Okay, so this sticker, it was supposed to be mass produced and distributed within six months. At least that's what I was told. Like I said, that was two years ago. How do I explain this? So, putting it plainly, it's for fruit. Kind of like the Chiquita banana sticker. Except this told the customer, stock boy, managers, etcetera when the fruit was ripe. It changes color."

Hayden asked, "You mean like Hypercolor or something?"

Luke grimaced and shook his head. "Yeah, but aren't you too young for that?"

"There's an infamous picture of me when I was a baby and apparently, I wet my diaper and also turned my onesie from purple to pink. My dad is a Vikings fan."

Luke laughed so hard he even snorted, picturing a baby boy in a pink urine-stained outfit.

"...and that's why I don't often tell that tale." Hayden was beet red.

Luke would have been rolling through the aisles if they had still been in the chapel. "I'm sorry but being nothing is or should be funny right now, somehow that makes it twice as comical. Oh man, that's good, whew!" He took a few moments to gather himself together. "To answer your question though, yes, it's the same principle." He lightly chuckled, still not over the story. He wiped the tears from his cheek. "Well, it turns out that's not all it was good for. It could also be used for vegetables. In the early testing phases during the trial and error portion of creation there was a small hiccup. Any time that grocery stores would spray their produce with their irrigation systems to keep it fresh, the stickers would bubble up and fall off. With even the faintest amount of condensation. It was frustrating. The scientists reported that one of the chemicals in the compound vital in the color change also had a wax-like consistency. It was imperative we kept that specific chemical. So, our engineers went to the drawing board and found a workaround. The answer was to make it stickier. To do that they added an ingredient named Cloniquin. That's going to be important in a second. Is this making sense?"

"Yes," Hayden said, "they needed to adjust the viscosity, keep going."

Luke's brow lifted and he placed his hand on Hayden's shoulder. "Okay, now, have you ever heard of Coronavirus?"

"No, what's that?" Hayden asked.

"Sorry, it's basically consumed my entire life the past three weeks. I didn't realize that it hasn't everyone else's. Mark my words, everyone will know of it very soon. It's a new virus strain. Technically it's known as Covid-19. Hayden, this thing is a completely different animal. It started in China and it's spreading faster than anything ever has before. They still don't know enough about it, including exactly how it's contracted, but it's extremely deadly. It's infecting almost everyone but killing mostly old people." He paused only momentarily to get his bearings. "In the next two weeks it's rumored China is going to shut down, as in everyone in the country locked down in a type of quarantine. Other countries, including ours, will likely follow suit. That's how crazy this thing is. Not only that, but I've yet to hear anything from our government and I know they've been told, which is extremely disconcerting."

Luke stepped down from his soapbox of information and came back to Hayden. "I know by what I've told you about myself that you have absolutely no reason to believe any of this. I must seem like an old kook spewing crazy, but this is extremely deadly."

Hayden stopped him. "My best friend died, possibly the love of my life is going to die and now you're telling me everyone is going to as well?" The part about the love of his life was a little difficult to get out considering who this man admitted he was.

"Not exactly. When I say deadly, I mean like two to five percent of those that come down with it will die. It doesn't sound like much, and they don't have a ton of faith in projections right now, but they're thinking like 2 million dead worldwide in a worst-case scenario within a year or so."

Hayden sat down to get his bearings. *How can this be possible? How wouldn't people know about this? Why isn't every news outlet on the planet headlining this right now? Is Luke a crazy conspiracy theorist and got ahold of some end of the world type propaganda from one of those nut-job chat boards online?*

It all seemed too contrived and over-the-top insane. It seemed as if Hayden would have a better chance of winning the lottery than everything that has happened to him in a matter of days.

Luke continued, "A month ago the Chinese government were quickly trying to get a handle on the who, what, when, where, and why. They started in high traffic areas. Apparently open markets and grocery stores were like ground zero. They saw how easily it was spreading and immediately knew how massive and deadly it could get on a global scale." His posture had completely changed. Luke was wrenched and twisted, almost tormented. "They found it everywhere. That was except for one singular place that it was completely void. The fruits and vegetables using our stickers contained no signs of the virus. We had been in the infant stages of distribution and one of our test markets was the Wuhan province in China, which is where this all started."

If terror and curiosity had a love child, that would be the face Hayden currently exhibited. Despite the overwhelming bad tidings, he listened intently.

"It's a cousin of Chloroquine, which is an arthritis and Lupus medication that showed some promise for Covid-19. The problem was it only kept this particular strain at bay for a couple of days and then it would come back with a vengeance." He puffed his chest out. "Cloniquin eliminates all traces of the virus." Luke's fists balled. "A group of Chinese government scientists under the direction of Jinping himself attempted to rip us off by synthesizing our product. Well, they failed and it didn't work. That call I got, was from my guy Marcus. China expedited an order to my company to mass-produce

Cloniquin on a scale the likes of which even I can't begin to comprehend."

Luke looked Hayden up and down and leveled with him. "Hayden, Rae called me on her way here and told me what happened. It's not by chance I was in that chapel. What I'm about to ask you is so far beyond fair. I can't fathom asking a stranger I met less than an hour ago that has gone through what you have. If I had any other options, I'd be exercising them at this very moment." He paused. "This is beyond me, you, Rae, Sloane, all of us." Luke reached out and laid a hand on Hayden's shoulder. "I have to leave *now*." Luke gestured outward with his hand and extended his index finger in the direction of the hospital while looking directly into Hayden's eyes. "All those two women in there know of me has been walking out on them when they've needed me. Now, more so than ever, they need me and here I…" he stopped and choked down his saliva swallowing the lump in his throat hard and continued. "Here I am…"

Hayden stopped him dead in his tracks "Yes, I will."

"But I haven't asked you anything yet."

"Can I be frank, sir?" Hayden extended him the respectful title that he was sure Sloane would have spat at.

"Of course."

"You're asking a guy you met to take care of your family and smooth it over with them, so they understand you're not abandoning them again. I know you've given me no reason to trust you, but an incredible young woman not that long ago trusted me and I kind of owe her one. Now you're going to owe me one."

Luke started tearing up. A colossal smile crossed his face. "I will never forget this, Hayden. I will return as soon as I can, I promise." With that he whipped out his phone and took Hayden's picture. Then handed him the device. "Here, put your number in."

Luke walked into the building directly toward the head nurse. He placed his hand on her arm as he spoke to her. Being Hayden was still outside he could only see part of the exchange through the large, windowed revolving door. The discussion he had with her was very brief. He smiled at her, pivoted, and b-lined for the parking ramp.

Hayden started walking toward the nurse in the lobby. She gave a nod of recognition and closed the gap. He asked, "What was that all about?"

She responded, "He told me whatever you and her mother decided regarding the surgery, he would pay for all of it. He wanted me to tell you so that you could tell the rest of the family. This goes against all HIPAA guidelines, but I'll follow you into her room. I've been told that I should trust you in his stead to make any financial decisions on his behalf. I can't do that as that's up to her mom, but he ran off before I could tell him that, so here we are."

She had Hayden walk ahead while she went to refill her coffee. He walked somberly through the cold and quiet tan-tiled corridors back to Sloane's room where she was surrounded by her family and friends. He knocked on the heavy brown oak door and peeked his head in. He felt completely out of place. He could read the looks from many of their faces. They nodded one at a time. They were packed into nooks and crannies all over the room. He didn't care and walked right over to Sloane. He couldn't care less about their judgmental stares. He would have never left her side, but for visiting hours. Now that he had a duty, not even a wrecking ball could have moved him. He reached for Sloane's hand as the nurse was arriving in the room. The moment he touched it there was a jolt of energy that flowed through her to him causing her eyelids to flutter. It was akin to the phenomenon of a static electric shock but amplified. It was resoundingly powerful.

Hayden composed himself. "Whoa, did you guys see that?"

Everyone looked at Hayden like he'd lost his fricking mind.

"Seriously, no one saw that?" His voice rose in frustration.

"Saw what, Hayden?" Heidi spoke up.

They hadn't exchanged but mere pleasantries. It's likely she was still harboring some ill-will in his direction for landing one of her best friends, her sister-from-another-mister, in here. Sloane was laying comatose in that hospital bed.

Heidi had heard the story of what happened. Granted they'd all concluded there wasn't any funny business, but it didn't change the fact that Sloane wouldn't be here had it not been for him. Yes, it was unfair he'd lost his best friend. No one said complicated and intense emotions made any sense or showed fair rationale. PG and Hayden were innocent, but Heidi, Kristi and Rae weren't ready to be fair-minded yet. There was a resentment that only time could heal.

Hayden turned to her and looked at the nurse who had come to rest beside him. "Have you ever heard of anything like this before?"

"Like what?" She was confused to say the least.

"I felt, well, I don't exactly know what I felt. Maybe like a jolt of electricity that ran from Sloane to me."

"It's possible you built up some static I guess."

"Maybe, but this felt different."

"Maybe you wanted it to feel different?" The nurse made a disheartening, yet good point. It's possible with everything that has and is happening that he's a little, well, off. This all ran through his brain in the briefest of moments. He also realized if he didn't let it go the "wackadoo" stares he was getting weren't going to subside.

"That's definitely a possibility." Hayden cleared his throat and changed subjects. "Rae, can I talk to you outside for a moment? Luke wanted me to talk to you. Well," he looked over at the nurse again "he wanted us to talk to you."

The ten to a dozen people in the room looked at each other with a flash of recognition. They all knew the name Luke. The looks screamed "does he mean that Luke?" Rae knew it was. "Hayden, if there's something that man wants to tell me, he can tell me himself!"

"That's the problem, he's no longer here." In a strategic move, he stopped himself from saying the word gone. He already knew how the information was going to be received. Hayden was treading on thin ice, as the northern turn of phrase went. On his walk through the corridors of the hospital, when figuring out how he was going to deliver the news of Luke's departure; he'd realized the straight-forward, honest approach like a Band-Aid rip was probably the correct choice.

"Typical, of course he left. Why should I be surprised? What else did the asshole have to say? These people can hear it."

Then Hayden gave them the facts. He delivered them as candidly as possible. He wanted to champion for Luke's cause based on his generous offer, but Hayden read the room and knew his audience. He repeated what he was told and decided to let the chips fall where they may regarding people's opinions. It was only fair considering they'd known him or at least known of him for considerably more time than Hayden had. Then he told Rae of the promise to cover the surgery, no matter the cost. It's a remarkable thing to see someone's opinion of another human being go from one extreme to another. While it didn't put a smile on her face, she did ask Hayden to repeat that last bit.

Rae had immediately given Sloane's care team the green light for the surgery. It was a pretty quick procedure of a couple of hours at most. All those in Sloane's corner were now in the waiting room.

The doctor came out just shy of the full three hours and delivered them the news. "The number one thing here is for me to manage your expectations. The surgery was a success. Everything went well." The room erupted in elation.

The doc had delivered this exact speech too many times not to know that this was an important moment of relief for the families. He paused until the hugs and tears subsided and the room could hear him again. "Like I said, my job is to manage your expectations. Yes, the surgery went well, but relieving the cranial pressure and blood from her brain was step one of about five. The brain is an extremely difficult organ to explain and even more impossible to understand. There is so much that we, in the medical community, still don't know about it. It's fragile and it's not like anything else. Her brain has been bruised. Bruising of the brain isn't like smacking your shin and a purple welt shows up tomorrow only to disappear a few days later. It takes much longer to heal, and the after-effects can be wide-ranging and, in many cases, permanent."

The energy in the room took a stark turn. "Sloane has a long uphill battle now. She's still in a medically induced coma. I know if this were my loved one, I would want my doctor to shoot it to me straight, so that's what I'm going to do here. While the surgery had an eighty percent success rate, the overall chances of a full recovery with something like this are much different. Though she didn't have one, these cases are like those of a stroke victim."

The silence had become unnerving when Rae finally came forward. "So, what are we looking at here?"

"The probability that she comes out to be the same Sloane you knew and loved is somewhere around thirty percent."

The use of past tense and the numbers put a lump in Rae's throat. "What else?"

"She could have loss of memory, motor function, or may very well never regain consciousness." Rae's cane fell and Hayden caught her as one of her knees grazed the floor. Slowly Rae regained her composure and let go of Hayden once she regained her feet. Everyone started to understand the dire situation for what it truly was, and a heavy cloud descended on the room. Everyone except for Hayden and Justine. This was old hat to them. They were pros. In this moment, it wasn't something they wanted to shout from the rafters. There's no pride in this knowledge.

The doc continued, "Now, I know you have a lot of questions. When it comes to the brain, there aren't many definitive answers or odds. There are kind of 'rules of thumb.'" He even used the air quotes. "They aren't written in stone and there are always exceptions, but the answer is really three to five days. After five days the chances diminish to about twenty percent. Meaning one in five people come back to us. Every day after that we drop by about five percentage points. At ten days it drops to low single digits. The best thing that all of you can do right now is go home, rest, and await word from her medical team and immediate family."

Distressed looks of concern proliferated the room. "We'll be giving her a day or two for healing and then start incorporating a vigorous routine of trying to wake her up. That part is difficult for loved ones to deal with. It's a lot of hard prodding and poking."

Rae looked at Hayden, Kristi, Heidi, and Justine, who had congregated near each other and said, "You're handling that part." It was a minute moment of levity in this chaotic storm. It was also Rae's own therapeutic way of putting Hayden on the spot and challenging him. If he wanted to court her daughter, she needed to know he wasn't going to bail. He gripped her hand tightly and gave her a look that said "Yep, I've got you." In that moment they shared something. She smiled through tears and squeezed his hand back.

The doctor concluded his speech, "We won't have any further answers for you until she wakes up. Then we can discuss the next steps based on how she's responding."

It all seemed so matter of fact to him. He had a decent bedside manner and Hayden knew the man obviously knew what he was talking about. It seems like something with this gravitas and importance would require more. Again, maybe that was what he wanted.

Rae told everyone to go home. Justine said she'd catch a ride with Heidi and Kristi. Rae exchanged numbers with Hayden. He'd wanted to stay by her side, but he also knew that his presence there was awkward to begin with. He didn't want to compound that by being stubborn, so he relented knowing obviously she was in good hands with her mother. "If anything changes, at all, please call me. Anytime day or night. I'll stop by every day to check in for a while if that's alright?"

"Of course, it's alright. I hope that you do. It will give me a chance to grill you a little." He caught her smirk and smiled back while reaching out his arms in a come here and hug me motion. She accepted. It wasn't one of those quick pats either. This was a real hug. The variety that included Rae's hand on the back of Hayden's head and it didn't end quickly. Their embrace conveyed so much more emotion than spoken words could right now.

Hayden Foster walked alone outside into the night. Also into a blistering snowstorm. He was well underdressed, having only a single layer tank top undershirt on, and yet it was the very last thing on his mind. It was fourteen degrees below zero, snowing heavily, and the wind speed was at least forty to fifty miles an hour. His truck was nearly frozen. The wind chill factor, now referred to as the "feels like index," had to have been well over sixty below. He turned the key and she slowly came to life. He waited about ten minutes in the driver's seat with the front and rear defrost turned to full blast and his seat warmer cranked to high. He blankly scrolled on his phone through voicemails, missed texts, and social media messages. In this type of cold it's extremely hard on an engine to start it up and take off. You had to give it sufficient time to warm up. Frequently he'd thought it would have been a wise investment to have installed an auto-start, but he also wasn't really built like that. He was pretty simple when push came to shove and for the most part lived a minimalist life. Physically and emotionally the darkness started to cascade over him, and he cognitively realized he was completely drained. Nearly void of all energy. He turned the radio on, and his hand went to the transmission column.

Dave Matthews *Stay or Leave*, coincidently one of Andy's all-time junior high favorites, came to life in the middle of the first verse. Andy had mentioned to Hayden once that he wanted this to be the first dance song at his wedding.

The road conditions were terrible, the visibility was worse. He was transported to another place and time. He was going through the motions as he drove back to his house. A house that no longer provided shelter and comfort for his best friend, for the person more than any other on the planet he really could have used right now. Hayden was a shell of a man. He'd put on the false vibrato for Rae and everyone else, but now his walls came crumbling down from the inside. Pessimism about all that had transpired hit all at once. He zoned out as the snow created the strangest phenomenon of hypnotic swirling. It's a sensation that really can't be described. Yet, if you've experienced it, you knew exactly what he was encountering. To someone that didn't really know snow, I guess you could compare it to those 3D prints from his childhood that were popular. The kind where if you skewed or blurred your eyes right you could see something hidden, like a sailboat. Except here you only saw the blurry part. The snow danced and played tricks on his eyes. It would have been tough to concentrate merely due to the weather conditions, but when you factor in the numbness of losing his best friend and possibly the most amazing woman he'd ever met, he didn't stand a chance. The tears streamed.

He hurt. He hurt so badly. He wanted to scream and pound his fists. Instead, he silently let the moment overtake him. Through bloodshot and blurry eyes, the waterworks wouldn't turn off. Not even his mother's early passing had shaken him in the devastating manner that he was experiencing now. He yelled as he slammed both hands on the steering wheel, "It was one damn night!"

CHAPTER 27

"Shut up!" She pushed Andy by the shoulder.

He laughed. "Maaan, you are one pathetic loser." Andy did his best Jim Carey impression.

Sloane would have been hurt had it not been for the sarcastic tone and comical delivery. She completely understood why Hayden shared him in such a positive light. There was a smile on his face in that booth every time he'd mentioned him.

She slammed him back, "Hey, I can't help the fact your gender sucks!"

"Touché and more than fair. Really, though, you couldn't have found a better guy than Hayden." Andy beamed.

"Yeah, I got that. Nothing like rubbing salt in the wound, eh? Now there's nothing I can do. I found him and just as fast I lost him." She wanted to scream with frustration. In that very moment, her conscious and subconscious melded into one and she gave into the temptation. "Damn it!" She shouted and pounded both fists into Andy's chest as hard as she possibly could.

There was a flash of brilliant white light that acted as an echo would, but without sound. It was like some type of otherworldly EMP. It blew them off their feet. They could see it continue far off into the distance until it was eventually out of sight. Andy looked at Sloane like she was an alien. "What in the hell was that?"

"I don't know, but it was powerful."

"Understatement of my lifetime. Well, deathtime, whatever."

They were both still a little dumbstruck as they slowly regained their feet. As Sloane once again approached Andy. She couldn't help but notice the imprints remaining where she hit Andy on the chest. They appeared like healed burn marks. Her hand went to her mouth in shock. "Did I hurt you? Are you okay?"

"No, it didn't hurt at all actually." Then without pausing, yet seemingly out of left field he followed with "Did you ever do those giant balls?"

"Andy!"

His face contorted and then he realized what he'd said and then he cracked a smile. "Not what I meant perv, but I like where your head's at." They laughed.

"Those giant inflated balls where you climb into them and only your legs are sticking out and you run at each other as fast as possible and then hurl yourself at the other person. You collide and both go flying backward, but you're not hurt.

"Nope, never had the chance. I saw videos of them."

"Well, it was like that." He thought a moment. "Do it again."

"What? No!"

"Seriously, try it, it was pretty cool."

"It freaked me out."

"Come on, it's something new and different. I need that right now. In case you forgot, I was here all by my lonesome before you stumbled along. Sorry, maybe that's a bad choice of words. All I'm saying is let's investigate this thing."

Andy sensed the walls of her reservations slowly collapsing.

"Ahhhhhh, fine! What do you want me to do?"

Then without warning he pounded his chest, as if pledging his loyalty and sword to his king in the upcoming battle. Nothing happened.

Sloane started chuckling. Then she couldn't catch her breath when he did the Tarzan call. Everything he tried was to no avail. She was finally able to speak again when she grabbed his wrists. "Andy, stop, it isn't working." Sloane took a step back and realized this would have been one of the stories Hayden would have told her. Now she got it.

"Here, let me try it on you," Andy said.

Sloane covered her chest. "Don't even think about it!"

"Come on, you prude!"

"Andy! I'm Hayden's girl, how dare you? You're supposed to be his best friend!"

"First of all, I wouldn't. I said it for comic effect. Secondly, I'm not letting that comment go." He furrowed his brow. "I thought you guys were only together one night?"

"We were." She swallowed hard. She had come to a pretty stunning revelation. "Andy, wow, how do I say this? How can I even be thinking it?" Her eyebrows rose and slanted.

"You don't have to. I knew with Justine too. I get it." She blushed and believed he did. "Try it again on my chest."

She walked up to him and lightly tapped his pecs with her fists balled up and sideways like last time. Nothing.

"Come on, girl, I'm not made of glass. Like I told you, it doesn't hurt."

She raised her fists and brought them down hard again and bang, there it was. The ripples flowed again like before, but it felt like much less of an impact, as if it wasn't as powerful. She reeled back and gave it everything she had. While the anomaly was still strange and something unlike they'd ever known, it didn't pack the same concussive wallop, no matter how hard she smacked him. Without regard she kept pummeling him.

"Okay, okay, okay, ease up Donkey Kong."

Sloane blushed and stopped. The therapeutic by-product of Andy's chest acting as a stress ball of sorts got away from her. "Oh, sorry."

"That's cool. We know that it only works when you hit me. Does it work on other parts of me? Sloane, smack my ass." He winked.

"Ew, no!"

Andy now turned around and bent over and started smacking his own ass. Again, she doubled over laughing. "Come on, baby, spank me!" He broke the comedian's cardinal rule and began laughing uncontrollably himself. Sloane punched him hard in the arm. There was no anomaly.

"Ow, what was that for?"

"Scientific advancement. Now we know it's only your chest with my fists and I can hurt you everywhere else."

"In comparison, your theory proving sucks, Dr. Knox."

CHAPTER 28

❄

It was ten A.M. sharp on Monday the 20th. Hayden was in Dan Murphy's office. Dan had been the CEO of his agency for a year longer than Hayden had been at the company. He knew of Hayden from several VPs impressed with his rather meteoric rise. He knew what Hayden looked like, but always misremembered his name. It wasn't always the same wrong name either. Last time Hayden had briefly chatted him up at the office Christmas party a little over a month ago Dan had called him James. Some people would consider this a power move. When in all actuality, it was the one big glaring weakness that he had. Self admittedly, Dan was terrible with names. That was one of the reasons why he wasn't on the big-pitch team.

A week ago this meeting scared the living crap out of Hayden. Now it barely registered on his to-do list. The original calendar date, the 13th, had been circled for weeks in large red marker. He had put together decks with charts and graphs that all added up to his case for making Vice President of Sales and New Business.

He walked up to the desk that Dan was standing opposite of and shook his hand.

Dan held his arm out extending an invitation. "Take a seat please, young man. I've been looking forward to this for a couple of weeks." It was a nice way of ribbing Hayden about rescheduling their meeting. Most people jockeying for a position like VP wouldn't have the audacity to inconvenience someone like Dan. If they did, they rarely got the opportunity to reschedule.

"Now, Hayden..." Hayden did a double take, shocked he had remembered his name. Dan smiled knowingly. "I didn't know what you were dealing with outside of the office, but I did do some digging. Rebecca..." Hayden cringed at the mere mention of her name, which Dan picked up on. Hayden noticed this and was disappointed in himself. Dan chuckled. "Yeah, I know she rubs some people the wrong way. Rebecca told me she fixed the problem a week or so ago with Sampson's."

This time Hayden thought quickly and didn't even flinch. Why you might ask? Probably the leaning in body language and interrogative tone Danny boy had delivered that last sentence in. His inner monologue scolded him for ending a sentence in a preposition, but damn it, sometimes words out of order have a greater effect and are more fitting to convey the proper emotional depth. In the text of this conversation, now was one of those times. It was almost as if Dan was asking Hayden if Rebecca had done this. He was baiting him. Dan wanted him to lose his cool with over-enthusiastic accusations of Becky's dishonesty.

Hayden saw right through it and didn't bite for a second. "Is that so?"

Dan smirked. "Well, that's what I understood until Tammy out there forwarded an internal email from your team that somehow made it into her inbox." Hayden had always liked Tammy. They shared funny jokes, stories, and memes when he was on that side of the building. "Not exactly following company policy or the chain of command, but I understand that sometimes going over someone's head is necessary."

Hayden guessed right, Dan knew. He also didn't show any tells when Dan divulged this info.

"I haven't spoken to anyone about this matter Hayden, not even the team member it came from." Hayden immediately guessed it was

Faith. Now the corner of his mouth had a slight upturn, Danny had cracked him. "I'll save you all the details, but the email suggests that the inevitable resolution was all actually your idea. It went into specific detail of how you had returned to work and swooped in "like Superman' I believe is how it was put, to save the day. It also imparted some additional info that I hadn't known. Is it true you've been coming in at three in the morning for some time?"

"Yes, just Fridays." It was a short solemn response as he knew Dan was planning to continue.

"Hayden, most of the time my responsibilities keep me focused on the future. The next big deal or opportunity. I don't often enough take stock and look at where we are and how we got here. You have not only been towing the company line, but you've been excelling at it I'm told." Then he did something that shocked even Hayden, He threw Hayden's presentation in the trash. "I'm sure that was an exemplary presentation, but I'm a man of efficiency and that…isn't important." Hayden was still too beside himself to register what he'd been saying. "This meeting is long overdue and for that I am sorry. I almost feel, I don't know, guilty, I guess. That I've overlooked you and the job you've been doing. Well, I'm sure you've been frustrated by that. I know I would've been. Yet how did you respond? You kept your nose down, kicked names, and took butt twice as hard." Hayden knew he hadn't misquoted the idiom.

It was a seller's jargon, which was also Dan's background. They spoke in clichés and shock terminology. In the office people called them DMs (as in Dan Murphyisms, not direct messages). Everyone had their favorites. Hayden's was "don't lift up my skirt and tell me there's nothing under there." Crass yes, but funny and ice breaking. "Hayden, I did a lot of digging on you over the week you've been gone. I know about your friend and the girl. No one knew you were seeing anyone, neither did Kent."

Hayden's mouth fell open and his face was void of expression.

Dave continued. "I do my research. I reached out to every one of your clients." Hayden could use a stiff cocktail. Dan continued before Hayden had a panic attack from the intrusion into his personal business. "I know you have been through a lot this past week. I can't fathom the pain and heartache you must be experiencing." Dan shook his head. "And yet I also know you have stayed on top of communication with your team and clients while you've been gone." Hayden's ears perked up, the slightest amount.

"I won't beat around the bush any longer Hayden. Here's what I'm going to do for you and only because you have more than earned it. As of today, you're getting a pay increase. How does a hundred thousand base with a $50k commission bonus structure in place sound?" Hayden's mouth was agape. "I'm going to take that as a positive response. We're going to give you a company car. We're bumping you to a new benefits plan, a seven percent matching 401k and you're getting six weeks of PTO." Dan tapped his dimpled chin. "It feels like there was something else."

"What else?" Hayden knew this had to be a joke. "Are you serious?"

"Yeah, but there's something else I knew I needed to tell you and I can't..." he trailed off. "Oh yeah, speaking of Kent, when he heard about what happened he put together a little two-week vacation package for when your girl gets out of the hospital. Speaking of that, I know it's none of my business and I apologize for not knowing, but what's happening there?"

This guy is for real, I'm impressed. I suppose that's how you become CEO. "Thanks for asking. She's has been in a medically induced coma for four days now. We don't really know. Fingers crossed."

"I know this isn't probably PC in the workplace, but you and me, we're sales guys. We're cut from the same cloth and sometimes we don't exactly play by the rules when it comes to professional communication." Hayden knew he was right and felt a twinge of pride with the comparison. "I'm really sorry and my family and I will be praying for her, and you."

Hayden brushed an unforeseen tear from his face. "I appreciate that, sir." He didn't add more yet since he hadn't wanted to accidently cut off Dan and the never-ending treasure trove he kept dumping in Hayden's lap. Every time Dan opened his mouth it was more good news for him, and Hayden didn't want to interrupt that.

"Just a couple more things." Yep, he was right, and excited to hear how there could possibly be more.

"One, I almost forgot this and for some people it's kind of a big deal. The corner office, it's yours." Dan stopped waiting for a reaction and nothing came for a few moments, Hayden merely produced a broken stare.

"Well? Cat gotch yer tongue?" His Scandinavian was showing.

The corner of the right side of Hayden's mouth lifted. "You were on a roll and I didn't want to stop you." They both laughed. "Dan, I can't begin to tell you how grateful I am right now. This is what I've been dreaming of for years here. I feel like all of that hard work was worth it. I don't feel deserving. Don't get me wrong, I'm never going to let you take any of it back." Hayden extended his hand over the table. "Really, truly, I want to say, thank you. This mean's the world to me."

"Now that's more like it!" was Dan's retort. "Look, I wasn't looking for accolade or praise because you did this, not me. Your work ethic and leadership have earned this. I need to know that this is exactly what you want."

"Yes, Dan, this is exactly what I wanted."

Dan stood up and walked around the desk. "I'm going to preface this with I'm going to touch you, but there is nothing sexually suggestive about it."

Hayden quipped back, "So ignore the coming ass-grab, got it."

It was a powerfully emotional moment for Hayden as Dan came over and gave him one quick heartfelt, yet professional hug. This was something he'd been working toward for a long time. One could say his entire life.

Dan concluded, "By the way, there was one other thing. This might possibly be your favorite part."

"I don't see how anything, other than my friend waking up, could be better than the news you gave me, but yeah, go for it. I ain't gonna stop you." Hayden used friend because seriously, who wouldn't think he was a three-ring circus, bouncing off the walls, nut if he called a girl he spent one night with his girlfriend.

"Here's the thing. We had a board meeting this morning and it's pretty obvious Rebecca lied and from what I gather, has been for a while now. So, we're going to have to let her go, Hayden. I want you to do it before end of day. I know, it doesn't seem fair, but firing is one of the day to day hats you'll have to wear as a vice president. This is an atypical situation. Think you can handle that?"

"Yes, sir."

"Good, have a good remainder of your day Hayden and let me be the first to congratulate you, VP."

"Thank you so much again, sir."

As if the smallest beam of sunlight had peeked through a crack in the clouds of a nuclear winter, Hayden felt a sliver of pure joy for the first time in he couldn't remember how long. Wait, he could pinpoint it to the exact moment. He'd heard the sentence, "I don't know about you, but I'm almost queasy from that emotional roller coaster." It had come from a smart mouth behind a butcher counter. How he wished she was here right now.

Hayden strolled the hallway across to the other side of the building where his team resided. They were all in a meeting in a dark conference room hosted by Rebecca regarding another client of theirs. Hayden calmed himself and lowered his shit-eating grin, well, for now anyway. He quietly ducked undetected into the back of the room and had a seat. Only when the lights came back on about ten minutes later and people were standing to exit did his team turn and see him. The girls rushed to him and threw their arms around him. Well, most of them that is.

Rebecca said, "Hayden, how good of you to join us. Hopefully, you're ready to get back to work after your week off."

He glared at her, as if to ask, "Why? Why are you this way? Who hurt you?"

Rebecca paused briefly and looked away after seeing his look. She realized she'd gone too far.

He decided not to even acknowledge it and said, "Based on what I'm seeing here I need to reach out to a couple of papers to see if I can get them to budge on rate. I have a strategy regarding that, but I need to need to schedule a quick conference call with the client yet today to see if we can make it work. I'd like it if we could all be on that call. Let's see if we can get something scheduled before five. Does that sound okay, Rebecca?" It wasn't the right time. He could be a narcissistic unfledged immature jerk, or the consummate professional he always had been that earned him his new position. His smile briefly returned. Just once he wanted to be petty, once he wanted to be satisfied, but that isn't how he was raised. After his mother's passing, he'd promised himself that he would always try his best to live his life in a way that would make her proud. That included always taking the high road.

* * *

THERE SHE SAT at the far end of the long maple table Hayden now approached. She had a look on her face that he instantly read. She knew she was getting sacked. That surprised him. Also, why was his inner monologue using terms like "sacked?" He was so nervous. He'd never had the authority to fire before. Now, the day he was given this power to wield, he was expected to give his own boss the axe. In all the scenarios he repetitively played out in his mind, this little twist of fate was definitively not one of them. He wasn't a fan, but also didn't want to appear vindictive. He considered the information that he held and the weight of the responsibility that came with it. This is going to change this woman's life forever.

Rebecca sat there in silence for an uncomfortable amount of time.

"Rebecca, I need to tell you a story." She looked at him perplexed. He advanced, despite her sneering gaze. "There was this woman who tragically died. Before gaining entrance into heaven an angel wanted to take her to see and experience hell, so they popped down. It had this lake of nutritious stew. It was an enticing medley of baby carrots, crisp celery, red russet potatoes, and juicy roast. It was as if Gordon Ramsey himself created the dish from scratch. There was one problem, the people only had ten-foot spoons. They were so frustrated trying to feed themselves." Rebecca had a look of righteous indignation. He knew he was testing her patience and she was getting, well, pissed off. He lingered, "So the people were miserable and starving. Then the woman was taken to heaven. Amazingly, heaven had the exact same stew and ten-foot spoons as well, but there was one glaring difference. Here the people were well fed. The woman asked the angel, 'why are they so different?' The angel replied with a smile 'because here they feed each other; these people have learned the way of love.' Do you know what I'm saying Rebecca?"

"Is the moral of the story that I'm fired?" She was going to own her reputation to the bitter end. She had one of those voices that grated on a person.

"I see your veneer, Rebecca, and not once did I bite. I gave you every ounce of respect when you started. Somewhere down the line, previous of your time here, someone treated you poorly and it spurned you. However, we both know that was never the case here. You needed to let that die there. Yes, you are fired. I take no solace in this. I'm happy to write you a letter of recommendation."

"Oh, I'm sure you would." She rolled her eyes and drew out the word "sure."

"I already did." Hayden handed her a two-page document.

Rebecca had a knowing smile on her face as she snatched them away. Slowly but surely the contours of her face shifted as she scanned the stolen document. Her patronizing grin lazily lowered to a resting face as she read more. Her eyes lightened and began glazing over. "Why would you write this? We both know I don't deserve this from you Hayden. Is this some sick twisted plot to get revenge?"

"No, Rebecca, it's not. Though I think some of your ways are very misguided, I do think you're management material. You have to believe that you deserve to be where you are like everyone else does. No more firing people because they disagree with you. Treat them as they would you. Collaborate rather than bicker. From here on out, co-workers are working with you, not against you. Understand?" She put her hand to her cheek. What was he saying? What did from here on out mean? "Rebecca, just so you know, I'm calling you Becky from here on out." A huge grin appeared on his face. "It's the one thing that is non-negotiable."

"Hayden, what in the hell are you talking about?"

"Becky," he paused for a substantial amount of time, "have I ever been anything but respectful of you? A week ago doesn't count, you were asking for that."

"No."

"So, you would say you can probably trust me?"

"I don't trust anyone, Hayden."

"I know, that's what got us into this mess to begin with. That's all changing about right" —he looked down at his wrist as if there were a watch on it— "now and here's why. I had gotten off the phone with JBass to ask what times a conference call today would work for them. During it some new information came to light. They let go of Matt." During the "courting to earn their business" portion of their relationship both Rebecca and Hayden had both gotten to know Matt Fish well. "I guess he wasn't getting it done over there. What I found out is he was plagiarizing the media plans we put together and then pawned it off as his own. I confirmed with James they were our plans. I could hear in his voice he was still pretty upset and despite that he asked who put them together. Well, it turns out he was impressed. We both know that's partially your work, Becky."

She gave him a sideways glance.

Hayden sustained. "So, I asked James if they've filled the position. He put two and two together and he asked if I had someone in mind. I gave them your name Rebecca and that letter. I told him that I hadn't spoken to you yet and I'd get back to him shortly."

To say that Rebecca was flabbergasted would be a colossal understatement. "But why?" She couldn't comprehend.

"For several reasons, not all selfless." Hayden smiled. "Here is their offer." He pulled the slip of paper back quickly from her outstretched fingers. "This is contingent."

There was that knowing smirk again. "Oh yeah, on what?"

"All the media is bought through us."

"But I—"

He cut her off, "Don't deserve it? Yeah, I know."

"Then why?"

"A conscience, altruism, trying to be a better man." Hayden sighed. "Who knows?" He knew. This staunch digging of his heels into the sand of morality wasn't mere coincidence. His character was growing stronger for a woman that may never know she truly did make him a better person. It turns out it wasn't a cliché men use to come on to women. It defied logic and reason. Either way, he decided to take the high road less traveled. "Maybe I'm hoping some pendulum of karma can swing my direction for a change." The way Sloane grabbed him at Perkins ran through his mind. His heart and other parts of him yearned momentarily.

Rebecca pleaded, "I know you have zero reason to believe me, but I'm sorry. I heard what happened. I can't apologize enough for my rude comment before."

He rebutted, "Let's not act like we're going to be best friends here and keep this transactional. I am still harboring some feelings on behalf of people that are no longer here thanks to you. You haven't been held accountable for any of your actions to this point. You do not deserve this. I'm a decent person, but you have been terrible to everyone."

She was choking up a little bit. "I know, I know. I admit it. I'm sorry."

"I'm doing this for the company, not you, so we're clear." With that he handed her the slip of paper. Her eyes grew to the size of kumquats. "Yeah, I thought you'd like that." Referring to her entire compensation package. "They'll even pay for the move. Also, your lead will be Faith."

"But I don't think—"

"Rebecca!"

"Sorry, old habits."

"Agreed? This is a one-time offer Becky and it ends when I walk out that door, so what will it be?"

"Yes, are you kidding me? California and a huge raise? Yes, please I agree."

"Great, you start in two weeks. I even took the liberty of putting together contact info for you to gather shipping bids."

"Boy, you can't get rid of me fast enough huh?"

He took one last jab while he could for good measure, "I would pay you for the chance to move you out tomorrow." She picked up on the sarcasm in his voice and let that comment slip by her defense.

"I guess I should say thank you, Hayden."

"Not exactly how you expected this conversation to go, was it?"

"You're like Ferris Bueller, aren't you? Nothing sticks to you."

"Oh, how I wish that were true."

She awkwardly hugged him. It was weird for them both, especially since he didn't really reciprocate it. He stood there with his arms at his sides being squeezed. He stepped back and shook her hand. They both respectively went on their ways.

Hayden walked back over to his team and asked if he could take them all out for a late dinner and drinks next door after the conference call. He said he had news. They all readily agreed, guessing what it may have been. I mean it was free food and alcohol. What more do you need?

He reached into his pocket and dug out his cell phone and hit Nurse Kodi's phone number and waited for it to ring.

CHAPTER 29

❄

He'd never even heard of the Anshun Bridge before its beauty took his breath away as they made their final approach that first night. The bridge was majestic in the foreground of this foreign land. The way the entire structure was illuminated and then reflected in the water of the Jin River should have made it one of the seven wonders.

After his conversation with Nurse Kodi, Luke was taken by police escort directly south to Terminal one at the MSP Airport. The undercover sedan drove right onto the runway and parked in front of an open hangar. Luke had never experienced that before. He was the sole occupant of a small jet from Minneapolis to San Francisco. They landed and came to rest directly alongside a Concorde jet. They had him deplane and quickly transfer. "Wait," he said aloud to the hostess quickly attending to his bags, "weren't those de-commissioned a few years ago?"

Her eyes widened and then landed in a firm stare that told him to stop asking frivolous questions, "Yes."

If they weren't allowing the momentary pause of re-fueling, that was maybe a half hour, then this has elevated way beyond what he thought. He struggled and spoke under his breath to himself, "It's really happening." He felt an enormous lump form in the back of his throat.

For the next six hours Luke was supersonic. Chengdu was as close to Wuhan that the Chinese government would allow Luke and his team to set up shop.

Luke's hamster wheel was spinning at the maximum RPM level it could reach without "seizing the engine" so to speak. He searched for the distance and realized they were at nearly a thousand-mile radius. That was insane. At this point it was thought that the virus' origins began in a market or possibly a laboratory somewhere in Wuhan.

While in the air Luke led a Zoom conference call for the company's board. They had been awaiting this meeting and all hands were on deck the moment they received the invite. His final words were "… and make sure you stay up twelve hours past when you feel like you need to go to bed tonight. I need you all adjusted to overnights as quickly as possible. We need you to be able to work in real time with the infrastructure team over here. Time equals lives people, it's really that simple. This is our moment. The world needs us, and we will give it everything we've got or die trying." They all looked around the table at each other nodding in silent agreement and pride.

The pilot leaned over his shoulder and told Luke he might want to get some shut-eye. After the whirlwind last day of his life with Sloane and now this, he watched the insides of his eyelids for an hour, max.

When Luke arrived at the airport, late Friday afternoon, he was picked up by a motorcade with at least a dozen vehicles. He was in a black, tinted window, bulletproof Cadillac Escalade. All he could think was "wow, they mean business." Inside of it were a man and a woman. He extended his hand to introduce himself. They retreated as if struck by a snake and gave him a double take. Their looks would have been less judgmental had he had a single horn protruding from his forehead.

The woman merely waved and threw a mask at him matching those they were wearing. "We aren't touching. Don't touch anyone!" Luke pulled his hand back and rested it in his lap. The man was to be his translator. His name was Bryan and looked to be about forty. Kate, the recently candid woman, was serving as the ambassador from the U.S. Embassy and Consulate. She spoke again. "Mr. Harder, I've been asked to take you straight to your new lab and warehouses."

"That's fine, during the drive can I make some personal calls?"

"Go right ahead, we'll be there shortly, so please keep it limited to ten to fifteen minutes. We literally have no time to waste."

Luke pressed the icon with Hayden's face and got caught up on Sloane's surgery. He was very pleased it was a success.

"She's not out of the woods," Hayden said. "She's more like entering them."

Luke sat silently as he listened to everything Hayden explained regarding the details of Sloane's case. "Hey, I am only going to be here for ninety-six hours. I've agreed to get the infrastructure set up and kick out the first batch of product. Then my buddy is going to take over and I'm headed right back, okay?"

"Alright, how are things going there?"

"Hayden, I can't begin to tell you how crazy this is. We'll sit down in the atrium and talk about it, okay?"

"Sounds good."

"If anything happens…"

"Don't worry, Mr. Harder, I'll call you the moment I see or hear anything."

"I'd say you can call me Luke, Mr. Foster. I think you've earned it."

"So long as you call me Hayden."

"Deal." They finished the conversation with pleasantries and wished each other "good luck".

CHAPTER 30

❄

The virus was given many names, but its official name is "severe acute respiratory syndrome Coronavirus 2 (SARS-CoV-2)." At Rikr's headquarters they called it Covid. Symptoms included fever, cough, and difficulty breathing. The people most susceptible were those with weakened immune systems and prior respiratory issues. For the most part, it was killing the elderly at an alarming rate and in a very condensed timeline once contracted. In most cases of death, people had three weeks to live once they started to feel slightly warm.

Two weeks ago, they had been one of a handful of companies in the world given top security clearance for a private videoconference held by Chinese leadership in Beijing. Their company, Rikr, was asked to do their part in saving the world. Rikr was a condensed combination of the words "Ripe" and "Sticker".

During the briefing, more than a few times, people looked around the room gauging if they understood the momentousness of what they were hearing. After logging off, Luke stood and addressed the room. "I think this is the perfect time to use the phrase 'smoke 'em if you got 'em'." No one laughed. It was an ill-timed attempt at humor. When he was extremely nervous Luke would say the most inappropriate things. As if his filter no longer functioned when he got too riled. "Everyone take a fifteen minute break to get your bearings and meet right back here."

Luke walked out a side door leading to a small walkway between their building and the company next door. He leaned against the building, puked into a nearby trash can, then slowly slid to the ground with his head buried in his hands.

Pandemic. He barely knew what that word meant a half hour ago. The emotional equivalent of an atomic bomb was delivered to everyone in that room. Two million. That couldn't be right, there was just no way. Two million people dead in twelve to eighteen months? That's a city nearly the size of Houston. Imagine if Houston were to drop off the map. Easy to imagine in terms of a map, but the cataclysmic shift to people's lives should something like that happen was incomprehensible. Everyone in the world would be within two degrees of a Coronavirus victim.

There were so many numbers and projections thrown around it was hard to stay focused, but that number, will be impossible to forget for the rest of his life. There were a multitude of variables to consider and ways to drop those numbers significantly, but the world needed to act quickly and drastically. But that wasn't really happening.

Our lives would drastically change. The only way for us to contain this was two-fold. One, was staying a safe distance apart from one another and only leaving the house for essentials. This would "flatten the curve." Another phrase that would soon become typical household vernacular. The other part, was how quickly they could manufacture and distribute Cloniquin.

The description of what Covid was going to look like on U.S. soil made America appear like China during the bird flu, swine flu, and SARS, but much worse than all of them combined. Everyone wearing masks everywhere.

When the host of the video conference switched from Mandarin to English, everyone quickly sat up and gave him their undivided attention. "A lot of people are going to die, and we only need serious people right now that understand the severity of what we're dealing with here. This is "Real News." The world is basically about to shut down. A cluster of pneumonia cases in the Hubei province will be announced in the next day or two. Everyone will downplay it. This is no joke. This is why you are here."

After Rikr's hour-long meeting that took place after the conference call; the board set up a timeline for response and implementation. They needed to work their butts off for the next two weeks. So when the call came from the Chinese government everyone would be ready.

Luke had been given a contact named Marcus Rondo that was serving as a liaison between Rikr and the Chinese government. He was already on the ground in the Sichuan Province. He was to be Luke's "jack of all trades" guy that was ready to address any needs prior to Luke's arrival in China. Marcus had already secured the location for the lab and inventory storage. He had hired and established temporary housing for the team of scientists and labor force the Rikr board had contracted for the foreseeable future. Luke made it a point to adamantly request that the workers were paid double what they should have been with plush accommodations to work in. The company didn't need sweat-shop allegations swirling as they were about to take off. Then once Luke got the infrastructure in place they would then handle the production in China. The Chinese government would be hands-off from that point.

China would pay for their own and only their own vaccines. They also realized that despite the best efforts that could be implemented at this juncture, Covid-19 would be a global pandemic. The National People's Congress had a special secret session where under cloak and dagger they unanimously passed laws that expedited and relaxed all red tape on Cloniquin. Essentially China waived every drug trial, tax, and tariff for Rikr.

The People's Republic of China needed to squash all perceptions of profit. They were going to take a beating on the world stage regardless. They didn't need an even bigger black eye. Covid was already being called "The Chinese Virus" by many.

The WHO and NMPA, the Chinese equivalent of the FDA, granted

Rikr immediate clearance for mass production and gave the delivery contract to Amazon. Usually there was a lengthy process which would take a year and a half before the general consumer would be able to get their hands on a medication. There were clinical trials and animal testing, but Rikr already had the NMPA's highest seal of approval for the stickers. They were deemed completely safe. That's one big hurdle the company didn't have to deal with.

It was a sticker, but the engineers back at Rikr knew they needed to make modifications for consumers to slap it on themselves rather than produce. The process moved quickly once a mysterious email with the schematics for the NicoDerm patches miraculously landed in Luke's now fully encrypted email server. After they combined their formula with the patch all Rikr employees slapped on the first available patches off the line as a sign of solidarity and patriotism. They were now all in this together.

From a business standpoint, it was known as a homerun product. When the company realized exactly how vital they were in all of this, Luke made some big, quick decisions. He needed the advice, intelligence, and wisdom of those he trusted the most. There was no one Luke trusted more than his old naval buddy Keith. They'd been through everything together in each other's lives since basic. He was the first call Luke had made after receiving the news about Sloane from Rae. When Luke called him after having been in China for less than a day and told him to hop on a plane, no questions asked in three hours, his only reply was: "I can be ready in two."

Keith Harrison was an actuary. While Luke didn't know much about the profession, what little he did know seemed like vital information right now. Actuaries were good with numbers. Not good at just numbers, but good at evolving complex numbers. Most of the time they work for industries like insurance, financial investment, and accounting firms. They're like prognosticators.

Keith was great at evaluating the numbers and seeing all the variables to accurately predict the future. He saw depth and breadth the likes of which could be compared to Gretzky with a puck.

He had one all-important, yet seemingly impossible, task. Determining the price of Cloniquin. He came up with an algorithm and plugged in every variable he and his team could come up with. Now that he was in China, two days after Luke, he could paint a much clearer picture of the overhead numbers and figured out nearly everything this was going to entail. It needed to be affordable enough for governments to purchase it for everyone. It seemed like the only way to avoid free-market nightmares of who would get it and who wouldn't. Keith landed on $53.66, so they rounded it off to $55.

CHAPTER 31

❄

It had now been four days since Luke had left his daughter's bedside. He was half a world away now headed back to the airport to return to her. Luke rode in the back of a stretch limo. It seemed like a big waste to him. The only passengers were himself and a small box about a foot high, deep, and wide. He wasn't worth all of the hubbub and grandeur, but the contents of his little "friend" were.

As the jet was taxiing the runway, he called Hayden. He picked up after a couple of rings. There was a lot of noise in the background. "Hayden, Hello? Hello?" He was louder the second time.

"Luke, hold on a minute." You could pick up on the rustling of a phone and Luke could hear him moving. "Let me walk outside to talk." Finally, there was silence on the other end of the line. "I'm in the parking lot of the restaurant next door to my office. I'm taking my team out for dinner. We had to work late. Sorry about the noise."

"How is Sloane?" Luke would check in with Hayden at the hospital every day.

Hayden exhaled deeply. "I got off the phone about an hour ago with Kodi. Unfortunately, we're rapidly approaching day five." He choked up a little bit, "There's still no change."

Luke had feared as much. Even though he knew not to get his hopes up, he was still heartbroken every day when he learned that nothing had changed.

Hayden continued, "I knew I'd be working late. I asked Kodi if it would be okay if I stopped by after visiting hours today. Otherwise I wouldn't get to see her."

"What did she say?"

"It took some sweet talking, but I'm headed out from here in about five minutes to go see her."

"Then I'll let you go since you're busy with more important things. Please give her a hug and kiss for me. I'll be back by Tuesday night."

"Will do, sir, and safe travels. I'll see you soon."

"Yep, thanks, Hayden. You're my rock."

* * *

IT FELT NEARLY impossible at times to gather the gumption to go on. Every time he wanted to give up and remove himself from his own life, even for a day to sleep, he thought of her. He really wished he would have gotten a picture with her. Some visual aids would come in handy for inspiration. Right now, all he had was his memory and with the drowsiness now seeping in, it was hard to retain the acuity her beauty deserved. She was perfect to him. Easily one in a billion. There it was. There was the motivational push he needed. He summoned the little energy he had and sucked it up. Hayden wondered if she would do all of this for him? Probably not, considering the last thing she had said. He wished she knew the truth.

Hayden walked over to his high barstool and without sitting down laid down a couple hundred dollars on the table. I want you guys to have a great time and eat and drink to your heart's content. Be responsible, okay?

"Where are you going?" Kirk asked. Kirk was one of Hayden's rock stars. He'd been basically covering for him back at the office during all of this.

Hayden put his arm around his upper-back and his hand gripped Kirk's shoulder. He whispered in his ear, "Do you trust me?"

"Yeah, without hesitation, why?"

"Dude, at least hesitate, what if I'm wrong? I don't need the pressure of being on your pedestal." Hayden's face cracked and Kirk reciprocated the arm shoulder gesture.

"You know what I mean." Kirk corrected himself with the look of feigned frustration.

Hayden smiled. "Good, because what's about to come to light here would cause most to question. Don't, I got you. I'm not going to say anything yet. You know how superstitious I get. You're going to have to lend me some of that blind faith." I'll do everything I can to pay the debt in full and then some. Kirk cast him an incidental look of bewilderment.

With that Hayden raised his hand in a gesturing manner toward his team. "Faith, can I talk to you outside for a minute?" Faith's face instantly wrenched like a dog curling up about to get hit. Nevertheless, she followed behind. Hayden thought briefly, *maybe that's why I have problems with women, I keep comparing them to dogs.* Women loved being called dogs. Sometimes he would shake his own head in disbelief at his absurdity. If only people knew what went on in that head of his they'd probably run for the hills. By the time that thought finished, they were back in the same spot in the parking lot where he'd been about five minutes ago.

Faith started, "What's up?" The delivery of the question wasn't overly confident. As if she was worried about the response. Her extremities were lightly shaking.

Hayden observed the stress she was under. "Relax. Breathe. This is the opposite of bad."

Faith's shoulders dropped as she exhaled loudly. "Hayden, holy, you were freaking me out!" She punched him in the shoulder. "Don't do that!"

"Hey, you were the one that got all contorted for no reason. This is me, don't treat me any differently than you have before. It's weird."

They chuckled and hugged. He always loved hugging. It broke the ice on a friendly level and helped ease the stress of a first encounter. He and Faith had gotten close.

"Okay, Hayden, spit it out! You're killing me here."

Hayden began, "A lot has happened since you and I last spoke."

"One could say that." If sarcasm was peanut butter, this would have definitely been chunky. Faith winked and it eased the tension for both of them.

He was about to plow through when she interjected, "Did you get the VP or not? I mean that's what this was all about here, right? Hayden, is she gone? Did you kill the wicked witch of the west suburbs?

"Whoa, slow down." Hayden could see how riled up she was getting. He knew how to shift her gears rapidly. "This happy hour slash dinner here has nothing to do with me. We're here for you." She gave him her typical Faith triple-take. They all gave her a hard time for it, and they all had their own impressions of it. She knew they did because they'd done them so many times for her. She was always a good sport about it. Now Hayden enacted his. He took pride in his delivery.

She chuckled and punched him again "Stop it, I do not look like that!"

"Faith, I have good news and bad news. Which would you like first?"

Her brow furrowed. "The bad news, of course."

"You're still going to be working with Becky."

Her eyes got huge and without realizing she was speaking, she spat out, "What the?"

"I know, I know." He was still smiling delivering this info. Faith was wondering why.

Hayden reverted to a seven-year-old for a minute and raised his hand emphatically. "Ooo, ooo, ooo, pick me, pick me!" She laughed as she gestured at him like she was his teacher calling on him for the answer. He beamed. "Guess why?"

"Why?"

"Cuz you're her new boss!"

Faith's face went blank. "What?" was all she could muster.

Hayden did a weird little shuffle dance that looked like the offspring of an excited baboon and a leprechaun. "Becky, and that's her new name officially, not even joking, will be the new Marketing Director for JBass. She'll be booking all of their media through us. Here's the best part, she leaves in a few days for City of Industry California."

"How? Why?" She was unraveling.

"Tell me it wasn't you that 'accidently' forwarded that email to Tammy?" She looked down at the white paint dividing the parking spaces in the lot their office complex shared with this restaurant and a Country Inn & Suites. She obviously couldn't deny it. "For my second act I'm making you a team lead and JBass is your first client. Don't fuck it up!" He said it in a loving big brother way that said, yeah, I swore, but right now you love me so get over the shock that your boss swore at you and move on lady.

"I don't know what to say. What does this even mean? Can I tell you what to do?"

"No, you pretentious bitch!" He could help it; he was enjoying this too much right now to stop yet. She gave him a look that said he was being an arrogant prick. "Too far?"

"Ya think?"

"Sorry. You know how I get wound up sometimes." She knew. "You are taking over my cube. I worked JBass' human resources for you."

Faith asked "Which means? You're so obtuse sometimes!"

He knew he was ruffling her feathers with the overly dramatic elocution of her news. "It means I explained to them I was saving them forty grand plugging Becky in at the position. Between recruitment firm fees and the two to three months it would take to properly back-fill the job. They agreed and said if everything with her checked out they'd be willing to pay. So now. Faith, you get a little signing bonus. After Becky passed the background check, they wired the funds. Then I went to payroll and had them cut a check to one Faith Sharper for…?" He trailed off as he reached inside his suit coat pocket for the check. "The full twenty grand!" He handed her the slip of paper and Faith started bawling.

Hayden had called Dan and received approval once he had explained everything that had happened with JBass and Rebecca. "Hayden, as long as you're making money in a respectful way for the company, I'm giving you pretty much carte blanche. On a completely unrelated note, do you know of anyone else like you? Feel free to forward me their resume." Hayden chuckled and imagined he was going to love working more closely with this man. They really were alike. As he handed her the check her hands went to her mouth, like back at Henry's.

"From what I hear that will cover like half of what a wedding will cost. Sorry, it's the best I could do."

"Hayden, I love you."

"I know, but you're already taken, and I respect Dustin too gosh darn much."

She scowled. "But how did you know?"

"I was there."

Instantly a full facial flush overtook her with embarrassment. "You were not!"

"Yeah, Tony and I 'cooked up' your upside-down cake."

"You *were* there!" She realized he was telling her the truth. "Did you see how nervous Dustin was?"

"The look on your face when he smashed that cake down on the table, that's what I'll remember the most," he lied.

The satisfying look of sheer joy you had on your face is what I'll always recall. That and what happened right after it.

"But, Hayden, that's your client."

"No, it's *our* client."

Faith pointed out, "Yeah, well you landed it."

"I was a part of landing it."

She gave him a sideways smile.

"Don't worry, I'm good. After all, I'm a vice president." Hayden beamed, he couldn't hold it back another second.

"I knew it."

"Really though, this is about you. I have to go."

Faith's gaze shifted straight into his eyes. "I'm so sorry." He realized she knew. The remainder of the conversation was taking a turn for the ominous deep end of the pool. "How did you—?"

"You've been out for over a week. For a guy that doesn't really take vacations, there's been a lot of speculation about what you've been up to. I hope you're not upset, but we were worried about you and did a little digging."

"So, Kirk told you?"

"I mean we had to tickle torture him, if it paints him in a more respectful light." Hayden hadn't told Kirk not to tell anyone, just to keep it on the down-low. He didn't need everyone knowing his business, so he left it up to Kirk's discretion for those that needed to be "in the loop."

"I would have thought he could hold out at least until he saw the waterboarding apparatus." Hayden entertained himself with his cheesiness more frequently than others. It was one of those weaker references Sloane would have considered cringe-worthy.

"Hayden, we all loved Andy. I hope you know that. He was one of a kind. He was the life of the party. From the after-work happy hours he would crash to your crazy birthday party. There isn't one person here that met him that didn't adore him and his energy. I can't imagine losing my best friend. And she's not even that fun." That got him to crack a tiny smile. "And I'm so sorry for you. I want to hug you and never let you go." She reached for him. They embraced for a long moment. The tables turned as she now comforted him. She pulled back and wiped her face one final time. "Now get out of here. I won't be the reason for one more second you're not with her."

He grinned like an idiot and opened his door, hopped in, turned the key, and rolled down the window. "Congratulations, Faith, you deserve it. Now go in there and celebrate with the team."

She blew him a kiss he'd never see as his taillights dropped out of sight before the on-ramp to 494.

He was headed to her.

CHAPTER 32

Stealth was the name of the game.

Kodi was specific in how she explained the rules. "If we catch you after visiting hours which are nine A.M. to eight P.M., we're required to ask you to leave and return the following day." He had heard her emphasis on the word "catch" and "ask." He would need to sneak from the front door of the East Bank Hospital to Sloane's room. That included two nurses' stations located smack dab between himself and the end zone. He approached the first one and stoked up a conversation out of thin air. He was in his outgoing element. Hayden always spoke to his ability to read people as a by-product skillset he'd picked up after having talked to forty different people on the phone every day for the last few years. Frequently he knew what people were thinking or going to say before they said it. He swore he'd missed his calling as a therapist. The random things people would tell you on the phone about their personal lives in such a short window of time knowing them, was astounding.

Most of the time the key was speaking first. Oh, and flattery, flattery got you everywhere. More specifically, undetected flattery. That was the key. If you could butter someone up without them knowing, the world could be your oyster.

If these tactics didn't work, bribery tended to do the trick. He held behind his back two cheesecakes that he stopped to get at Lund's grocery. They were those individually divided by wax paper types. There was Oreo, strawberry or cherry swirl, turtle, hot fudge, chocolate chip, and then like three plain vanilla scattered throughout. It was nearly a guarantee there would be something here they'd like.

Hayden sauntered up to the desk like he had important business to discuss. Then, he flipped the situation on its ear. This was where Hayden shined. Instead of bullshitting his way by them, he was dead honest. Somehow, and he had no real idea how, it usually worked.

"You gorgeous, gorgeous ladies at the end of your long shift. Your feet must be killing you and I'm sure your patience for BS is wearing extremely thin. I'm going to be straight forward with you. I know it's after hours and I know that I'm not supposed to be here." He cracked a big smile.

One of the nurses, likely a head nurse by her attitude, butted in. "And you thought we were gonna let you charm your way by with those dimples, didn't you?"

Usually when most people were called out like this they would retreat and back down or feebly try some other plan B type of tactic. Hayden wasn't like most other people. He never had a plan B. He would push his chips all-in. It would either work or he'd go down engulfed in a ball of flames.

"Me, oh hell no. I don't stand a chance with you two." She was giving off the "don't' mess with me" vibe via her standoffish disposition. However, she couldn't help but smirk at his self-deprecating humor. He knew her type. Hayden needed to convey to her that he knew she was in charge. He shouldn't mess with her or she'd kick his ass.

It was the opening he needed to bring forth the cream cheese delicacy. He gulped. She tilted her head in the direction of Sloane's room. He smiled and grabbed her by the wrists to express his appreciation, before she could protest the physical gesture, he had let go. The other nurse was giddy over the dessert. About ten steps down the hallway she peeked around the desk and yelled "Thanks Hayden, Sloane's a lucky girl!" He did a pivot to an about-face and gave her a knowing look. The hard-ass nurse yelled at her in an amusing tone to shut her "big damn mouth". Everyone knew.

There were three nurses at the next stop. They must have come on for the overnight. They were chatting amongst themselves. "So, I told him that if he wanted me to come over, he was gonna need to call me before ten. Girl, you know this doesn't happen like poof." She was presenting herself in the style of a model and snapped her fingers.

Her colleague cleared her throat with an imaginary cough as Hayden approached. "Ah ha hem, Ali." She turned around, her eyes went wide, and her hand went to her mouth.

Rather than employing his ninja skills at this station he merely walked up, placed the cheesecake on the desk, and said "Ladies, it seems as if you were all given prior notification of my arrival." They acted nonchalant and oblivious in an overtly obvious way. They couldn't even make eye contact with him without blushing. "If it's okay?" Hayden pointed in the direction of Sloane's room.

The last nurse scurried around before he was out of sight and stopped him to give him a hug. "We all know what happened and what you've been through Hayden." She kissed him on the cheek. "We're all rooting for her to wake up."

He simply smiled and thanked her.

He approached her suite and peeked through a crack in the door. There was an overhead TV on across the room from the foot of her bed. An old re-run of Password had created a white noise in the room.

The curtain was blocking her bed. He walked in and peeked around the fabric. He stood gazing at her angelic face. If nothing else, he thought, he had a beautiful girl once upon a time. Even if it was impossibly short to legitimately reference her as his.

Rae must have fallen asleep in her chair at her daughter's bedside. Then he picked up on motion. For the briefest of moments its source was imperceptible since he'd only caught it peripherally. Hayden's spirit rose. However, as quickly, he realized Rae was rubbing Sloane's shoulder with her thumb. She was still barely awake. He lightly rapped three times on the table next to Sloane's bed. The knock startled Rae enough for her to pull back. "Oh no." He piped up with an outstretched arm toward her. "Don't stop on my account. I didn't want to startle you."

Rae smiled at him. "Hayden, I didn't think you were going to be able to make it."

"Are you kidding? Our Sloaneside chats are my favorite." Then it was her turn to reach out for him. She hugged him tightly. This was likely taking quite the toll on her. No parent should have to see their child unresponsive in a hospital bed. She gestured for him to take her chair next to Sloane. Though every part of his upbringing told him not to take the chair of a disabled woman, the overwhelming need to feel Sloane didn't make him balk even momentarily. Rae took his hand, placed it on Sloane's and squeezed.

The moment their skin made contact he was blown back into the seat. It must have scraped along the floor two to three feet making one of those horrific screeching sounds. Rae gasped at the event. "What was that?"

"Didn't you feel it? It's exactly what I felt last time. Remember I was trying to tell you guys? It's so difficult to explain. It's a shock through my entire body, but it doesn't hurt. You were touching me though this time when it happened. You seriously didn't feel that? It's so powerful it's like I'm getting shot in the back with a shotgun and no one can see it." Rae responded, "No, I didn't feel anything. It's really weird." Hayden realized he was sort of freaking her out with all of this. "Look, I know how strange this is, but I also can't help but feel like it's not nothing. That I'm feeling this for a reason." He scooted the chair now back beside Sloane. Then reached, albeit very hesitantly, for her hand again. He kept about an inch from her epidermis looking for an arch of electricity or some type of similar phenomenon, but to no avail. He slowly once again intertwined his fingers with hers. Now there was nothing. It looked and felt normal. Granted, a replacement definition had taken over his life's version of normal as of late, but there was no longer a sharp distinctive sensation.

He watched her intently for about a half a minute. When no new fireworks erupted, he closed his eyes to see if removing his sense of sight might heighten his other senses, like touch, and he would feel it again. It's not like this feeling was faint. It was one of the strongest things, if not the strongest, he'd ever felt. When nothing happened and he allowed himself to relax a little.

"I spoke with Luke about an hour ago. He's on his way back now. He'll be here by this time tomorrow." Hayden was half expecting a smile, an affirmative reply, something. She was too set in her ways and had been let down too many times by this man. Maybe once she could give him the benefit of the doubt, but that would likely mean at least once he would have needed to come through. She wasn't going to get caught holding her breath.

"Oh yeah, what else did he have to say?" Rae was at least attempting not to convey true disdain at the mention of his name. After all, he had paid for the surgery that at least prolonged the life of her daughter. Hayden looked down and reached for Sloane's hand.

"He asked me to give her a hug and—" He was cut off. Not by anyone, but one specific thing…or in this case three specific things. Rae could visibly see him jolt each one of the three times. They were very distinct. In that moment, he also concluded this wasn't electricity. Static was never perfectly successive like this. It was random and sporadic. This phenomenon that he was experiencing, the one that he couldn't explain, it had, well… a pattern.

CHAPTER 33

❋

"Dr. Knox," she repeated. "I kinda like the sound of that."

"Keep dreaming! I think you have to have at least two brain cells rubbing together upstairs to pull off the extra letters." Andy was referring to P, H, and D in this case.

Sloane smiled, thinking Andy was pretty darn witty himself. Her mind went on a bit of a bender for a few thinking about male and female friendships and how they work. The rule of thumb here was universally known or should be. A woman could be friends with a guy, but guys couldn't be friends with girls. Something seemed to always get in the way. About ninety-nine-percent of the time that thing was a penis.

However, with every rule, there are always exceptions. Other than being gay, they are as follows:

- Those where one of them is dating or have dated a friend (Check)
- They have too cool of a personality to keep out of your life, subheading excessively funny (Check)

- They remind each other too much of themselves. (No one wants to date themselves, self-gratification aside. Check)

IF THE TWO individuals in question share those things in common, then true platonic friendship was possible. They asked one another the darkest secrets about each other's best friends. Then funny drunk stories started to come out. They would both laugh until crying at one another. Then they would cry and hug and the whole unhealthy cycle would fire up again. Sloane's favorite was the story about how Andy met PG's dad.

"It was our first night together and we were both loaded. I mean bent sideways. I remembered one thing before we poured ourselves into bed. I asked her if I could borrow her charger so I could call an Uber in the morning. Pan to seven A.M. and the phone snaps me out of a deep, drunken slumber. I swipe right. "Hey, Dad, what's up?' To which comes a reply of 'who the hell is this?". I had grabbed the wrong phone and swiped right on the wrong dad. Basically, verifying his daughter was a tramp." They both laughed so hard at that one. "To this day, I've still yet to meet him in person. I guess he's like five foot six and one forty sopping wet and I'm truly scared to death of the guy."

Sloane's head tilted back in hysterical cackling. She reached for Andy's arm to steady herself. He started telling her something about undergarments and then bam! Another energy wave with the same impact of the first landed on them both. They tumbled backward ass over teakettle. There was never any pain associated with this sensation. It was all-consuming. Sloane was the first to her feet, followed shortly thereafter by Andy.

They walked the fifteen to twenty feet that now separated them and stood before one another. "How?" Sloane rubbed her head to clear the cobwebs.

"Like I know." Andy shrugged.

Then something hit Sloane like a smack square to the face. Andy saw the look on her face. She hadn't said a word, yet this idiot was agreeing.

"What are you nodding at, you moron?" Sloane smiled.

"Hayden is the luckiest SOB. He always has been. We would have been good friends." She embarrassingly smiled back at him. "What's this would have been shit?" She knew what he meant. "PG didn't do too bad herself." There was a mutual respect there.

"New development, Sparky." It was a new nickname she had conjured for him. "It would seem there are a couple of other options we missed regarding our mysterious EMP friend. I think there's something we may have missed or not scientifically proven wrong yet."

Andy agreed.

"Thanks, Captain Obvious!" She rolled her eyes at him as he continued.

"Well, what do we know? What has been the common denominator every time it's happened?" Andy asked.

Sloane extended a hand in his direction in explanation. "That's something I wanted to discuss. Listen, I've been thinking a lot about this. What if this isn't as simple as what have they had in common?"

"You're confusing the hell out of me girl."

"I know that's *so* hard to do." She loved giving him crap nearly half as much as Hayden. "What's the best way for me to explain this so we're both on the same wavelength? I have an idea. This is probably going to get a little technical. What was your best subject in school?"

"Anatomy and Chemistry, baby." Andy's grin proved he was proud of himself.

Through true giggling amusement she begrudgingly retorted, "You are hopeless…and funny, Andy. Justine was really lucky."

"Thanks." He got serious for the briefest of moments. "It was math, I've always been pretty good with numbers. I encountered this gangly little piss ant that always sat next to and annoyed the hell outta me in math class. He ain't too shabby himself. Obviously not as good as me…"

"Wait did you just give me your bromance meet-cute?"

"What, No!" His cheeks flushed.

"Andy loves chick flicks; Andy loves chick flicks!"

"Shut up, someone will… Oh wait, no, go ahead, get it out of your system! Andy loves chick flicks! Andy loves chick flicks." When he joined in on the chant it ruined it for her.

"Are you gonna shut up now so I can explain this?" She gave him a tilt of her head and judgmental stare.

He acted like she was an overbearing man-hater. "Ooo, maybe Hayden lucked out. Hell hath no fury, woman."

Sloane rolled her eyes and instead of waiting for him to be done bulldozed through the rest of it. "I'm going to be serious now for a minute, can I do that?"

"I don't know, can you? I think you meant to say may I be serious?" He was reverting to elementary humor now. She knew it was to extend the moment and conceded temporarily to give it to him. In all the time they had been here, there weren't a ton of good times to reflect on. It was a lot of remorseful reflecting.

"I hate you." She could barely form the words because her cheeks hurt so much from laughing.

"You love me, and you know it!" Andy replied. He was a pretty likeable fellow. Pretty gosh darn fun and awfully funny to boot. Andy was also real when he needed to be. He was exactly everything a best friend should be.

"A little," she admitted, "but strictly as friends, so don't go overboard and get cocky about it."

"Good thing we don't have any doors in here, I would need to grease the frames to get my huge head through them." They both laughed one last time.

They gave each other the 'alright enough' look. They both understood when to stop too. Most times people that had a totally different gear were missing that one fundamental cut-off valve. The one that said "ok, I'm flirting with the too far line, time to pull back on the reigns a little." Well, these two had it. Imagine the tour de force game partners they would have been together on double-date nights. She knew they would have dominated.

"Your best subject was math, so then you have some experience with spreadsheets, like excel?"

"Yeah, I know excel well."

"That's the exact reference I was hoping for. Now, anytime that you're trying to do something complex and need to write a formula for it, what do you do?"

Andy humored her. "I type the problem into Google and look for someone else that's asked for the same thing. Then I click on the most applicable link, go to the page, and copy and paste it."

"Exactly, okay good, then you'll completely get this. If you do that and it still doesn't work, then what's wrong?"

"I either copied it wrong, haven't plugged in my own specific row and column numbers, or there's some additional variable that's off, so I typically need to dig deeper."

She was damn impressed. Andy was intelligent too. Then she thought Justine's parents really missed the opportunity of knowing this great guy. There was no way once Andy met Bruce he would have been intimidated. "Right. So, I'm thinking there's something wrong in the formula." She stopped briefly, realizing how crazy the thought she had in her head sounded even to her. Sloane shook her index finger in the air. "Let's think about this. One time it happened hard when I hit your chest. That was me plus you." Andy wasn't about to stop her now that he could see she was on a roll. "Then I hit your chest again and they were a lot lighter, but still distinguishable, right?"

"Right, but right now you weren't touching my chest," Andy pointed out.

"No, but I was touching you. So, me + you = send EMP."

Andy's muscles went ridged. "So, you think there are different formulas for send and receive?"

"Yes! Well, kind of. I'm thinking a better explanation would be like different file directory paths on a computer. Hear me out. My theory is that we don't have all the variables involved in the equation and therefore we're working off an incomplete formula." She was pleased with Andy following her chain of thought so far. This next part might either lose him or throw him for a loop. He knew enough about her by now to know that she wasn't crazy, so that eliminated one response.

Sloane dropped the first breadcrumbs in hopes of cluing him into her entire hypothesis. "I'm saying we know that A + B = Small Surge, right? You'll agree the sensations, though on a different level of intensity, are still alike, right?"

"Yeah, so?" He wasn't there yet.

"So, based on that, we can likely conclude that A + B + X = Big Surge."

In a baffled tone Andy sustained, "I was with you all the way to X. But I thought you were 'A' and I was 'B?' That doesn't make sense since all variables in an equation have to be equal."

"But it does..." She began leading him. Reiteratively she intentionally trailed off. She was entrusting him to get there on his own. He didn't want to let her down.

"It can't be though."

"Unless..."

"Unless X is someone else."

It was at that moment when Andy's pupils dilated to the size of saucers that Sloane realized he had arrived at the same conclusion.

She chimed in, "What if it's you and I that can produce the small surge..." She left a statement one final time hanging.

Andy physically staggered. "So, you think...?" In perfect reciprocal fashion he let the sentence die with its rhetorical tone. He understood.

"Yeah, I needed you to get there on your own. If I came out and said it, you probably would have thought—"

He cut her off, "You were bat-shit crazy? While the ship hasn't left port on that one yet; I'm willing to entertain about anything right now. What in the hell do we have to lose?"

Sloane grinned. "I'm happy to hear you say that. I think we're both a little desperate."

"Let's do this." He gave her a look and she immediately knew what they had to do. They needed to figure this out right here and now and they were going to do it together. As if they were both met with a new responsibility or awareness of something bigger than themselves that they were now a part of. The depth of what they were experiencing washed over them. They were now partners in possibly the greatest escape room ever created. Sloane grinned.

Andy asked, "Any thoughts?"

"There is something I wanted to try, stand still." Sloane walked over to him and successively hit him on his left pec, his right, and then in equal time his left again. After the pulse flashes had reached the end of the corridor she stood with her ear at an odd angle, pointed down. She closed her eyes hoping to drown out everything. Andy realized what she was doing and in perfect time he also stopped speaking, moving, even breathing. They both waited for what seemed like at least an hour but was more like only a minute. Andy was getting impatient, had inhaled deeply to speak his thoughts, and then it hit. Three back-to-back-to-back huge pulses reverberated through their bodies and Washburn.

It was a shattering excitement they could read in each other's eyes. They were silent and sobbing uncontrollably. The tears began streaming down her face first, quickly Sloane scooted forward on her knees toward Andy. Also, on his knees, he held his arms out and she embraced him hard. Neither spoke for a long time.

Then they broke out of their elated trance and quickly conversed. "What should we do or write, or whatever?" She was trying pathetically to regain her composure through what was still the biggest smile she'd ever produced. Sloane hadn't thought what would happen if she proved her theory right and needed to communicate any further with X.

Andy spoke first. "That could have been a coincidence. It likely wasn't, but let's make sure."

"Good idea. So how many? Something random?"

The previously established incandescent bulb in Andy's cranium immediately upgraded to an LED. He grabbed her wrists and waited for her to ball them.

He winked at her and hit his left, right, and then left again in short sequence. Then he briefly paused. He matched those by hitting the middle of his chest with both of her fists, waiting two beats, repeating with both fists again, another two beats, and then they both beat his chest one last time. Then he repeated the three successive, once again alternating her hands.

Sloane's curious furrowing brow slowly ripened to a smile.

CHAPTER 34

Though he wasn't knocked backward, the look on his face Rae would have described as stunned to say the least. "What in heaven's name was that?"

Hayden gasped. "Did you feel it?"

"No, but I could see that you did." Every portion of Rae's face emulated astonishment. The slack jaw, the step back, and big eyes.

"That's the thing I was trying to tell you all about before! When I touched Sloane when she was first put in this room. It was before I told you that Luke left. Do you remember?"

"If you said something in close proximity to my good-for-little…" she caught herself and changed it from 'nothing' to give him the tiniest sliver of respect he had earned by footing the bill for once in his useless life for Sloane's initial surgery. She thought she may want to work a little harder at retracting those claws a bit before he got back. She repeated herself so as to continue her thought fluidly, "If you said something around the time you mentioned he was taking off, my mind may have drifted out of focus for a moment or two. I was slightly frustrated." That was way too gentle in her mind, so probably about the right tone to take when he returned.

"At that time, I only felt, whatever that was, once. I've felt the sensation a total of four separate occasions. The first two times was once. Then three times."

Rae interrupted, trying to get to the bottom of it all. "And how many this time?"

"Nine."

"Nine?"

"Yeah, nine, but not like in succession. It was almost as if it were…" he looked at her with realization. "…an S.O.S."

* * *

"WHAT?" She passionately believed the sleep deprivation had finally caught up with him. He couldn't have seriously said what she thought she heard.

"I know how crazy that sounds, I really do. I'm explaining how it felt."

Not wanting to be the pessimist, Rae replied, "Well, do it back."

Hayden's eyebrows angled at forty-five degrees. "Do what back?"

"The wave thing!"

"Oh, yeah, of course. Let me fire up my wave generator over here." She saw his look of frustration. "I don't know what's happening. I have no clue as to what that was or how to replicate it."

"Relax, calm down. I'll help you get to the bottom of this." She felt as if she was humoring him. "Well, what was happening both times that you felt it?" To Rae it seemed obvious.

Hayden frowned. "I guess I was holding her hand both times."

"There you go. Hold her hand and reply in Morse code," Rae replied excitedly.

"But I don't know Morse code," Hayden shot back.

"I beg to differ."

"I mean everyone knows S.O.S., don't they? Sorry, but that concludes my proficiency in the language."

Truthfully, Rae did remember learning something about this in grade school. She knew it meant "Save Our Ship," but she didn't know the code itself either.

"Well, what if you duplicate it then?"

"Gotta be worth a try, right?" With that he reached for Sloane's hand and squeezed it three times fast, then three times slow, then three fast again.

They both impatiently waited.

Their wait was disrupted less than ten seconds later as Hayden's eyes fluttered nine times. Rae had specifically counted this time. As she got to seven, then eight, and finally came to rest on a ninth and final time, she began sobbing uncontrollably. She hugged Hayden and with one arm he reached around her and pulled Rae close.

They had come to terms with a paranormal phenomenon and realized that Sloane, was alive and communicating. It was impossible, wasn't it? How could this be happening? Rae asked him to attempt it again and he fired off the message and it returned again. One piece of knowledge that he'd gained over the past minute or two was that the power was so intense, it was becoming overwhelming. Before he hadn't noticed because the number of waves were limited, and his constant lack of sleep didn't allow him to differentiate between the waves sucking the life out of him and being tired. After Hayden had explained this to Rae, she had the idea to keep their communication spread out until they figured out exactly what to say.

The two of them slept in chairs in Sloane's room that night and not a single staff member said a word. Every couple of hours Rae would wake Hayden to repeat the distress call and receive its return.

They discussed amongst themselves about what they were going to do with this new knowledge. They expeditiously agreed to keep it between them as discussing this with anyone else had better odds of landing them in strait jackets than anything else. They knew how unbelievable this was despite the fact in real time it was happening to them.

Later that next day as they were nearing their wits end and getting tired of grasping at straws, a knock came at the door. The two expected a nurse to be checking on Sloane's vitals. However, that wasn't the case. Before the visitor came around the curtain a bouquet of flowers, a dozen balloons, and a small box poked past. Two extended arms and the corresponding hands holding the riches hung there about chest high. It was as if it were a long overdue apology and only upon verbal confirmation or agreement from the current occupants would they be allowed to enter.

"Get in here, asshole!"

Only then did Luke appear.

CHAPTER 35

She was growing impatient. Her eyes would roll, and Sloane would throw her head back now every time they felt the message. She wanted Andy to try something different. She hadn't realized Andy was a step ahead.

"Why aren't you sending something different?"

"There is a reason that Morse code existed Sloan-E!" Now he was being a smart ass. "Morse code is the most efficient means of communication. So, by keeping the same message whoever is on the other end realizes that they need to give the correct response to move forward. It's like a magic password."

"Yeah, that's the problem, I'm not stuck here with Ali Baba and we don't know our 'Open Sesame'."

"Ahh, but see, that's where you're wrong." With a smirk forming, he swiveled his head in the opposite direction.

She had never been happier being incorrect. "I am? What is it?"

"Don't worry, we'll know it when we see it."

"You will? But how?" Sloane demanded. Then she realized Andy had a unique hidden talent. "Wait, you ole' sandbagging sunuvabitch! You know this stuff, don't you?"

Though they were both lethargic, he couldn't hide his beaming face any longer. "It will be one short, one long, and one short."

"Andy! You've been holding out on me. I could kiss you!"

"Hey, hey, hands off lady! I'm taken. It means 'r'."

Sloane retorted, "Just the letter r?"

"Yes, it stands for received, as in message received. That's what we're waiting for. Until then we keep sending the same message."

"How do you know this stuff?"

Andy replied with his chest puffed out in pride, "Eagle Scouts! My final project was on signs, signals, and codes."

"There's a merit badge for in limbo language?"

Andy smirked, "First of all, nice alliteration."

She grinned at his perceptiveness.

He persevered, "Actually, yes and no." Her look of puzzlement amused him. For one glancing moment he felt like he was the smartest person in the room. His bemused look acknowledged that, and it pissed her off at the same time. "Fine, I give, what aren't you telling me?"

Andy jocularly rubbed it in, "Yeeeeaahhh, Booiiiiiii!"

CHAPTER 36

Never in her life did Rae anticipate being happy to see her ex's face again. Anyone at this point would have been a sight for sore eyes, but someone invested in their situation was more than welcome, no matter who it was.

Hayden and Rae, without agreeing to break their pact of telling no one, instantly began a barrage of storytelling. They couldn't get it out fast enough. In rapid succession they rattled off the tale and all of today's events until he was caught up to that very moment.

Luke had a thousand questions, but also a thought. One he at least wanted to test. "Hayden, let me move in there for a minute." For the first time since this back and forth ordeal started Hayden released her hand and stepped away. It dawned on Luke it would be the first time he would ever touch his daughter as he hesitantly raised her arm and held her hand with his. He gathered his wits and Luke squeezed her hand short one time, then slackened his grip, then squeezed long one time, he loosened again, then clutched short one last time. He didn't know why he was surprised that there wasn't a response. I mean the story was preposterous to begin with, right?

Rae and Hayden looked at each other knowingly and smiled. Hayden let Rae enlighten him. "Luke, it only works for Hayden."

Whether it was disappointment at the prospect that her father couldn't be her knight in shining armor as he'd imagined in his mind thousands of times when daydreaming of ways to re-enter his daughter's life or a lack of belief, Luke's answer to the info was an aggressive eye-roll.

They sensed his skepticism. Not in the least did they blame him. After all, seeing was believing.

Hayden finally opened his mouth, "Luke, how about this? How about you squeeze my right hand and I'll pass the message on?"

Luke hesitated in response. "Sure."

Hayden shimmied his way between Luke and his daughter. He grabbed each of their hands and awaited Luke's message. He squeezed short, long, short. They both waited idly, for different reasons. As Luke was about to call him out Hayden began squeezing and releasing. Luke started laughing. He had just busted him.

"OMFG? Sorry, Hayden, but that makes no sense." Hayden and Rae's eyes lit up. Rae laughed.

Luke squinted as if his brain cells had gone out of focus. Hayden joined in the laughter that inevitably lead to tears of bliss. Rae's daughter was not only alive but communicating. As Rae shook her head back and forth she apprised Luke while at the same time thanking the almighty for giving Sloane her mother's street smarts. "Luke, it means 'Oh my God'!"

Luke paused momentarily then frowned "You forgot the F."

Rae finally interrupted him before he could make an even bigger fool of himself. Typically, she was against foul language and would cringe when people used it. But in this instance, with pure joy in her voice, she nearly sang it, "Fucking!" For effect she repeated herself. "For fuck's sake. Luke, The F is for fucking!"

CHAPTER 37

❄

Sloane wasn't too prideful to admit when she was wrong, but now she understood he knew what he was doing, she readily agreed with his plan. "What happens if or when they respond? Wait, also, who do you think is responding?" It dawned on her she hadn't evaluated the big picture of what was happening. Some large and pertinent information was hot off the presses here.

She hadn't thought of the big picture since her theory of A + B + X panned out to be correct. Another revelation struck her when she asked, "Who was responding?"

It hit her like a ton of bricks. She wasn't sure if Andy knew or not, and she wasn't sure enough to bring it up. If Hayden and PG were together that night mourning Andy's death, what if...she was... somehow alive? What if she was the conduit on the other end? She racked her brain trying to come up with other plausible explanations that maybe they hadn't figured out yet. Several scenarios, about as equally outlandish in nature as the next, populated her little brainstorming session.

As she started laying the pieces into place, the waves returned. This time was different than the previous. Three pulses rippled through them. One short, one long, and another short. Andy smiled at her, grabbed her hands, and hurled them onto his chest with three longs, pause, two longs, pause, two shorts, a long, and a short, pause, then finally two more longs and a short.

She wanted to know. "What was that?"

He answered quickly to not interrupt a reply that could come at any moment, "O-M-F-G."

She giggled. Sloane was rifling her mind for their most important questions so Andy could ask them when not more than a few split seconds later did the letters S-L-O-A-N-E get translated by Andy. They stared briefly at one another. While looking deeply into her eyes he grabbed her wrists once more. He began with three longs, then paused, then a long and a short, another pause and then finally three shorts and two longs.

Sloane asked, "What did you send?"

Andy's eyes welled up. "On three."

As what he'd said sunk in like a nail driving through a coffin; they both started crying. He knew. The first pulse echoed. She wanted to scream at Hayden to stop, to abort the launch, whatever it took. They both understood. It was too late. She quickly leaned in and kissed him on the forehead and then lingered there.

He spoke hurriedly "Tell her..." The second surge sounded. She could hear the deep emotion and sincerity in his voice "...my answer is yes!" On the beat of yes, he grabbed her arms and slammed them into his chest.

At the same moment, she screamed, "Andy!"

CHAPTER 38

It was 5:24 P.M., nearly a week had passed when Sloane Knox regained consciousness. It could have been more aptly described as screamed into consciousness. She bolted upright in bed as though she was having a nightmare, shrieked the name "Andy," and within five seconds passed out again. Doctors assured everyone that her vitals indicated she was merely sleeping and needed rest to regain her energy. Rae, Hayden, and Luke had called all of the relatives and friends back to the hospital telling them the miraculous news. They hadn't explained in finite detail the extraordinary circumstances of how it happened. People would have thought they needed to check into the psychiatric wing of this place.

Her wellness team now consisted of twelve different staff members due to the word of the miracle. All weighed in with their opinions. Medically speaking, they were in uncharted territory. They all had various philosophies on the matter, but one thing they all agreed with was how they were going to proceed with treatment. Since symptomatically this phenomena most closely resembled a stroke, they would continue with its standard protocol and treatments. Number one was plenty of rest and fluids. Step two would be evaluating her physical and mental health. To get an accurate depiction of her acuity, they knew they needed her rested, which meant cutting off all visitors. The families and friends once again were taken back to the same waiting room as they had been a week ago.

Just before she woke up the team of four medical professionals that comprised her wellness team at the time weren't holding out much hope. Statistically speaking, she was in the single digits for likelihood of waking up. The chances that she would still be the same person without any long-term effects caused by brain damage must have been mere fractions of a percent. The problems she could have were nearly innumerable. Most likely were speech and memory issues. Rae and Hayden had been educated about how she would need to relearn some fine motor and language skills and would need to work with her on those through intense therapy.

CHAPTER 39

It was nearly twelve hours after jolting awake when her eyes fluttered open again. Sloane's gaze drifted to her hand. Her fingers were interlocked with Hayden's. He lightly snored beside her. Sloane's eyes weren't sore considering they had been closed for the past week, but he was most definitely a sight. She wanted to wake him. Out of the corner of her eye she caught her mom's waving hand. She was making a "no, don't" gesture with her hand. Sloane understood it meant he probably needed the sleep.

Her eyes then directly rested on Rae, who saw her awaken. They sat staring at each other in silence as their tears welled within.

After nearly a half minute it had become too much, and it consumed them both. They started blubbering. It was disgusting and so beautiful at the same time. Rae stood up with the biggest smile and moved around to her daughter's other side. She leaned in and gave her an affirming hug. What did it affirm? Everything. It affirmed everything.

Rae withdrew and transported her chair to where she'd been standing. She ran her fingers through her baby girl's hair in silence and proceeded to wipe the gathered tears from her cheek.

Neither a single test, nor a word uttered. Rae smiled. Sloane was

Sloane. Her spicy and feisty, yet gorgeous daughter that tried her patience everyday was all there. Rae didn't need any so-called medical experts to tell her that. She had been more worried about that than anything else after she woke up. Having now addressed that final concern, Rae's mind was finally at ease. She could rest, relax, and crash. Between her lack of sleep, emotional taxation, and her own condition, she was beat.

About the time Rae was finally allowed to exhale was when the first nurse walked in to drop off a menu. She was told to give it to the mother in room #116. Sloane intercepted it from her while at the same time asking in a whisper if they had pancakes. She confirmed they did in fact and said she'd send the nutritionist in to get her order. Sloane rifled through all the options. Not one of them sounded bad as a yawn escaped her mouth. She was starving. Rae whispered at her, "Honey, I'll order them, you're still tired, go back to sleep. You need lots of rest now."

The bags under Sloane's eyes had bags. Luckily she was only figuratively dead now. There was no time in Washburn, so she really had no way of knowing how long it had been. She had one last sentence in her. "Make sure they give me enough syrup." With that her head had barely hit the pillow before she was out. Rae didn't put the pancake order in. By the time Sloane came to again, they would be cold.

Through the entire exchange Hayden remained out. To Rae it was perfect. She knew their lives were about to get crazy. Especially with the Coronavirus Luke had told her was coming. Yeah, she and Luke were at least talking once again. Rae was smiling ear to ear recalling the mother daughter moment they'd shared. It meant the world to her. For the first time in the better part of a month, all three of them were now getting much needed, peaceful shuteye.

Luke took this time to meet with the hospital's board of administrators for an early morning meeting. He spun his package to the middle of a very cool looking large rectangular conference table. It was one of those wood and blue resin river numbers. Luke would eventually order a few of them for his offices. The company's board was able to gain approval from the city council to expedite some construction permits. After all, with Rikr poised to be the company that saves the world, it's only fitting they're headquartered in a place with a name as apt as New Hope. He began the meeting by typing in the number for one Christopher Redman from Luke's contacts into the intercom system.

This man would soon be a common name across the planet. He pushed the speakerphone button allowing them all to hear the conversation. Chris, as Luke called him, picked up. An answer came at the other end. "Luke, we good?" Chris was a stickler for efficient communication. It was an admirable trait for a man in his position.

"Yep, Chris, go ahead. You have the undivided attention of the hospital's entire board." With that the room suddenly went silent. It was the non-confrontational way of saying "shut up!"

"Ladies and gentlemen, my name is Christopher Redman. You may or may not know of me. Either is inconsequential. I am the Director of the CDC. I am currently emailing you my credentials. You are hereby ordered to do exactly as Mr. Harder has directed you. If you've been reading our weekly newsletters, back in November you would have noticed that we began notifying people of a new virus strain known as Coronavirus or COVID-19. We are calling it 'Covid' for short. In the same attachment you'll see the studies and data to support what I'm about to tell you. We have never and likely will never again see a pandemic of this magnitude in our lifetimes. Yes, I did not misspeak, I said pandemic. Nothing will ever be the same again after this is over."

Forty-five minutes later Chris concluded his briefing to the board. Luke recognized the looks of traumatization. "Luke Harder is officially one of the top experts on Covid on the face of the earth. He knows the ins and outs of the strain, the current state of projections, and guidelines for how we proceed forward to be able to survive this. Oh yeah, and I'm told he's got a box in front of you. Fellow medical professionals, I'd like to introduce you to a new life-saving drug called Cloniquin. This box he brought with was only the second created. He put the first on himself and the entire team working in the Rikr's satellite headquarters, now located in Chengdu. First off, you have no clue how valuable those patches are. Second, as per his instruction, get them on everyone coming into and exiting all facilities. Patients and staff alike. Otherwise it will be four to six months before you see another one and you will have saved at least a dozen lives with that one little box. That's a guarantee. This is not a drill folks. Luke, it's always a pleasure, but I've got to get back to it. Members, you have no clue how fortunate you are that he chose your hospital for treatment. Make the most of it now." Luke wondered if any of them could read between the lines and ascertain what he meant. He opened the box and started handing out the moist-toilette type foil packaging with Rikr in large and bold purple letters. As a tribute to its Minnesota heritage, Luke spelled Rikr using the same font as the Minnesota Vikings. He grabbed a handful, held them up, and said "I'll personally deliver these." They all knew where he was headed with them. Though it had only been a few hours, they had all heard of his daughter's miraculous recovery. It was already well-known throughout the halls of the hospital. Luke thanked everyone for taking such great care of his daughter and that is why he was gifting them this life-saving medication and information before the federal government made it officially known.

* * *

HAYDEN SLOWLY AWOKE early Sunday afternoon. For the first time since karma had begun taking a 2x4 to his life he slept pretty well. Lately it was always some type of nightmare that would startle him awake in a cold sweat. Now there were no remnants of any bad dreams. He sat up and looked at both Sloane and Rae still sleeping as he rubbed his eyes and stretched. It was pretty peaceful. Almost serene. He stood up and looked out the window to the Mississippi River. It froze over at least two months ago. The ice had to be at least a foot thick by now. Which was enough to handle pretty much any vehicle safely, shy of tank that is. There were pop-up single-man ice fishing shanties all over the ice.

Hayden thought he'd probably need to head out soon before he was kicked out by a nurse enforcing visiting hours. First things first though, he was starving. More promptly yet, nature was calling. The caffeine in here ran through him almost instantly. He must have passed out from exhaustion right after Sloane screamed "Andy" as she woke up. This was the first chance he'd gotten to even contemplate it and what it meant.

He trudged slowly out of the room and ducked past one of the nurse's stations without notice. His appearance was more than a little disheveled. As if he had fallen asleep on eighteen different seatbelts, he had lines all over his face. They originated from Sloane's tubes. His hair looked as if someone had cut the wrong wire in a bomb defusal. It was somehow everywhere. He kept his head down as he walked past open doors of other patient's rooms. He passed the coffee station and decided to take a quick minute to start brewing a fresh pot. Then he could grab some for himself and Rae on his way back. Hayden imagined she'd be waking up soon as well and he knew he wished he'd had a cup a minute ago.

Inside the bathroom he washed his hands and then brought himself to look in the mirror. What stared back was something resembling if Ian Somerhalder was beat with a sleep-deprived somewhat ugly stick about a half dozen times. He was always his own worst critic. It wasn't that bad truthfully, but he decided he could use at least an Irish shower. He filled the basin with cold soapy water and thrust his face in the ice bath. For good measure he also dunked his head. Then he wiped down with hand towels and spritzed himself with cologne from the small bottle in his pocket. He checked his appearance one last time and concluded what stared back wasn't terrible, possibly bordering on somewhat presentable.

On his way back to room #116 Hayden stopped and grabbed three coffees. He dropped one off at the nurse's desk and winked at the ladies behind the table. Hayden Foster was in a good mood. He hadn't really analyzed it or even thought to analyze it until this moment. He wasn't sure why. Yes, something had changed last night Hayden thought. Sometimes he'd get quite the dialogue going inside his own head with himself. He shook his head again in a lighthearted nature.

He was "quite the character" as his mother used to always say. He always thought it was a nice way of saying she thought he talked too much. Later in life he determined she was more likely saying he was an "odd duck." At least sometimes. This was one of them.

    He was doing a little happy dance type of shuffle with the coffees in hand when suddenly extreme heat singed his leg hair. Soon it would seep down into his boots, which would inevitably soak his socks.

CHAPTER 40

Sloane's eyes fluttered open. She sat up in her bed and took in her surroundings. She briefly recalled a scene this morning with her mom who was now resting over the end of her bed while simultaneously sitting in the chair next to it. In truth, it looked somewhat uncomfortable. Sloane was experiencing déjà vu with her lack of memory. She was confused and disoriented. Where was she? Why was she in this bed? Who put these wires in her? She started freaking out and became restless. This woke Rae.

"Hey, baby girl. Sloane, relax!" Rae reached for Sloane's hand to use as a grounding force. When Sloane continued she got up and went to her. She hugged her tightly like when she was a little girl and something or someone had hurt her. Sloane would get so red-in-the-face and riled up. It would build to such a crescendo. If she didn't breathe, she was either going to pass out from a lack of oxygen or her head would explode like a bottle rocket on Independence Day. Rae shushed and rocked her daughter for a good half minute as she came down from her panic attack and calmed herself using her mother's heartbeat.

Rae pulled back. "Are you okay? Should I get the doctor?" There was worry in her voice.

"I don't know for sure. Give me a minute to breathe here." Sloane was doing her level best to collect herself.

"Maybe it would help if you could explain to me what you're feeling?" Rae suggested.

"Like there's something I need to get off my chest or get out, and I can't figure out what it is. My memory is all over the place."

"Maybe if I get you some ice water?" Rae suggested. "Let me run and I'll be right back." Rae grabbed the bucket and left the room.

Sloane pushed the button to adjust her bed and tilted her upper body forward. She gazed out the window and watched millions of snowflakes fall peacefully in the hospital parking lot. A small portion of the flakes were illuminated by the lampposts. It had been an overcast day so none of the campus lights had turned off overnight.

Then, once she'd been thoroughly hypnotized by the picturesque arctic scene; movement caught her peripheral vision and she turned her head toward its origin. Sloane's attention instantly tapered to a fine point as her primary motor cortex caught up with her optic nerves. Hayden.

Her hands slowly covered her mouth. Sloane remembered reading an article once or maybe it was a podcast she'd heard. It was about a group of researchers studying the phenomenon of contextual binding. Ever forgotten portions of a night of drinking only to recall them when you're drunk again? Same thing, well, basically. Hayden was her context. He was her beacon. A house of light she could follow like a port in the storm. Her pupils dilated and everything came flooding back. It was so thick. She remembered it all. Hayden dropped what she presumed were cups of coffee on the floor and the backsplash landed all over the bottom of his pants. She barely registered it.

Now with her hands covering half of her face the tears reached her fingertips. She shook as an uncontrollable sobbing commenced. They were no more than twenty feet apart staring in disbelief at each other, frozen in place. Now Sloane felt as if there was a canyon between them.

Hayden's top and bottom lips hadn't reconnected yet. His posture wilted. His mouth opened and closed several times before he was able to form words. The first were in the form of a question. "How do you know Morse code?"

"I don't." Sloane let it hang in the air. She wanted to keep her answer condensed to prolong any sense of normalcy. She knew the silence would become too unbearable for him. She waited until Hayden could no longer. She bit her bottom lip. As the muscles surrounding his mouth elevated slightly to form a new word Sloane astonished him with two words that would change their lives forever. "Eagle Scouts."

His eyes widened. Sloane saw the realization on this face. He dropped to his knees. His lips pressed tightly together as his head fell forward, shaking back and forth in disbelief. Hayden Foster was a strong individual. He could take-on, deal with, and handle more than his fair share and typically didn't crack. Now though, he didn't stand a chance in hell. Hayden was succumbing to the unbridled tally of the last month. Emotionally it had more than taken a toll. To what extent hadn't been realized until this very moment.

Within seconds he was forced to come to grips with all of it and the dam broke. Like an overhead waterpark cone that finally reached the point of critical mass and could hold no more H2O, something had to give. Now it was all cascading down on top of him. The weight punishing him into the tiled floor. What he was experiencing was known as therapeutic tremoring. It's the body's natural way of releasing tension. Like a babe not able to catch its breath, he shook.

It broke her heart seeing him in that pain. She knew it because in real-time she was experiencing it as well. Sloane's guilt now got the best of her knowing that she had only added to his despair. She threw the covers off her body and quickly swung off the bed. On unsteady legs she ran to him with her monitor in tow and covered him with her body, placing her arms around his entire frame. Deep silent sobbing continued for several minutes while Sloane comforted him.

About this time Rae came around the corner down the hall and saw Sloane grasping Hayden in a fierce embrace that defied time, space, and comprehension. The nurses from both stations were now populating the hallway about fifty feet ahead. They were wailing in joyous praise. Their commotion drew out other patients, staff, and all of their family and friends from the waiting room. All inquisitive about the pandemonium.

Hayden, to this point, had merely been the recipient of Sloane's embrace. The improbable moment was here. Hayden rectified their predicament and clutched at her with desperation.

He kept repeating through deep sobbing, "Thank you, brother." To everyone else in that hallway it made zero sense. To Sloane and Hayden, it meant everything.

He had vowed to himself if she ever woke up he would never let her go again. This was the beginning of him making good on that promise. Eventually they would draw apart from one another and the world would go on spinning.

Just not yet.

CHAPTER 41

Hayden gathered up Sloane in his arms and carried her back into her room and laid her back on the bed. "Hey, this is only date number two. Don't be taking me to bed thinking you're gonna get anywhere this soon." God, he loved this woman.

Hayden finally spoke through his cheeky grin, "We need to talk. There's plenty of time for that. Right now, I think there are some people here that would like to see you." God, she loved this man. It nearly killed him to put his personal feelings and questions aside to appease all of her loved ones and their need for connection.

All of their family and friends gathered again in her room. This time no doctors would be attempting to "manage their expectations". They were going to celebrate, and no one would dampen their spirits.

After about forty-five minutes they all laughed, cried, and hugged Sloane. Relieved that she was alive. Amid the tears of joy her medical team came in and evaluated her. To their surprise, she showed zero long-term damage or effects. Every poke, prod, and question resulted in a positive response. They decided to keep her overnight for some further testing, but if she was given the all-clear in the A.M. she would be allowed to be discharged. Her primary neuro physician did tell everyone they would need to take off. Though healthy and mentally acute, she did need a lot more rest. The ordeal she had been through had drained her batteries and they needed recharging.

Heidi and Kristi squeezed her and kissed her forehead one last time with tears in their eyes. Then they went over to Hayden and gave him hugs and kisses on the cheeks. "Leave room for Jesus ladies!" Hayden's chin was on top of Heidi's head looking straight at Sloane. The look and smile he gave her warmed her thoroughly from head to toe. Hayden's eyes crossed the room pointing Sloane to the room entrance. There he was. Sloane's father. All the girls took this as their queue to skedaddle. They snuck past him without paying him the respect of even a glance. He was still a deadbeat in their eyes. They waved and blew kisses to Sloane on the way out. She caught them and blew them back. As they left the room Sloane's eyes shifted to the foot of her bed where Luke now stood.

He had a look of pride in his eyes that he hadn't earned. She frowned at him. The tension in the room was palpable. "Sloane."

"Luke," she snapped back.

He wasn't going to get a lot of slack here, so he needed to make what he was about to say really count and get it out quickly. Short and sweet was the name of the game. "I am here for a few reasons Sloane, but none more important than this. I am sorry. That's it. I have no excuses that are worthy of being considered. I was selfish and stupid. I am not asking for forgiveness. I need you to know that I know, I was wrong, and I have no one to blame but myself."

In an extremely cold and emotionless manner she countered with, "Is that all?"

Hayden tried not to judge Sloane unfairly when it came to Luke. He really had no right from the cheap seats to adjudicate their relationship. He knew from her own words that her father had hurt her deeply.

Luke simply countered with "Yes." His face winced in pain. "Hayden, can I steal you away here for a few minutes? It's time for that walk."

Sloane looked at Hayden with surprise mixed with a dash of hurt. Both Luke and Hayden had seen it. Hayden leaned down next to her ear and whisper to her, "You told me you trust me, right?" He withdrew a few inches until he was looking in her eyes. She was blushing while looking at his lips. He knew exactly how to put her mind at ease. "I'll be back shortly and then we'll talk Sloane, I can't wait."

She bit her bottom lip. "You kill me, you know that?"

"Yeah? How's it feel getting a dose of your own medicine?" He said it in such close proximity to her she could feel his warm breath on her cheek.

Sloane was acutely aware of the fact she hadn't brushed her teeth in who knew how long and covered her mouth with her right hand, cupping it in front like a mask.

Hayden thought she'd never been more beautiful than that moment. She saw the look he gave her and whispered back, "later." One word sent shivers down his spine.

Luke cleared his throat. Hayden jumped to attention and nearly died of embarrassment. The dynamic is unique to say the least, but this was still her dad to him. Hayden kissed her on the back of her hand and told her he'd be back in about an hour. That would give Rae and Sloane a chance to get caught up.

Luke walked in front of Hayden and held the door open for him as they left the confines of the building. As they began their walk through the breathtaking greenery toward their path Luke looked up and laughed. He had reverted to the mindset and innocence of a five-year-old and started hysterically laughing.

Hayden asked, "Am I missing something?"

"Oh, it's funny, is all."

"What is?" Hayden asked.

"Hayden, you may not be able to process this, and likely only time will resolve that for you, but you're a hero. A pretty big one too."

"Thank you, I guess?" He had no idea where Luke was going with this one.

"When the Chinese Government contacted me again with the green light, I was going to refuse. I didn't fully understand the implications and what was and is at stake then."

Hayden interjected, "But why wouldn't you help all those people?"

"I had decided for once in my pathetic existence I was going to do the right thing by my daughter. At the last minute I called my man Marcus back and told him I was pulling out because Sloane needed me, and I wasn't going to disappoint her any longer." He paused for a minute as his eyes and voice softened. "When Rae called me and told me about Sloane, Hayden, I was right there. He extended his right index finger pointing to one building to the left of Sloane's. "But isn't that the cancer wing?"

"Yes."

It struck Hayden with a resounding chord. He put his hands behind his head and looked to the sky. "Of course." He shook his head. "There's never anything so bad that it can't get worse."

Luke frowned. "Huh?"

"Nothing, something my dad used to say." Hayden now looked up into the sky and again pondered the universe, fate, a greater being up high, everything. "So how long?"

"They'd given me six months about three months ago."

"I don't know what to say."

"There's nothing to say son. You've been my rock. You afforded me the one thing that no money could ever buy, redemption. I am forever grateful and indebted to you for that Hayden. Those two may never forgive me. I wouldn't blame or hold it against them for a second if they didn't."

"Sir—"

"Luke"

"Sorry sir, Luke. I am so sorry. What can I do?"

Luke pointed at him while reaching and grabbing him for a hug. "That son, that. Keep being the amazing young man your parents taught you to be. The type of man that other guys should aspire to be. A person that always puts others needs and wants above his own. One that any father would approve of for his daughter." Hayden looked him in the eyes as if to confirm that he had heard what he thought he had. The wink Luke gave him was confirmation enough for Hayden. "Prove that altruism is real and be a much better father than I was. Somehow find a way to make this okay for them. Help them through everything that is coming. I'm not demanding anything of you Hayden, on the contrary, I'm a dying man with one final wish."

Hayden smiled with his head down recognizing Luke's tone. Also the guilt laced sarcasm he was presently using to lay it on thick. "Low blow."

It was now Luke's turn to smile. "Hey, you can't blame a guy for tryin', right? Blame it on the day job." Without missing the profound depth of the way that statement landed on Hayden, he spoke. "Luke, you have my word. I'm not going anywhere."

"I already know that."

"What?"

"Never mind, we'll get to that. As I was saying Hayden, that's why you're a hero. Eventually the numbers will start tallying up in big bold black ink. The number of cases of the virus and the number of deaths. Remember one number for me. Whatever the eventual tally is in both, multiply that by four.

"Why four?"

"Because the difference between the multiple of four and the number they list will be the number of people that you and I saved. When you boil everything down, it'll be a fact. As I said, I wouldn't have agreed to go do what needed to be done in China had it not been for meeting you in that chapel. There's no way. So that's why I'm laughing Hayden. Because it's pretty darn ironic I can save the lives of well over a million people and in comparison to earning my daughter's trust before I die, well let's say it's not even close."

Hayden decided it probably wasn't the optimal time to discuss the nuances of the term ironic. He did however add, "But you did save her life Luke and I'll never let her forget that."

He put his arm around Hayden. "We saved her life, son. We did that."

Hayden returned the gesture to Luke. "Yes, we did."

"Now, let's talk turkey."

Hayden started scratching his head "Huh?"

"You're in marketing, right?"

By the end of the conversation Hayden didn't know if his

threshold for crazy drama could be pushed any farther. He was flirting pretty hard with it. The swings of his life right now were way too big. The pendulum needed some Zoloft to chill out. These wide swings were going to kill him.

Over the next half hour Luke explained his plans for his little company Rikr. They in fact included their own in-house agency that would also be its own separate entity. Then Luke offered Hayden a job. "How would you like to be CEO of this little new agency I've created called Foxster?"

Hayden thought briefly, "Why Foxster?"

"Foster + Knox = Foxster, simple."

Very quickly the name was growing on Hayden. Luke pushed on. "Do you think you could handle that?"

"Yeah, I think I probably could."

"Good, because you start next Wednesday working from home."

"Why from home?"

"We're all going to be working from home soon. I need you, Sloane, and Rae to stay home. Seriously, when you get back in the room slap these on Sloane, Rae, and yourself." With that he handed three patch packets to Hayden. Now, you're going to be safe, but people also can't know that you are or a lot of questions we really can't answer will start popping up. Like how and why you got them before anyone else. Heads will roll and you won't be safe."

"True. Not to be a stickler for details here Luke, but do you think that maybe you could embellish a little bit further on this new gig?" Hayden was strategic in ascertaining more information, since two minutes ago this man had divulged his impending death to him. Another redeeming quality Luke liked about him.

"Oh, now you're not so selfless?" He threw Hayden a goofy look that told him he was being facetious. "My man Keith will lay it all out for you. Essentially we're opening two businesses here. Rikr Pharmaceuticals and Foxster Media. You and your team at Foxster will serve on the boards of both companies. However, I don't know anyone with CEO experience for Rikr, do you?

Hayden replied, "Yeah, I think I've got the perfect guy for the job actually."

"Well okay then!" was Luke's next reply. "This is great!"

To this point in his life Hayden dreamed of landing an eight-figure yearly spending advertiser. He was closing in on one with Sampson's, but likely wouldn't be there for another year or two. Eight figures in Hayden's line of work was the gold standard of clients. That was considered a whale by anyone's standards. Luke handed Hayden a check written to Foxster in the amount of $1,463,000,000 for their media advertising buy. Rounded off, nearly $1.5 billion.

Luke's tone took on a quality of bemusement. "I thought you might like that. Here's the best part, that's for Q2! Oh, and I almost forgot." He began rifling through his pocket. He found a slip of folded paper and handed it to Hayden. It was a check written for $100,000 with his name on it.

"Though I don't want to seem ungrateful, I just got a raise at my current job and already make more than this."

"Hayden, here is your contract. Read it thoroughly. There's some fine print on the bottom you'll want to check out."

Hayden continued to read and dropped the pen when he got to the bottom. "Is that even a real number?"

"Yes, I give you my word, Hayden."

"I don't like this. I don't think deception is the right angle here, but it's your money."

"So, you'll do it?"

Hayden fidgeted and rubbed his hands together to give himself a few additional moments to think it over. "Yes." With that, he picked up the pen from the ground and motioned for Luke to swivel around. He understood his meaning and hunched over as Hayden used his back as a table. There in the middle of the atrium Hayden placed his John Hancock on the dotted line and their future fates were officially merged.

Now his tone changed from freaking out to nonchalantly stating the obvious. Like this was real life we were talking about any longer. Wait, this had to be real though. He had the tangible check *in his hands*! Luke smiled, likely due to the look of pure stupor on Hayden's face. "When you eventually share that with Sloane, make sure to tell her 'not bad for a fruit sticker eh?' She should have gotten in on the bottom floor when I first offered her the chance to invest." He smirked briefly. Hayden knew what he was referring to. It was the only real story Sloane had told him about her father. "Hayden, this is enough money to provide for generations. Be careful and smart with it. I told you I could never repay what you did for me. To know that my girl was in safe hands and you were at her side every moment you could be? This is the very least I could do. You once said I'd owe you one. I'd say we're now even."

Hayden's mind was going a mile a minute. A question popped into his head. "Rikr is going to have one hell of a start, Luke, but after this initial influx of cash how is company going to survive?"

"That is why you're on the board." Luke was sure he had made the right decision. "I put together a business plan and prospectus. It'll all be on your desk waiting for you. I do have some ideas regarding the future.

Hayden simply thanked him and hugged him one last time. "Luke, I won't let you down."

"You couldn't if you tried, son. Thank you, Hayden."

"You're welcome, Luke, and thank you!" They shook hands to establish the professional addition to their relationship.

CHAPTER 42

❄

She hated that her father had struck up any kind of relationship with Hayden. She wanted him to keep his filthy grubbin' mitts off her man! Was he trying to talk him into some Ponzi scheme? No matter what he had happening up there in his pea-sized little brain, it's safe to assume it wasn't good. Rae waved them out the door and turned back to her daughter. She saw the sour puss on her face and announced they needed to talk.

For twenty or so minutes Rae recollected everything. She explained the details of how she ended up in the hospital. What had transpired with the waves on their side and how technically, her dad saved her life. Actually, he'd saved it twice. After he'd left them both again. Before Sloane had the chance to ask any reciprocating questions Rae interrupted herself. "I can't believe I forgot about this until now. I've had one question to ask during this whole ordeal and haven't been able to ask the one person I've needed to. There's been an air or uneasiness for me here with Hayden and I have to have this cleared up for my own sanity." The line and angle of the question caught Sloane by surprise.

"What happened on that road? Can you remember?"

Sloane breathed a sigh of relief as she had gotten worked up with her mom's serious tone. "Do you mean did I see something happen between Justine and Hayden?" Rae nodded repeatedly. "Rest easy mom they were comforting each other, completely platonic mind you. They knew each other. Her fiancé and his best friend had died."

"Together? How?" Rae stopped and peered intently at her daughter.

Sloane laughed and shook her head. "No, that's the thing, it's the same person. Andy was his name. If you knew the entire story, there's a lot more to it than that, but it was completely innocent."

"You're positive?"

"One hundred percent."

Rae sighed with relief. "Thank God, girl, because I didn't know if I could dislike that boy, E." Sloane's smile was ear to ear. "I was seriously beginning to understand arranged marriages." Sloane cracked up. "I mean seriously, Sloane, what did you do to land that? You better put that on lock-down or you're going to have some stiff competition." Sloane's mouth was agape at how blunt her mom was being. "From me!" They cackled.

As the laughter died down there was a knock at the door frame. There stood a bright-eyed beaming PG. Again, the waterworks began. Justine ran in and swooped Sloane into a hug. They held each other tightly for a good minute or two. Sloane's mind was swimming with everything she needed to tell her.

During the hug Luke and Hayden had returned. "Justine, you made it!"

"Well, when someone texts you that your best friend woke up from a coma, you tend to take notice."

Hayden said, "Thanks for coming."

Through smudged mascara that she had reapplied, Sloane mouthed the words "Thank you" to Hayden for the gift of her best friend.

Rae piped up. "Hey, Luke, maybe we should go grab a cup of coffee in the cafeteria?"

"Yeah, actually I'd really like that, R." He smiled at her, attempting to gauge her disdain for him. She smiled back and started walking for the door. He couldn't keep back the smirk. He was wearing her down.

Before he'd gotten to the door a voice chimed in. "Luke?" He swiveled and caught the remaining utterance from his daughter. "Thank you."

He merely cracked a slightly bigger smile and tilted his head downward in a gesture of respect. An inaudible "you're welcome."

The moment they were both out of earshot Hayden pointed at Justine and the chair next to Sloane's bed beside his own. "Sloane, you need to know something about Justine and me."

"That you know one another through Andy?"

"My reasoning for asking Justine to come wasn't completely selfless. Mostly, yes, completely, no. I need to explain…" he trailed off.

"Hayden, Mom kind of caught me up and filled in most of the gaps while you were on your walk. I need to speak here, if you'll allow me the floor for a few minutes?" He had no intention of interrupting and extended his arm in a "please continue" gesture.

"I'm not sure exactly how to start here, but to explain my experience from the outset I guess." She started from the very beginning and explained the white, the fog, and the emptiness to begin with. "It was desolate and frightening. Amid my shaken and confusing state I heard a voice."

She was now looking at them both intently now. She needed them to see her face when she said it and she needed to see theirs when they heard it. "It was Andy. This is going to be nearly impossible for me to get through, so please bear with me." Justine looked at Hayden, expecting the same look of utter astonishment but was surprised when he smiled back at her with a knowing nod. Sloane continued, "You guys don't understand. I'm not saying like I heard his voice and he guided me out. As real as you two are here, right now, that is how real Andy was. Now, if I were you PG, I'd think I was nuts." Justine couldn't help herself now. "What about Hayden?"

"Hayden understands. Not completely, but you see, we have this connection." Sloane winked at him, grabbed his hand, and kissed it, and held it to her chest. "That's what I'm trying to explain. As I was saying, I would completely understand if you didn't believe me. I can prove it though." PG gave her a smart-aleck type of eye-roll and smirk. It conveyed nothing but doubt. "I know why Andy never met Bruce." Justine's eyes perked up until she realized she still hadn't really divulged any personal knowledge yet. "I'm sure I told you that."

"No, you didn't. Also, I know he was wearing your underwear when your dad called." Sloane began laughing.

Both PG's and Hayden's eyes widened, but only one of them was out of embarrassment. For Hayden he brushed it off like it was nothing. He didn't know that story before either, but he knew Andy…and that sounded like something that would happen to him. It also isn't one of those stories you randomly share with your bros. Hayden never would have let him live it down. Justine's eyes started tearing up. "Hayden, I know about the time you puked in the middle of the century club."

"I've told a ton of people that story," he said.

"How about the part where you finished the game?" He knew where this was headed, and he didn't like it one bit. "And then pissed in your sock drawer, didn't remember in the morning, and wore a damp pair to work the next day." There was that same look of embarrassment PG had. He shrugged and whispered "traitor" under his breath with the biggest smile. He also realized he could have told her much worse stories. "And he told me about Sarah with an 'h'."

"Damn it, Andy." Though quiet, he couldn't hold that one back. That one was going to be more difficult to explain. Maybe she didn't know the part about…

"And the fire-escape the next morning."

Hayden wanted to curl up and die. *Damn it, Andy!* Listen, Justine, just believe her already." They all chuckled.

Justine asked, "Why is it Sarah with an 'h' Hayden? Is there another story of…?" She paused and tilted her head at an awkward angle in thought until it hit her. "Holy crap, there's another story about a Sara without an 'h', isn't there?" The ladies were enjoying toasting Hayden's buns in the hot seat. Very much like their Friday night endeavors toying with the boys downtown.

Sloane knew better though. She actually loved all of Andy's stories about Hayden. It humanized him to her. Her mother had told her what Hayden had done for them the entire time she was out. How he'd come to the hospital every day and sat with her and her mom for hours. He was the one that figured out their connection. He had literally saved her life. Hayden was her hero. Sloane beamed with pure pride.

"PG, you have to believe me. It's extremely important you do for this next part."

Justine looked up at Sloane searching for the meaning in her eyes. "At the very last second he told me to tell you that he would have said yes." PG's eyes welled and she dissolved to tears. Hayden realized what she was saying as well. Sloane reached again for PG to hold and comfort her. "There's a lot more, but that's the most important part that he begged me to tell you."

"Thank you, E! Thank you, thank you, thank you!" Sloane pulled back from her friend and whispered, "You're welcome."

"Hayden, I spent the last week straight with your best friend. That night at King's my favorite stories were those of you and Andy. Now I realize why. We became pretty close friends. He saved my life Hayden."

He smiled while choking back the tears himself. He'd had enough crying for a lifetime. An unmistakable smile popped on his face and internally he thanked his friend again for what he'd done for him. He missed him so much.

"I am so sorry you lost your best friend Hayden. I am also sorry I overreacted and put you through even more."

He could see the sincerity in her eyes. "Sloane, my best friend saved *your* life."

"Other than Andy being here right now, I couldn't be much better." Hayden hugged both of them.

They all sat together for a while rehashing the entire experience. The three of them had shared this unbelievable bond. Justine had every right to feel a little jealous. Andy had told her "yes" though, she grinned. They would have gone to Chicago and built a life there and would have been happy, being together. Fate however had other dark plans in store for Justine that involved her staying put. Though her heart was broken once again, she could no longer be mad at the unknown. For the first time in history, Justine had been given postmortem peace from the source. A tear dropped from her cheek as she hoped Andy now had that same peace.

Once the catch up had pretty well concluded Hayden asked if he could talk to them in a more professional capacity for the next couple of minutes. "I wanted to know if I could interest the two of you in positions at my new agency." They stared awkwardly at each other and then back at Hayden.

"Ladies, let's talk turkey." He adopted the phrase in honor of Luke. Hayden went on to explain everything from the past two weeks. Coronavirus, Rikr, Cloniquin, her father's time in China, the campus going up in New Hope, and then in a left field turn of events, offered both of them jobs. He enlightened them on the details of the positions, benefits, PTO, vacation, and the finer amenities including company cars.

Hayden had promised Luke the three of them would serve on the boards of both Rikr and Foxster. Sloane blushed a little at the prospect of them being "shipped" in a permanent form before they'd even started dating. He looked at her and before she could speak, he spit out, "save it sweetheart, you're stuck with me!" She smiled coyly at him and fondly remembered Andy. Hayden knew her so well already and she absolutely adored him for it.

Justine interjected, "I'm just saying if the letters 'P' and 'G' are on any office door I'm associated with I'm out." The trio giggled.

"Oh, somehow I doubt it." Hayden was pretty sure of himself.

Sloane said, "What if I don't want the job? I mean I'm not going to jump at the prospect of working for my father's company."

Through a freshly formed lump in his throat Hayden decided now would be about the appropriate time. He handed each of them their contracts offers. "You're absolutely right, Sloane. I have zero right to speak on your behalf. Once you've read through these contracts, if you decide you don't want the jobs; then by all means, it's your life.

I've already given Luke my answer." While he'd been talking, they really weren't listening to what he was saying. They had been skimming the details and looking for the fine print. Eventually they got to the $250,000 they would each be compensated with; they were stupefied. No matter how many times he repeated that he wasn't lying or joking, they couldn't believe him. He found it *ironic* they had just proven another plane of existence, yet something perfectly tangible, like money, escaped comprehension. That's when he took out the check proving the validity to his claims and their mouths dropped. Hayden couldn't stop laughing.

* * *

At that same moment, across the building, in the hospital cafeteria Luke and Rae sat down at a table. "I apologized to our daughter Rae, but I haven't to you. With that he handed her a nearly identical contract to the one he'd given Hayden, though this time the hundred grand was treated as a signing bonus so she wouldn't have to work for it. She already had, by raising Sloane.

"But I don't understand, why?"

"Why? Maybe because you got your wish, I'm dropping dead." He giggled a little. She was even more lost, however now also concerned. "Rae, I'm sick. I have been since before you called me that night about Sloane. I only have a couple months." Rae reached across the table and grabbed his hand in a sign of respect. "I have rehearsed this speech a few hundred times. You'd think I wouldn't be so nervous." He lifted his water to his mouth with a shaky hand. "This doesn't make up for what I did to you and Sloane. That is not what this is about. Truthfully, it's probably still selfish. Trying to garner some charitable favor before I meet the big guy upstairs and all that." He smiled and she returned the gesture, still holding his hand.

Then she read the number at the bottom of the agreement. Rae let it sink in. She was still mad at this man. She was still hurt. He couldn't buy his way out of this. She refused to let the tears materialize in her ducts. Luke broke the silence, "There is a catch."

"Of course, there is." They both laughed through the tears that now united them.

"There is a small stipulation you probably won't like. Hayden already agreed, but I didn't really give him a choice." With that he showed Rae the fine print gag order she'd be agreeing to by signing.

"Let me save you the trouble. It says you can't tell Sloane about my condition, or you forfeit everything." Rae didn't want to agree like Hayden hadn't either, but on principle she felt he at least deserved the chance to earn his daughter's forgiveness before he died in an honorable way. She signed and thanked him.

"Rae, I'm not going to ask for your forgiveness. I can't because I know I don't deserve it. All I can give you is a heartfelt and completely true apology." He reached out for her hands once more. She reciprocated and her soft touch reminded him of that night so long ago. He looked her straight in the eyes and in the most serious voice he stated simply, "Rae, I am so sorry for everything. I will never have any idea of how hard it was for you. It's completely my fault. No one deserves being left. I know I was in the wrong. The job you've done with Sloane," he paused to collect himself before he cracked, "she's amazing. That's entirely due to you. I have no excuses or even an explanation. I have an 'I'm sorry'."

"Thank you, Luke." She gripped his hand tighter.

He gripped it back and said it again, one more time, for her. "I'm so sorry, Rae."

She closed her eyes and her chin trembled. A tear formed, but she wouldn't let it fall. The admission unexpectedly overwhelmed her as though she'd been waiting for those exact words for years without realizing it.

CHAPTER 43

They were now staring at each other constantly like two puppy-dog eyed teenagers waiting for the adult in the room to leave.

"I'm going to go celebrate, with Heidi and Kristi. You lovebirds think you can handle me ditching out on you for the rest of the night?"

The silence was deafening as she falsely waited for an objection she knew wouldn't be coming. Hayden spoke up without looking away from Sloane, "I think we'll be alright." Sloane blushed hard. Justine thanked Hayden profusely again, walked out, and shut the door behind her.

Hayden stalked over to Sloane's bed where he sat down at the foot. He approached her as a hunter would a whitetail, very carefully. As if he didn't want to spook her like a skittish doe diving for the underbrush. Hayden stared her straight in the eyes and held his arm out in a gesture that made her feel like a dog being told to stay. Usually she'd be offended, but she got it. If something good is happening to Hayden Foster right now, he wants to wrap it in bubbles and clouds, duct tape it, throw it in a safe, and throw away the key forever.

"Hayden, I want—"

Hayden burst in as if he was a balloon deflating that had been waiting for release for way too long. "I love you!"

She continued undaunted, "Hayden, I want—"

"I love you!" Again interjecting.

"Hayden, I want—"

He smirked and gave up. "How long are you going to continue and not acknowledge what I said?"

Sloane reacted. "Oh honey, I've acknowledged, basked, bathed, and revered every single word that escaped those delicious lips. Why do you think I keep repeating myself?"

"Sloane, we have—"

"I love you too!" She beamed with excitement.

They giggled like school kids. They couldn't do this any longer. They couldn't keep pretending. Their dry humor, wit, and sarcasm were gonna wait. They couldn't go another second without closing the gap and trying to suck the life out of one another. Desperate doesn't adequately describe the yearning these two were experiencing with one another. They went hot and heavy enough in the first thirty seconds to make the professionals blush. Then they slowed and found a more even and steady pace, their pace. Eventually it tapered to Hayden lightly kissing the entirety of her face. Forehead, cheeks, nose, lips, ears, chin, eyelids, you name it, he was laying claim. Then they simply hugged. This was like a plural hug though, like multiple hugs, but edited together seamlessly. They needed nothing more in the world than to hold and comfort one another.

"Hayden, I really want to be serious right now for a minute."

"Okay, me too. I have a lot I want to say, but even more I want to hear."

"Thanks. First off, can I say I'm rockin' the shit outta this dressing gown."

"This is serious?"

"Dead serious, Hayden, I'm killin' this look." He chuckled. "Alright, alright, sorry." She conceded. "Yes, I did apologize again to you after I said I wouldn't. I can't help it. Hayden, my mom told me what you did. I keep thinking that you're working some angle. But that's not it, is it?" Hayden shook his head swiftly. "This is *it*, isn't it?" Now he nodded emphatically.

He knew exactly what she meant. Of course he did. They shared a cosmic connection, soulmates was kind of a foregone conclusion.

Mountains crumbling to the sea, solar systems colliding, and souls eternally intertwining. This was full-fledged, nine alarm bell, real as it gets, head over heels, stupid crazy, intoxicating love. The variety that freight trains fear. The type that moves the hardest of hearts and leaps the tallest of walls. The standard of love that every other couple in a room is jealous of. Seventy years together without blinking, jump in front of a bullet without hesitation, rock-your-world, knock-your-socks-off inferno, love.

"Yes, Sloane Knox, it is."

CHAPTER 44

His computer dock, printer, telephone, office supplies, and calculator were all perfectly placed on this desk in corresponding location to where he'd had them in his cube.

The lion's share of the décor was Minnesota sports memorabilia. There was his signed and professionally framed Kirby Puckett and Joe Mauer jerseys from the Twins. Several footballs mounted in shadow boxes lined the wall. One signed by Carson Wentz and Easton Stick from North Dakota State. Then there was his prize possession, the autographed Stephon Diggs helmet from the Minneapolis Miracle. He'd won that one in a raffle at a charity golf tournament. He even had an autographed Mike Modano Northstars hat. He'd never worn it.

Corrie had given Hayden a framed photo of him and Andy together a couple of days ago after taking a stroll down memory lane. He dazed off looking at it and missed his friend.

He sat back down and reclined in his new comfy and deluxe looking office chair. If there were levels of office chairs, this thing had to be the Cadillac. It had lumbar support, no squeaky casters, and a hydraulic arm for raising the seat, it rocked. Not like metaphorically either, it literally rocked. It's the little things sometimes.

Hayden took in everything. The sounds, the smells, the lack of Rebecca, the feeling of attaining everything he'd been working for. For about two whole minutes.

Hayden stood up from his new desk for the last time, turned off the lights, and headed for Dan's office.

He had put this meeting with Dan on the books and this time wasn't going to miss or postpone it.

When Hayden sat down across from Dan, he couldn't help but notice a PowerPoint presentation in front of him. The cover sheet said "Rikr." Dan started clearing it out of the way for their meeting. "Hey, can I see that?"

"Sure, I was putting the finishing touches on it. It's close to finished, but there are a few sheets here and there I need to rearrange. We have a huge pitch for this new pharmaceutical in an hour."

"I know." That was all Hayden said and he threw the entire deck over his head behind him. When it hit the door it exploded into what must have been at least a hundred sheets that fell to the floor. Dan's face relayed that he couldn't process what was happening. Hayden saw the dumbfounded look on his face and quickly followed, "I'm sure that was an exemplary presentation Dan, but I'm a man of efficiency and that...isn't important."

As Dan started coming to he realized there was a certain familiarity about this speech.

"Danny boy, I've got a proposition for you instead." Hayden threw his own presentation back at Dan. "If I were you, I'd hold on to that one. Let me show you what I learned here." He winked.

Hayden walked Dan through everything over the next hour. The ins and outs of Coronavirus, Rikr, Foxster and finally, the second to last slide, his offer. Hayden had become quite the closer. "So, if you'll flip to the next sheet, you'll see a pie chart breaking out the media mix we're planning."

Dan stopped him. "I don't have any chart. I have a backwards slip of paper that looks like..." Dan flipped over the slip and saw it was actually a check. Written to one Dan Murphy. It was nearly ten times what he was making now. It was ridiculous and it turned Dan into an overgrown bumbling infant. Hayden explained how the hierarchy will work and the five-year business plan. None of which Dan heard or cared about.

At the very end after they'd drank a scotch together and smoked a stogie right there in Dan's office, there was a knock at the door.

Hayden perked up. "I almost forgot. I'd like to introduce you to my team. Barring clearance from you of course. I'm not too worried about it though." In walked his team he'd recently poached, from himself. Dan loved it. "There's one more thing, I quit."

Foxster started with a small staff of thirty-four people. They were an all-star team according to Hayden. His six-person troupe, comprised of Faith, Kirk, Jason, Greta, Suzanne, and Alana. Together they handled the on-boarding and first full year of business. They only had three clients, Rikr, JBass, and Sampson's. Hayden gave Kirk point on Rikr. After all, he was a man of his word. To say it was a decent first year would be a bit of an understatement. That was their favorite year. It was a lot of late nights and hard work, but they wouldn't trade it for the world. The entire company was tight-knit and celebrated all holidays with employees and their families.

CHAPTER 45

❄

It took everything they had to convince him, but Sloane and Hayden had somehow relaxed "dad's rules" for one last weekend before he was incorporating a company-wide lockdown and shelter in place order the following week. Basically no one was to go anywhere, and everyone would be doing their work from home.

By this time word had gotten out. There were two cases in the U.S., but the world now knew what was coming. Everything that Luke had predicted was coming true. The numbers in China were on the rise. Rumor in Luke's circle was that Italy and Spain had now seen a few cases that until now were still unreported.

Hayden plotted out the ultimate last weekend of fun. They started Friday night with Juicy Lucy's at Matt's and the 5-8 Club. They each had their favorite burgers. Hayden had her back to her house by eight and said he'd be back to pick her up at four A.M. He had every intention of kissing her goodnight like a gentleman. Once their lips touched; however, he attempted sucking her lungs out through her teeth. At least that was how Rae had described it to them no more than five seconds later through the Ring intercom. The camera had been recording all the juicy footage. Rae was watching with her popcorn. She was going to like this life of convenience and the perks that came with it.

Sloane blocked the camera by pushing Hayden hard against it, repeatedly. Unfortunately, this also kept ringing the doorbell. It was quite the comical scene.

Finally realizing she was the one causing all the ruckus, Sloane turned Hayden around and jumped him like a capuchin monkey. He pulled her off him and raised his head to the sky to break connection with her mouth to breathe. *One more day, that's it, I can do this.* Then she grabbed his face and brought him in for an extremely sensual kiss.

He was now putty in her hands. Putty with an awfully large knife looking to spackle something, or in this case, someone. They were teenagers at a drive-in theater, unable to keep their paws off one another. Sloane finally pulled away, "Stop, we agreed we were gonna wait."

"I'm not the one still dry humping me."

Through tight lips so as to avoid breaking out into hysterical laughter as she said it, "I realize straddling you doesn't really support my argument."

"I'd say it's that or the gyrating." Hayden flashed her those life-altering looks and she melted.

She responded, "Fine, truce, I give, whatever you need to hear, I'm quitting, done. Let me add it's under extreme protest." She bit her bottom lip in frustration and anticipation.

With that Hayden pulled away finally and kissed her forehead before he left. She loved that. She loved that so much. He jumped into his SUV and took off for home. He got there and packed the last few perishable items and threw the cooler in the back compartment of the Yukon. Then he went inside and attempted to crash. His mind was reeling for hours as he laid across the top of his bed.

Three in the morning came way too quickly. Hayden was still beat, but today trumped all of that. He was a giddy little child. He swung by her house by 3:40. Luckily, she'd gotten up early and was ready ahead of schedule. The plan was to head to the c-store for gas and goodies, stop at the butcher shop for the steaks, and take off for Lutsen.

Hayden had told her to grab whatever snack food she wanted for the weekend as he filled up. He topped off as she came out with four separate bags full of frozen pizzas. On closer inspection Hayden noticed the packaging and all the bells and whistles blast off in his head. "Where did you get those?"

Just one of Sloane's eyebrows shot up. "You're joking, right?"

"Really? I thought they didn't have distribution anywhere outside of North Dakota."

"You know this company?"

Hayden smiled, "Know them? They were my client for years back home. I know the owner and have made them multiple times myself. These things are like currency for all the people we're gonna see this weekend. I'm going to let you bring those into the cabin. You'll probably get mauled. I hope you brought some bear repellant." His mind was blown.

They pulled up to Best Cuts. Sloane had worked a shift at the shop yesterday and had marinated the steaks again for the same trip. Somehow it didn't surprise Hayden in the least it was Sloane's marinade recipe that he loved so much. She absolutely loved the "Liquid Heaven" marketing campaign idea. The store was quiet other than the whirring hum of the freezer. It was dark except for a couple of recessed lights near the front. As she had ripped off the last sheet of butcher paper Sloane looked in Hayden's direction. He was standing in the first spot they'd met and the last spot he'd gotten to speak to Andy. In hindsight it was a very bittersweet moment and location in his life.

"This is…"

Sloane nodded, sharing one and the same mind. "I know. He loved you so much Hayden. So do I."

He smiled past her. The memories swirled all around him in a tapestry of humor, friendship, and love. He paused momentarily as he watched Sloane drop off something in Robin's office. It was her letter of resignation. She smiled at the thought of inevitably how blessed they truly had become. They extended their fingers to one another and walked out hand-in-hand.

They hopped in his truck. People in the north call big sport utility vehicles trucks. Right or wrong, it's what they do. They drove the four hours north to the same cabin in Lutsen. The owner's had issued the first group a rain check due to their early departure and now they were redeeming it.

Upon arrival he introduced all of them to Sloane. She had shown up with T-Bones and Pizza Corner pizzas. All of Hayden's North Dakota transplant, Twin Cities friends had a new favorite. As a matter of fact, they chose to start the weekend with the frozen pizzas over the steaks. They were absolutely crazy, but Sloane loved and truly got along with every one of them. She realized how close they all were and how well they complimented and supported one other. She could only be so lucky to call these people friends someday.

That night, before dusk, Hayden asked if Sloane wanted to go on one more run. She was a snowboarder and could shred pretty hard. He was a decent skier, but in North Dakota there weren't any mountains, so finding any place to downhill was rare. The flat plains were only really good for cross-country skiing. They made it on the lift as the patrol at the bottom cut off everyone behind them. The last run of the night would be all theirs. Hayden was thoroughly impressed with her skills. He told her to wait up and he'd go ahead to the bottom of the last jump so he could record her doing some sick trick. She couldn't see him on the other side, just hear him. "Are you ready?"

"I've been ready since I first saw the hairnet."

"That's sweet, but also random. I mean are you ready for my sick backside 1080?"

"Yep, hit it!"

Sloane hit the take off ramp at a pretty good clip. She flew through the air while flipping and spinning. As she landed the trick she looked ahead in bewilderment. There was a semi-circle of lights about fifty feet ahead. Hayden was nowhere to be seen. There were camera phones recording her, but it had nothing to do with her snowboarding skills. There must have been a hundred people there waiting for her on the other side of the hill. They were all silent. Each of them holding a small candle in one hand and recording with their phones with flashes in their other. It was reminiscent of a Christmas candlelight service. She was discombobulated. Her glance darted to each of them and she turned her head as if looking for answers. Then she saw Kristi, Heidi, Justine, Robin, Rae, and Luke. She was so happy to see them. It hadn't occurred to her yet what they'd be doing here.

Her mom had a tearful look of pride on her face when she looked past her daughter. Sloane noticed and with a blank look and slack expression she turned around. There was Hayden, on one knee. In his hand he held a small, opened box. He held out his other hand to her and she took it.

"You are one in a billion Sloane Knox. I was put on this earth to find you. I'd say that's pretty much non-debatable. We have a proven connection so overpowering and undeniable. You are the sweetest, smartest, wittiest, sexiest, everythingest woman I've ever met." She rolled her eyes at the term "everythingest." "There's nothing I wouldn't do to make you happy. I truly mean that with every fiber of my being. The fact I know you would do the same for me, tells me that we were meant to be. For all eternity. I don't care we've only known each other for two weeks. So, I ask you simply as a guy who loves a girl more than life itself; Sloane, will you marry me?"

Her oversized mittens completely covered her face. She couldn't believe how much she loved this man. She spoke softly so only he could hear, "I'm only doing this once."

"I know, me too." He whispered back.

"Hayden, I really mean it."

He teared up and couldn't talk for about ten seconds. He glanced away and choked back the tears. Then Hayden looked back at her as he rose to his feet again. "So do I."

She literally couldn't say it. She wanted to; her closing throat wouldn't allow her to summon that singular, little word. Sloane opened her arms and welcomed him in. He whispered in her ear, for her, "I love you Sloane Knox. Will you be my wife?" All she could do was shake her head in the affirmative. An eruption of cheers followed, and she began laughing uncomfortably through the tears. She hated how embarrassed he'd made her, but absolutely loved the way he looked at her.

Hayden hadn't skimped on the 4C's. The round cut, multi-banded ring had extremely intricate beauty. It was breathtaking. It was an interlaced combination of both white and yellow gold and yet it flowed together flawlessly. It must have been three carats in total when you counted the smaller stones mounted in the band. She thought it was perfect. Anything bigger and it would have been gaudy. He slipped it on her finger and she again hugged him so hard he seriously wondered if she'd misplaced one of his ribs. Then she ran to her mom to give her the biggest embrace as well. In her haste, without thinking about it, she grabbed Luke too. Before it became awkward, she moved on to the girls who were pining over the ring and the incredibly romantic and elaborate proposal. They had nothing but tears of joy for her, especially Justine. "PG, come here. I want to celebrate this with you." She grabbed and embraced her tightly. "What do you say we all celebrate for Andy tonight?" PG pulled Hayden into a three-way squeeze. "I think that sounds like a fantastic idea."

After dark, back at the cabin, they built a huge bonfire and held an impromptu engagement party. They all knew this would be their last hoorah. They made s'mores in the middle of the snow, danced like crazy, drank from an ice luge, and played Hammerschlagen. Hayden pulled out a half-dead bottle of Jägermeister. It was Andy's. There was enough in it for one shot with Andy's old crew, Sloane, and PG. They'd lost a brother but gained two new sisters. Sloane loved all of their friends. Including those she believed to be borderline insane. Then again, in all fairness, she was the one rehashing stories told to her by a dead man.

The entire night was a huge celebration of life, love, loss, and friendship. Hayden cranked up the music as the bass beat hit for *Baby Got Back*. He grabbed Justine's hand and danced with her. This song now had a new place in his heart. It would always remind him of Andy. It wasn't the most romantic thing, but then again, neither was Andy. He was more fun than a barrel full of monkeys though and they were all going to miss him for the rest of their lives.

The festivities raged on until the wee hours of the morning. At about ten o'clock Hayden ducked away from the bonfire. Upon his return he spotted Sloane on the other side of the fire. He watched her interact with his friends. His gaze remained glued. Hayden took in everything about her like a sponge soaking up water. As if sensing someone staring, she shifted her gaze until her eyes locked onto his. They shared a smile. Hayden repeatedly curled his index finger in a come-hither motion. She willed herself not to look away, holding the connection. Several long strides brought her to his side. Every breath of cold air showed as a plume of white steam.

She pulled her coat tight as he reached for her. "Come with me." She accepted it and followed his lead back to the cabin. Once they were inside and had peeled the layers of clothing off at the entryway Hayden leaned his lips next to her ear and whispered "Close your eyes." A faint flush rose on her prominent cheekbones as her eyelids descended and held firm. He grabbed both of her hands and walked backward, coercing her toward him. He escorted her to the base of a spiral staircase. "Okay, open."

When Sloane opened her eyes, she saw a path illuminated with tea light candles on either side of each individual stair. The center path was adorned with thousands of fragrant red rose petals.

He gestured for her to take the lead from him. He stood at the base as she ascended to the loft. At the apex of her trek she stopped and took it all in.

The room had a simple color palette of gray and white with a few earth tone yellow accents thrown in for good measure. In the center, against a wall, was a giant California king canopy bed with white fabric drawn to the bedposts. At the foot, surrounding the bed, there must have been nearly a dozen lanterns of varying sizes filled with candles that dimly illuminated the room. In the corner there was an eight-person tub. It was turned on with the jets producing bubbles and more tea lights surrounded the outside of the bath. Opposite the bed was a large fireplace with a roaring fire warming and further illuminating the room. There was an intoxicating smell of lavender and orange blossoms. At the bottom of the bed was a silver platter of assorted delectable, edible goodies. Including chocolate-covered strawberries. In the opposite corner of the room stood a small nightstand. On top of it was an ice bucket with a bottle of champagne and two flutes.

Sloane's hands clasped together covering her nose and mouth. She turned around and stared at him with glistening eyes and an outstretched hand. Her face softened as he rose to meet her at the apex. Hayden reached her and she smiled and buried her face into his chest.

As she drew back, he swept the hair out of her eyes and framed her cheekbone with his hand. Her face leaned into it and she kissed the palm of his hand as she memorized every line and contour.

There, in that amazingly romantic setting, Sloane Knox and Hayden Foster made love. Mind blowing, hours on end, rock your world to its very core, earth shattering, double-digit orgasm, soulmate intertwining massive firework display sex. She'd never had sex close to this good. Neither of them had. At the conclusion they lacked the energy to do anything other than pass out entangled naked in each other's arms. Hayden caught a little half smile cross her face as he kissed her forehead and they drifted away.

They never did get to the champagne or food.

CHAPTER 46

❄

The next morning they all gathered together at the top of the mountain. Dave Tipton met them and presented a plaque at the spot of the horrible incident where Andy would be memorialized for all eternity. After a small ceremony to unveil it Dave and his son hosted a big brunch for everyone.

Hayden hadn't taken the opportunity to meet Dave at Andy's funeral. He was still hurt and couldn't handle it. This morning everything felt different, however. Hayden walked right up to him and extended his hand. "Dave, I don't know if you'll remember me…"

"Hayden Foster. I knew who you were at the funeral. I also understand it wasn't the best circumstances to meet."

"You ain't lyin'." Hayden spat out and they both chuckled. "You are an honorable man, Dave. Thank you for taking the time to make sure Andy isn't forgotten, it means a lot to me, his family, and the rest of our friends."

Dave's son was holding his father's hand. He was extremely shy.

Sloane got down on one knee, so she was at his level. "Are you Ryan?" The young man nodded affirmatively. "Oh great, I have a special message for you." Little Ryan was blushing at the pretty girl talking to him. "I was told to tell you Andy was so happy to know you were okay. Did you know he saved my life too? We have something pretty big in common I'd say." She held out her arms until he gained the courage to leave his father and hugged her. She got back up and turned directly to Ryan's dad who had a look of befuddlement being they'd never met before. "He wanted me to tell you 'not as much as losing a child would have'. Andy wouldn't tell me what it meant, but said you'd know."

Dave's eyes got big and his shaky left hand covered his mouth. He whispered "thank you" to Sloane and shook her one hand with both of his. When he composed himself, he spoke under his breath so only they could hear. "While he was unconscious, and we were waiting for the helicopter I kept asking the same question to try to get him to respond. I asked him if it hurt."

Hayden shook his hand again and proudly walked away. *Even in death he's still showing me up,* Hayden thought. A smile arose.

The rest of Sunday was spent mostly in windshield time. For Hayden and Sloane, it was valuable catch-up time. He needed her to keep talking to keep him awake. She was more than happy to oblige. Nothing right now sounded nearly as enticing as a nap. They had been up most of the night. She still made it a point on the drive home to occasionally brush his inner thigh.

"You're trying to kill me woman."

"But what a way to go, right?"

Hayden laughed. "So, what's your verdict? Did I pass the test?"

"I'd give you a solid C+."

He looked into her eyes like he was a puppy that had been abused. He was confident, but that didn't mean the woman who held his heart couldn't shatter his ego with a statement like that.

She was trying to rile him up and then realized how he responded. "Hayden, I'm completely kidding. You were there last night; you know how incredible that was." He exhaled a sigh of relief while Sloane forged ahead, "I'm seriously considering a new religion. It's called Haydenism. It's nearly identical to Hedonism.

"Thank God, I thought you were serious." His masculinity was officially still intact.

"How could you not know?"

Hayden flashed her a false smile. "I told you, I didn't have a lot of experience before you. It wasn't a line, I meant it."

"Let me put this to bed once and for all, okay? Think of this as an apology."

"What? Why?"

"Not a literal apology. I'm saying I'm going to tell you this once and then never again."

He hesitated with a response. "Oh, okay."

"Hayden, that's the best sex I've ever had. I mean like much better than anything before it. I'd say you were twice as good as anyone I've been with before. Then when you compound the fact that I am head over heels in love with you, it has a way of multiplying it. I've never orgasmed that hard or that many times before."

Hayden's head was likely getting huge by now, so she reeled it in. "If you can perform even half that well for the rest of our lives, I'll die a *very* happy woman."

"Wow, that good?" He asked.

She assured him, "Better. So, what about me?" She went fishing.

"Well, we need to work on your enthusiasm a little. You kinda laid there like a dead fish." Now Sloane feigned a look of resentment and hurt. That was when she realized he was pointing to his back. "Lift it." She did and an unmistakable claw mark with dried blood came into view. He was grinning from ear to ear. She blushed in embarrassment. "Nuff said."

When they finally got back to his place Sloane had discovered Hayden had cleared out a drawer for her in his bedroom and some hanging space in his closet. She looked at him in a cute, humoring fashion. Then she kicked him out of their bedroom. That was so weird for her to say, "their bedroom." She was alone in there for the next three hours. When she eventually let him back into his own bedroom, everything was put away and arranged nicely. He figured he'd gotten about forty percent of the space. That was more than fine by him. Remember, he's a minimalist. The cuddled together in bed and binge-watched *Tiger King* on Netflix while slipping into and out of sleep. Around a quarter after nine that night Sloane finally awoke to the smell of breakfast.

She crawled out of bed, went to the bathroom, and turned the shower on. It was a bigger shower than she was used to at her mom's place. *A girl could get used to lockdown with upgrades like this.* She smiled.

After she'd finished, she put on her silk nightgown and went down to the kitchen. Before she got to the bottom of the stairs Hayden spoke "I heard you turn on the shower. Your plate is on the island."

"How did you know I liked breakfast for dinner?"

"I didn't, but of course you do. Because I do."

"Not surprising."

Hayden gave her some time and space. She rifled through her phone messages and noticed a friend request was accepted and she had a pending tag from him waiting for her to accept his status change to "Engaged." He popped his head into the kitchen after another half an hour had passed, "You ready to go back to bed yet?"

A devilish smile graced her face, "Only if I get to be the big spoon this time."

"Absolutely, but first I wanna spork." He retreated up the stairs. Thirty seconds later she joined him, buck naked.

During the first few weeks of Coronavirus lockdown they made rabbits blush with the frequency and intensity of their coupling. They couldn't get it enough from each other. Sloane concluded there was nothing sexier than a man that told you he wants you and then took what he wanted. At bare minimum he wanted her at least three times a day. She wanted him more.

They were now realizing that saying "I love you" was only the beginning. Now they get to prove it and consistently show it.

Every morning during those blissful first couple of weeks Hayden would stare at her there in his arms when he woke.

At that moment he was taking in every minute detail of the tree tattoo that graced her left side. The length of the art had to be nearly three feet. It must have cost her a fortune because it was so beautifully detailed. The artist was talented, of that he was sure. It stretched from a few inches under her armpit to the bottom of her thigh, short of her kneecap. It was a long branching oak tree in the fall. Most tats like this stop at the trunk of the tree, but this one went further into the ground. The roots were intertwining with a heart that was pumping blood into the tree and producing red flowering leaves. Many were falling off and away from it while being swept up into the wind. It was so unique. Then again, so was she.

He'd count to at least sixty in his mind before he would climb out of bed. He always allotted himself that, as he called it, minute of selfishness. Sloane was an extremely light sleeper, so he knew once he even slightly shifted she'd wake up. She'd pretend being mad at him trying to steal kisses from her before she had a chance to brush her teeth. Finally, after he'd made her laugh, what he deemed to be a sufficient amount; he would brush and head down to the kitchen to start coffee and breakfast. Sloane in the meantime would shower and go get the paper. They would meet back at the kitchen island. Just before she would plop down onto her stool after pouring coffee for them, he would sneak up behind and grab her. He'd whisper the same words into her ear every morning and she loved it every single time. "It's not being in love that makes me happy. It's the person that I'm in love with that does." He would kiss her on the back of the head while she overlapped his arms with hers around her mid-section and then put her arm over her shoulder to draw his lips near hers and they would share a sweet intimate kiss. It was the perfect start to the day, every day. They were both deliriously happy.

They wanted this to be as real and raw as love gets. The no holding back soul-bearing kind. He knew that Andy more than approved of his new best friend.

Hayden asked if Sloane had gotten the mail recently.

She replied, "Yeah, I stuffed it in my hoodie pocket."

At the entrance he found the sweatshirt and all of the mail. There was an abundance of spam that he'd collected over the past few weeks. For some reason he had more important things on his plate and mail was pretty low on the priority list. He began sorting and then found a business envelope that had his name on the front. Hayden wondered how it had been delivered without the proper postage. It escaped him as he opened and unfolded what appeared to be a hand-written letter. He began trudging up the staircase to the living room as he read on. Once at the top of the landing Sloane took notice of him and what he had. It was a few moments before she really focused and inevitably realized what he was reading.

She yelled, "No!" He stopped dead in his tracks, but then continued aloud. "I thought we had something. I thought you were finally someone that I could be honest and let down my guard with." He broke his dramatic delivery. "Can you believe this drivel? Talk about pathetic. I mean, thirsty much? You thought wrong toots!" Sloane was instantly embarrassed and crossed her arms in a pouting manner when she realized he wasn't going to stop. It gave her a childish sulking appearance. She was attempting to elicit a feeling of remorse or guilt from Hayden for "outing" her the way he was. It failed miserably. He had her right where he wanted her and was going to press down on the bright glowing branding iron he was metaphorically prodding her with. She repeatedly explained the letter and the reasoning behind it. He would occasionally interject a crude statement with the intention of getting a rise out of her. "I'd lost my best friend, how rude!" She felt terrible. "Please don't read anymore, I can't take it."

"You wrote it and addressed it to me. It's mine and there are no take-backs."

She was honestly starting to have her feelings hurt when he grabbed her by the hand with his left and grasped her neck, head, and cheekbone with his right. "Listen to me, woman."

She gave him a look like "how dare you!"

"Woman, listen." She was really starting to get offended the way he was addressing her.

"Sloane." She stopped. "I want you to share everything with me. When you're mad, when you're happy, hell, even if you're indifferent. I love you and love everything about you. You had your time, now hear me woman. I love you more than anything I've ever loved before. More than I knew I could possibly love another human being. There will never be any cheating or even questioning. You own me, do you understand? It doesn't get any more real than this. Trust me when I tell you that if I can't be with you for the rest of my days that it would destroy me. Especially now that I know what true happiness feels like. I am yours in body, soul, and mind. As I pray that you are mine. When I said, 'So do I', it's my way of saying I'm all in. My life is no longer mine. It's ours." She grabbed all the mail, flung it in the air, and kissed him as hard as she could.

For the next eight months they experienced the honeymoon phase of their relationship. They moved past the constant pawing at each other and began laying the foundation for a once in a lifetime love. Their love, respect, and admiration grew every day for one another.

CHAPTER 47

❄

Sloane was by herself at the back of the procession. She was the last to walk down. Under her veil she kept her eyes focused on the tile beneath her feet. Sloane was waiting to hear the familiar first notes of *Cannon in D* when something hard smashed her in her shin. She started wincing in pain and looked down to see the source of the smart. It was her mother's cane.

She looked beside her and there stood, unassisted, her mother with her elbow bent, waiting to usher her beautiful baby girl to her next step in life. Sloane's hand went to cover her mouth. Rae danced a little jig in place. "How?" That's all she had. She grabbed both of her mom's hands with her own and held a look of shock that lead to tears of joy.

Rae lifted her daughter's chin. "I didn't want to give you false hope. Your dad told me it may help my Lupus. I went to the doctor on Tuesday and they gave me a clean bill of health. I couldn't help it Sloan-E, right then and there I forgave him. I hope you can too. Granted your dad wasn't the greatest father, but he did kind of save the world. So maybe we can cut him a little slack?" They gave each other a squeeze of one another's forearms in an act of reassurance. Sloane threw tradition out the window. She lifted her veil and let everyone see her mascara smear and flow all down her face. She was magnificently hideous, and the humanizing effect lent her a softness the world fell in love with. It especially made her stunningly gorgeous to Hayden.

The music began and Rae proceeded to walk her daughter down the aisle. Surprisingly however, the melody wasn't Pachelbel, nor was the music being performed by the orchestra. From the pulpit Sloane could make out a man with a guitar. He leaned into the microphone in front of him and spoke, "This is for Andy and Luke, thank you from all of us." The bewitching tones of a beautiful hand-crafted Martin acoustic guitar rang out. As Dave Matthews popped out from behind the lectern and began to sing. Her mother extended her elbow and Sloane accepted.

At the front of the church there was a table with three large candles burning brightly. One for Hayden's mother, one for Andy, and of course one for Luke.

Luke Harder had rewritten history books. When Ph.D. prognosticators came along offering death toll and infection projections, Luke's Cloniquin defied the odds. Rather than the two million forebode initially, Rikr had blanketed the world's population in less than a year. Nearly half a million did tragically lose their lives due to the Coronavirus worldwide. However, there would be no fall or winter resurgence. Soothsayers, doctors, and scientists predicted a second coming of Covid to take nearly three million more lives. Luke essentially rid the world of one of the deadliest pathogens in the history of our planet. Daily for the first couple of months before his health began deteriorating, he was on TV with the president and heads of the CDC, including Chris Redman. He traveled the world helping heads of state across the planet coordinate their global response. He was the captain that led the second ark through the stormy waters and would forever be immortalized for it.

Only Christopher, Keith, Hayden, and Rae knew of Luke's condition when he passed in early September. He'd asked them all to keep a lid on it in one form or another. He wanted their work to be about others and what they were doing collectively to save the world. It was never about him.

Everyone he'd shared his health condition with kept the secret until the very end. In true Luke Harder fashion, he defied the odds of the experts and lived three months longer than expected.

In the end, there would be no miraculous cure. No divine phenomenon would clutch him back from the grasp of the grim reaper. Luke went peacefully in his sleep. Exactly two days after everyone's Amazon Rikr packages arrived. As if he was finally allowing himself peace after accomplishing all of his self-appointed responsibilities. He only had one more on his list, but he'd never know if it would come to fruition. Luke Harder was given a state funeral and every flag on the planet flew at half-mast.

Then, about a week following the funeral a *60 Minutes* special with three shadowy figure interviews came out. Everyone now knew Luke's entire story and it fed the beast. Once word of Sloane's miracle made its way through every media outlet known to man, the worldwide legend of Luke Harder reached nearly biblical proportions.

He was the imperfect hero. Luke was the flawed and unlikely errant father with all odds stacked against him. A loveable sucker with a beautiful tale of atonement. It was a story for the ages.

The event wasn't just memorable for those in attendance. It was being carried live on every streaming device and platform known to man. In all, more than four hundred and fifty million people watched the wedding of Sloane Knox to Hayden Foster. It was watched by nearly four times the previous record for eyeballs of a single televised event in history.

CNN, Fox News, and MSNBC all preceded the wedding with hours of pomp and circumstance coverage, almost like pre-game shows leading up to the big game.

Since those in Luke's circle were the first vaccinated, all of their families and friends were allowed to attend. As well as the entire staffs of Rikr Pharma, Foxster and the University of Minnesota East Bank Hospital. About 400 people in total attended the affair at the Basilica of Saint Mary.

This wedding, held on the 10th of October 2020 would inevitably become known in history textbooks as: "The Day We Picked up the Pieces." For Hayden, it had been about ten months now since he'd lost Andy and his world was shaken to its foundation. This was the very first event since the world had gone into lockdown with a planetary quarantine back in mid-June. Just a few weeks after the George Floyd worldwide riots broke out. Multiple countries and states tested the waters by defying medical and infectious disease experts and ended their shelter in place orders back in May. Instead of the dipping of a toe, they opened the floodgates. They didn't take the proper precautionary measured steps and it was disastrous. It was too soon and had catastrophic consequences. The laxing of the laws resulted in tens of thousands of additional needless deaths. People were putting comfort and way of life above actual life. It was that old adage of not seeing the forest for the trees.

This union was being broadcast two days prior to the conclusion of the global shelter in place order adopted by all the world's leaders. Before their first dance Hayden looked into one of the cameras and asked everyone to join them in their living rooms...and they did. It was the world's last moment together. It was this generation's "you remember where you were when it happened" moment.

Instead of a reception, they rescheduled the annual Basilica Block party and broadcast it worldwide. Dave Matthews, U2, Billie Eilish, Jay-Z with Beyonce, Taylor Swift, and Eminem headlined an amazing night of music.

Two days later when the world was waking to its freedom, Hayden and Sloane boarded a plane for two weeks in Jamaica with Kent and his wife.

What people didn't realize until much later is that this was the first time in the history of humanity that the world truly worked together as one. Everyone did much more than purely stay indoors. They all became heroes and saved each other's lives. Putting others before themselves. The world reimagined altruism and redefined family.

From that point forward, the second weekend in October was the planetary holiday known as "World Weekend." It became the second most traveled weekend of the year behind Christmas. Families would come home and shelter in place for two days. They'd play games and binge-watch movies and TV series in their pajamas. All while eating fatty food and re-establishing their alcohol tolerances. They remembered what it was like "Once Upon a Time" and the family that saved them all.

EPILOGUE

There was a knock on Sloane's office door. It was *him*. "I've been meaning to discuss something with you. I'm actually pretty pissed about it." His concern grew over her tone. "Well, tell me what it is, and we'll try to figure it out."

"I'm sorry, but I don't believe this problem is really 'solvable.' Unless you've figured out how to unscrew me." A big grin crossed her face. "Hayden, look what you've done to my feet! They're like dirigibles down there! Well, they feel like it anyway. I'm not quite sure since I haven't seen them in about a month!" She grabbed his hand as he offered to help her up. It took quite the maneuvering to get her belly around the side of her desk.

He kissed her on the cheek.

"Hey, Hay, you know the company policy on PDA." He loved when she called him that. She loved his little kisses sometimes more than the big ones.

Hayden extended his elbow to he spoke. "Ready for dinner?" They began walking toward the cafeteria arm-in-arm.

Sloane retorted, "Are you kidding me, it's the best part of my day!"

"Hey, c'mon now. What about this morning in the shower?"

"Fine!" she said with a cheeky grin, "It's *barely* my second favorite."

"That's more like it!" Hayden chuckled.

Two weeks ago, the company expanded its options and added a pizzeria to the campus' food court. Every single day since they'd met each other at "their table" for made from scratch Pizza Corner pizza. Sloane grabbed the hot sauce and parmesan cheese. "I tell you what, Andrew Lucas Foster loves him some heat!" Hayden laughed picturing an actual baby eating the fiery concoction.

He couldn't wait to meet his first born. When the time was right, he would take him out in his old F-100 and teach him how to drive stick. He'd tell him of his namesake best friend and all of their adventures together.

On their way out Hayden and Rae walked through the newly completed tranquility garden they named "Redemption." Hayden never explained its origins. His relationship with Luke held such a deep place in his heart. This was his little piece to keep.

On their first Christmas Eve after the pandemic Rae was sitting in a recliner relaxing and cuddling with her new grandson. The fire Hayden had built began to crackle. The entire house smelt of sugar cookies and pine.

The Foster's continued Sloane's childhood tradition of opening one present the night before. Rae knew which one she wanted to give to Andrew. Technically it was a package addressed to both Andrew and Sloane. It was in her father's handwriting. It was a copy of *'Twas the Night Before Christmas.* It was one of those Hallmark audiobooks. Luke had finished recording it a few days after he'd been told of his daughter and Hayden's imminent bundle of joy.

Rae looked at Hayden and then subtly shifted her gaze to the stockings hung over the mantle place. They were all connected by a piece of garland that was illuminated by a string of battery-operated lights. There were business envelopes in two of them.

Hayden crossed the small living room, reached into the overgrown footwear, and read the names on the envelopes. They were his and hers. As he was about to hand her the one labeled "Rae," he recognized the handwriting. Rae saw the look of recognition on his face and nodded affirmatively.

"Hey babe?" He called out to Sloane who had been in the kitchen putting together a platter of gingersnaps and snickerdoodles Hayden had made earlier today to bring over. She grabbed her mug of hot chocolate and blew on it to cool it down, as she carried the dish in and set it down on Rae's tiny little end table. It was right next to one of those old ceramic trees with the bulbs made of multi-colored pegs at the end of each branch. "Yeah, what's up?"

He threw the envelope haphazardly at her. It landed in her lap.

With an almost frowning face she asked pointedly, "But this has your name on it."

"Yeah, but it's really for you. It's from your dad." Hayden replied.

This entire time Rae was as quiet as a church mouse. She'd been waiting for this moment for months. Sloane opened the envelope. She withdrew the contents. It was a slip of paper, what looked to be a backward check, wrapped in a letter.

She began reading aloud:

"Dear Sloane,

I realize I am now gone. Once again, I've left you. However, this time you're in good hands. Hands of a man that will protect, support, and love you better than I ever could." She looked at Hayden and reached for his hand. "While I can honestly say I did my very best in the winter of my life, it was important to me that you understood I wanted to make true amends and earn your trust and faith. It couldn't appear that I was trying to buy your love or guilt you for it out of empathy."

SLOANE TOOK a deep breath and let it out again slowly as she continued. "While that may be confusing right now, your mom and Hayden can fill in the gaps." Lines formed between her eyebrows and Sloane scanned them both. "I am so proud of you and proud to have known you. When you popped up in that hospital bed Sloane, it was the greatest moment of my life. You would think the satisfaction of saving millions of lives would have been it, but it didn't even hold a candle to you.

Tears welled from deep inside and coursed down her cheeks.

"Posthumously, I'll never leave you and your mother high and dry ever again. I love you, Sloane. You were the best thing that ever happened to me and I blew that for way too long. At the end, I did it all for you. So, I could leave you with something. A legacy that made you proud of your father. I hope this accomplishes that."

I'm sorry I didn't tell you I was sick. I hope you can forgive me one, final, time.

Love Now, Forever, and Always,

Dad"

WHETHER HE MEANT his apology solely for his earthly departure not allowing him to be there with them now or as her father growing up, she didn't care, the answer was yes. She forgave him.

…and Luke's final box had been checked.

With that Sloane flipped the check over and saw what had to be a fake number. The zeroes were written in the tiniest of handwriting and barely fit on the slip of paper. Rather than imagining where each of the comma breaks should be, she read the words on the "Dollars" line. "Ten Billion" she mumbled. "This can't…" She looked back and forth and up and down each of them for any signs of a prank or joke that would keep her grounded.

Rae had already opened hers, which was a check, minus the letter. She didn't complain as she held up an exact replica, with her name in the "Pay to the Order of" line. "It's real honey. Hayden and I didn't want to go about it this way or keep anything from you, but your father made us sign gag orders that we couldn't tell you."

"Tell me what?"

Hayden chimed in, "We knew back in January he was terminal."

Her mouth dropped and for a second she started to get upset.

With a nervous smile Hayden added, "Not bad for a sticker huh?"

Her somber face broke into a gleam of joy as she reached out to him, "You're lucky I love you so damn much!"

All the major streaming services had created movies and docuseries of their entire epic tale.

The Foster's became "The World's Sweethearts." There was no escaping the media and judgmental people that had their own perfect vision of how they should be living their lives.

Sloane and Hayden felt as if it was a no-win situation. They bought a ridiculously large cabin on Lake Minnetonka and lived the rest of their lives there retired. They had a fantastically normal little family. Three boys, one girl, and two dogs they named "Covid" and "Quinn". They were healthy and happy. Which in terms of the upper Midwest, was a fairytale ending.

Sloane and Hayden hosted every major holiday and friend gathering. Every year on the 11th of January they would throw the biggest party in honor of Andy. This year PG brought Kirk.

Thanks to Luke, the world spun on Coronavirus free ever after.

THE END

ACKNOWLEDGMENTS

This book never would have come to fruition had it not been for the second to none, incredible work of my editor, Tiffany. Simply put, you are amazing. You turned a dream into a reality.

Dedications:

In loving memory of my dear friend Andy and our friends and family in North Dakota and Minneapolis. We love and miss you all.

My wife Rochelle, my Sloane. She has always supported and loved me unconditionally. She is truly the best person I've ever met and an unparalleled mother to our three boys, Oliver, Archer, and baby Remy. Her faith and love are something I thank God for every day.

* * *

Thank you for purchasing *Love in the Time of Corona*. If you enjoyed this book, please consider leaving a review.

Find the author online:
www.cjloomis.com

Made in the USA
Columbia, SC
12 June 2020